THE
CRESCENDO

FIONA PALMER

ABOUT THE AUTHOR

Fiona has been writing rural stories for Penguin and Hachette for years and is now indulging in her love of YA. She is a full-time writer, farmhand, speedway racer and mum of two fabulous teenagers, from rural Western Australia.

www.fionapalmer.com
@fiona_palmer

The Recruit
The Mission
The Deception
The Crescendo

The Family Farm
Heart of Gold
The Road Home
The Sunburnt Country
The Outback Heart
The Sunnyvale Girls
The Saddler Boys
The Family Secret

Secrets Between Friends
Sisters and Brothers

ACKNOWLEDGEMENTS

I couldn't do this without Jim, big hugs, thank you for always answering my questions and helping my creativity along. Also to my friends and family who read my work, thank you so much. Thanks to Rach Johns for your support and friendship. A huge thank you to Cathryn Hein for being the reason these stories are available in print. Thanks to Claire De Medici for being such a fab editor for this series. Big thanks to my family Darryl, Mackenzie and Blake for their understanding. And as always, thanks to the readers who make all this possible. Thank you.

For Jim Jim

CHAPTER 1

VIBRANT RED WAS splashed all over her hands, her chest, her jeans and quite possibly her face, like a preschooler dabbling with paint. Only, it wasn't paint.

It was blood.

The smell of it drenched the air in the small car, raw metal in a sickly gut-churning scent.

It wasn't Jasmine Thomas's first foray into having other people's blood on her skin, nor her own. Having been shot in the leg not that long ago, one would think she would be used to this, or at least wouldn't feel so panicked. Then again, it could have something to do with the person who was sprawled over the back seat, blood seeping through his clothes like spilled wine on a tablecloth, as she pressed her shirt against the bullet wound in his shoulder.

Ryan Fletcher's normally tanned skin looked like glossy white paper. His dark eyes watched her carefully and were crinkled at the edges, the only sign he was in pain. He winked and gave her one of his sexy smiles.

He was the love of her life. Also a secret spy with whom she was definitely not permitted to fall in love.

Too late.

Far too bloody late.

You can make soldiers but you can't tell them whom they can and can't love. Well, maybe you could, but Jaz's excuse was that she hadn't been with the Agency for very long; she'd only been recruited at the start of the year. She still had to sit her year twelve exams, soon. This year had been a crazy ride, and it showed no signs of slowing down.

'Jaz, how's he going?' Tay glanced in the rear-view mirror as he drove on the freeway.

Taylor was one of her two best friends; Anna was driving the car behind them. Jaz could see Anna's worried face through the back window, her freckles standing out on her pale cheeks, her strawberry-blonde hair almost red and her white knuckles gripping the wheel.

Taylor and Anna had recently been recruited into the MTG Agency as well. She felt responsible for them, because they now swam in the deep dark waters of danger. But they wouldn't have it any other way. It was nice to know they had her back, and if it weren't for them – well, she and Ryan might not be alive right now.

'He's okay,' said Jaz with a lot of hope as she glanced at Ryan.

At twenty-four, he was a man of strength and menace. His physique was muscled and lean, his body scarred from knives and bullets; Jaz had known the first time she saw him that he was dangerous. Maybe it what was had drawn her to him, yet even though she was wary, she was also attracted like a moth to a flame. Finding out he worked for a secret agency, and then having him recruit and train her, had only made him more awesome in her eyes. She had fallen in love with him and yet she couldn't be with him. It was not permitted.

Ryan lifted his hand and brushed her long raven hair back over her olive skin.

'In your honest opinion, Doctor Jaz, do you think I'll live?' he asked, shooting her a smile that melted her insides.

The short stubble that covered his lean jaw, along with his clipped short hair, made him look as sexy as hell. She wanted to kiss his full lips but the smell of blood and the red splattered up his neck reminded her this was not the time or the place. A wave of panic washed over her again and she masked it by replying to his question.

'Of course. This is just a scratch,' she said, repeating what he'd said when she'd been shot in the leg not that long ago. 'How long till we get there?' she asked Tay.

'Just a few blocks away.'

Ryan tried to sit up and glanced out the window. 'Pax will go ballistic if I get blood all over his car,' he said with a chuckle and a wince. 'But it wouldn't be the first time.'

Pax was her adopted granddad. He ran the local gym The Ring, which was a front for his real job as the Agency's top computer guy: fake IDs, passports, rap sheets; you name it. Pax had been doing it for years, long before Jaz was born. Only, she had never known, until this year.

Then, to twist her mind even more, she found out her mum had been a part of the Agency in a previous life. In fact, it was her mum's family, the Montenegros, that helped set up the MTG Agency with the government's backing. But when her mum discovered she was pregnant with Jaz, she gave up being a secret agent and, with help from Pax, made a new identity and disappeared to Western Australia to live a normal life. Jaz had recently met James, who ran the Agency and he didn't know that his sister was alive, nor that Jaz was his niece. So yeah, this year had been full of surprises. Dodging bullets was just the tip of the iceberg.

And to think Jaz would be none the wiser if Ryan hadn't come into Pax's gym to train. Which in a way irked her, because she'd never have known about the huge secrets they kept from her. But now she kept one from her mum. Tasha had no idea that Jaz knew about the Agency, much less was part of it. Pax had sworn her to secrecy for fear of what Tasha would do to him.

It was a big, intertwined bundle of secrets that you couldn't even begin to believe, but that was her life. And funnily enough, she could live with the secrets because she knew the work she did for the Agency saved lives, saved innocent people, and she liked making a difference in the world.

Okay, sometimes she ended up in deep shit, like right now. Running down a lead on drug smuggling, Ryan and Jaz had followed the drugs to the source, Salvatore De Luca. The agency had been unable to pin anything on him, but Jaz and Ryan had come face to face with him and his goons in a shoot-out in his airplane hangar. Ryan's bleeding shoulder was the result.

Jaz still couldn't understand how they'd got out alive. She glanced down at her chest, where her medallion usually sat. It had been her biological father's, the only thing she had of his, made more precious with her mum refusing to speak of him. Now Salvatore had it, torn from her neck as she'd been pushed down onto a black plastic body bag.

'Just drop Jaz and me off and take the cars back to the gym. Check you're not being followed. Like I showed you,' said Ryan as Tay pulled up by his house.

'Got it. Can we come back?'

Jaz could see that Tay was worried and wanted to help, but she knew it would be too risky for them to stay together.

'No, stay there. Jaz can keep you updated.' Ryan tried to slide his body to the door but paused halfway for a breather. 'Oh, and thanks, Tay. You and Anna saved our arses back there. We appreciate it.'

Jaz caught Tay's nod in the rear-view mirror before he took off his shirt. 'Jaz, put this on.'

Ryan held his padded wound while she threw on Tay's black T-shirt. Then she opened the door and helped Ryan out. They tried to look inconspicuous as Tay drove away. Anna slowed down in the Commodore behind but Jaz waved her on to follow Tay. She nodded, her face grim as she made the hand sign for 'Call me'.

'Let's get you inside before your neighbours decide to look out their windows and report weird stuff in their hood.' Jaz put her arm around him as they quickly headed to his tall fence. She unlocked the gate and soon they were in the safety of his private yard.

'Thanks, Jaz.'

Jaz unlocked his door; she knew where his spare key was hidden. This wasn't the first time she'd been to his house. Only this time, it was Ryan who was bleeding all over his bathroom floor with Jaz trying to fix him up.

'This is quite the role reversal,' she said teasingly as she pulled out the scissors from the drawer by the sink and cut away his shirt.

'Hmm, as I recall, I wasn't wearing a shirt.'

Jaz did recall that, vividly. Even now it still brought chills of pleasure as she studied his chest, scars and tattoos. That fact that Ryan had used a needle and thread on her up made the memory even sharper.

'Don't think I'm going to be stitching you, though, and I've already had my shirt off.'

'Hmm, I remember,' he said. Dark eyes dropped to her chest.

Ryan wasn't normally this flirty; if anything he always tried to downplay anything between them as a slip-up, an accident or something they shouldn't do. Maybe being shot was having an adverse effect on his mental stability. Or maybe it was because they'd recently had sex? Her body exploded with tingles just thinking about it, but she pushed it from her mind to focus on Ryan.

Jaz heard a bang as the back door swung open and slammed shut.

'I'm here, how bad is it?' said Tilly as he came into the bathroom at a rate of knots. His arms were filled with medical supplies and a bottle of scotch.

'Hey Tilly,' said Ryan with a smile. 'Brought the goods, I see.' Ryan used his uninjured arm to gesture that he wanted a drink.

Tilly gave him the bottle then put the bandages down on the sink bench beside Ryan. Jaz stepped back and watched Tilly work. Tilly was older, thirties she guessed, scrawny like a bag of bones and had nicotine stains on his fingers and teeth. He looked like someone who'd had a hard life; he wore the scars, and not just on his body. She'd first met Tilly when she accompanied Ryan to Pakistan to retrieve vital intel. Soon after, she'd witnessed her first death. It had been horrific, a slit throat from a knife welded by Ryan, no less. She'd been a little traumatised but since then she'd seen more. Like watching *Game of Thrones*, Jaz was starting to feel numb towards the violence and blood.

Realising this, she stepped forward and asked Tilly if she could help.

'Good on ya, kid. Doing this stuff could save your life,' said Tilly as he cleaned the wound and checked for glaring problems. 'It's close to the bone, mate; not sure if it nicked it or not but I guess time will tell.'

Ryan grunted as he took a swig from the full bottle and grimaced more at the potent liquid than he had at Tilly's poking.

These two blokes were like grizzly bears, or more like Bear Grylls. Tougher than nails.

Tilly passed her the bloody gauze and she tried to keep them in a neat contained spot, but soon Ryan's bathroom looked like the scene of an Alfred Hitchcock movie. Red dots were splattered up the mirror and across Ryan's white tiles, making vivid contrasts.

'Why is it one of you is always getting shot? What were you up to this time?' asked Tilly.

'Us? What about you? You've been shot enough times to make a submarine out of the bullets,' said Ryan.

In Pakistan Tilly had been shot in his arm, but he'd carried on as if it were no biggie. Tilly getting shot was probably like Jaz getting pimples: annoying but unavoidable.

Ryan put down his large drink and began to relay their mission.

'You know we went north and staked out the beach, watched the drugs float in on the waves. They collected the drums, we followed.'

Jaz listened carefully when Ryan got to the stake-out part, no mention of nearly getting caught and having to improvise. Just the c of that improvisation brought a flush to Jaz's face. It had been the best moment of her life. Ryan's eyes avoided her as he continued the story.

'They went to a storage shed, then some guys split straightaway, talking about an urgent shipment. We followed and ended up at Salvatore's plane hangar.'

'No way. You finally caught him?'

'Kind of. We walked in but caught a worker after he'd just capped a bloke. We saw his gun and blood. He couldn't let us go then, so he marched us inside and lined us up next on the black plastic.'

Tilly grimaced.

'He doesn't like loose ends, and as innocent as he thought we were, he couldn't have us out and about. Cold-blooded death. We had to wait for our moment to strike, and then there were shots going everywhere, we barely got out of there alive,' said Ryan gesturing to his bullet wound. 'Lucky Jaz managed to get word out to Tay and Anna, and we got away.'

Ryan looked deep into the bottle he held, as if searching for answers to the questions she could see swimming in his dark eyes. She knew he had many, so did Jaz, but neither of them spoke about these to Tilly. Neither had mentioned 'that moment' to each other but it was there, lurking like a shark hungry for fresh blood.

'You two are lucky bastards. A bit like me,' Tilly said with a chuckle, and ended with a smoker's raspy cough.

Jaz used a flannel to wash the blood from Ryan's body, cleaning him without getting in Tilly's way. Soon they had him patched up and clean.

'Righto, I think you'll live, Fletch,' said Tilly.

Ryan's colour had come back a fraction, more due to the alcohol; they couldn't fix the blood loss.

'Let's get him to bed before he passes out.' Tilly took away his bottle of liquid painkiller and handed it to Jaz while he positioned himself under Ryan's good shoulder. 'Come on, mate.'

Jaz put the bottle on the coffee table in the lounge room before getting to Ryan's room to turn down his bed. It took all her willpower not to climb in there and wait for him to join her.

Ryan got into his bed, mumbling his thanks, and as he lay back, the pressure on his shoulder caused him to groan. He closed his eyes and started to breathe deeply, while they watched him. He looked so peaceful lying without his shirt, and Jaz couldn't help but admire his gorgeous body and the scars marking it. She searched out the word 'forever' tattooed under his arm. Under a black light it had more detail to it. It was a memorial to his mate Chris who was killed by Salvatore. Hence Ryan's decidedly personal interest in taking Salvatore down. Today would have really tested him, bringing him face to face with the man he'd been hunting for over a year. Trying to take down a cunning man like Salvatore wasn't easy.

Her eyes moved across to his chest; there was no visible tattoo, yet Jaz knew the Southern Cross marked his skin there with invisible ink. It was her favourite. It was Ryan's way of reminding him of home when he was overseas on missions.

'He'll sleep for ages. Do you wanna drink ... ah, I mean a cuppa?' said Tilly. 'Then maybe you can fill in some blanks about this mission.'

Jaz nodded and Tilly headed off to the kitchen. Jaz stepped closer to Ryan and bent down to kiss his forehead. His eyes fluttered at her touch but remained closed.

She wanted to say so much but couldn't. Once you opened that can of springy worms they just never went back in the same way. Sometimes life was just a bit tricky. With a sigh she stepped softly from his room and went to clean up the bathroom before joining Tilly for that much needed drink.

CHAPTER 2

JAZ CHATTED TO Tilly for a while until he was satisfied he'd heard enough about the mission, but all the while he watched her closely, as if feeling he knew she was omitting something, but he didn't pressure her. Yes, she had left out a few things, but right now she didn't feel like over-sharing.

Jas heard the rumble of Tay's Mustang and headed for the door. 'Thanks Tilly, let me know when he comes around.'

'Will do. I'll be here for a few days, I reckon. He'll be fine,' he added with sincerity. 'I'll pass on your mission details to the boss, you just go and rest up for a bit.'

She shut the door behind her and made her way out through the front gate. She slid into the back of the Mustang, but before she could even shut the door properly, Taylor was driving off. Already he was programmed not to hang around for too long and risk being recognised.

'How is he? How are you?' said Anna, turning around in the front seat. Her green eyes were huge and full of concern, reminding Jaz of the big sage lanterns that hung from the ceiling in their favourite coffee shop.

'He'll be okay. Me?' Jaz shrugged. Her brain hurt and yet she couldn't grasp a single thought from the thousands whizzing around her head.

'Wanna go to Molly's for a coffee?' Anna asked.

'Can you drop me off home first? I need a shower.' She'd washed off Ryan's blood, but still she felt a full scrub was in order. 'Then a coffee sounds great.' Plus she needed to check in with her mum after being away for a few days.

Tay pulled up at her house and Jaz snuck in quickly, worried she might have missed a spot of blood or that her face might give her away. But, as usual, no one was home. Her mum and stepdad were no doubt at work and Simon, her half-brother, was either in his room pulling apart a computer, playing a game on it, or with his dad learning more. Their dad. Paul was the only father she knew. At least he was who he was, unlike her mum who had a whole different identity. She often wondered if Paul knew. Paul was as far from a secret kick-arse agent as one could be. He worked in computers, a bit of a geek but so loveable. A lot like Pax.

Jaz frowned. Pax. Might he have answers to some of her questions? Man, her head was driving her nuts and no matter how hot she turned up the shower it didn't relieve the tension in her muscles.

In ten minutes she was back downstairs, wearing black cargo pants and a white tank top and her commando boots, her wet hair tied up. But something wasn't right. She touched her neck for her missing gold medallion. It was a circle, the front showing an image of Saint Michael, and her father's first name engraved on the back. At least Salvatore couldn't trace it back to her, because it didn't have a last name. Not even Jaz knew her father's full name. Her mum had kept it from her, and pretty much any other information about her biological father.

'Ready to go?' asked Anna, who sat beside Tay at the kitchen table. They had helped themselves to apples from the fruit basket.

'Yep. Can we get coffee to go and head back to the gym? I think I need a workout.'

Anna bit her lip. She was doing a great job of trying to give Jaz space when she knew she was dying to ask her a million questions. Jaz walked straight up to her and gave her a hug.

'I will tell you everything, just not yet. I need time to process.'

'I know. We're here when you're ready.' Anna smiled, her expression said she hoped it was soon. Anna hated waiting for anything, good news, bad news, any news.

Tay stood beside them in jeans and a blue singlet.. His muscles were looking even more defined than usual. Tay had always been fit, good at sports, but since he'd started training to get mission ready he'd really bulked up. The girls at school had noticed; Tay was already popular, but now he was reaching superstar status.

If only some of that could rub off on Jaz, who was still the scary freaky one no one went near, and Anna the smart computer nerd. But they'd been friends since they were kids, and it didn't change no matter what others thought.

They got their coffees from a McDonald's drive-through on the way to The Ring. Tay pulled up outside the large shed-like structure. Paint peeled off the old tin and the broken footpath didn't improve the feel about the area, but to Jaz it was home. She liked that it wasn't in a fancy neighbourhood like her house and that the area was a little dangerous. Danger was fast becoming her friend.

Yet Pax had lived in the little house connected to the gym for as far back as she could remember, and Jaz had been coming here to train since she could walk. Her mum the first one to teach her to fight. At some point Pax took over her training while her mum integrated into her new life after meeting Paul. And that's how Pax became the closest thing to a grandfather figure she had. He was also Anna's grandfather's brother.

Anna pushed open the old door, framed in wood, fading white paint and glass in the middle. The familiar scent of the leathery, sweaty gym eased her muscles more than the shower ever could have, and no sooner had she stepped inside than she heard her name shouted out.

'Jaz! Hey, girl.'

Tick waved from the floor mat where he was fighting Bags, who wore boxing gloves. Both were classed as Pax's gym family.

'Hi guys. Bags, don't let Tick get you with a lead kick,' she warned.

'Never do, Jaz,' replied Bags, who only just blocked a knee from Tick. He pulled a face and Jaz smiled for the first time in a while.

'Hey kids, what are you all up to? Looks like trouble.' Pax walked out of the office in a Hawaiian-style shirt over a white singlet and long shorts, topped off with sandals and glasses up on his balding head. He sniffed the air. 'Bring one for me?'

'Sorry Pax,' said Anna. 'I'll go make you one, though.'

Anna gave him a hug and Pax kissed her forehead. 'That would be awesome,' he said, trying to speak like them. Tay laughed as he followed Anna. No doubt he would be looking for Pax's secret stash of Tim Tams, which was never very secret.

'How are you?' Pax asked, stepping towards her.

Jaz couldn't get her mouth to work and just blinked. Pax pulled her into his arms and breathed out.

'The kids told me what happened. I was so worried. How are you feeling?'

Jaz let herself sag against Pax's soft teddy-bear body. He was a familiar smell of coffee and cinnamon – a sure sign he'd been indulging in his love of pastries again. After a recent heart attack he was on a new diet, but right now Jaz wasn't in a hounding mood. If anything, it was nice to smell the old Pax.

As they stood embracing, neither moving, Jaz tried to piece together her thoughts. How was she feeling? Everyone kept asking but Jaz didn't have an answer. Did she want to cry? Not really. Was she scared? Not anymore. Was she confused? Hell yes. But she couldn't tell Pax that without the whole story and she wasn't ready to share yet. Too much had happened in such a short time.

One minute she'd spent the best time of her life with Ryan, making love to him, and the next she was lined up on black plastic awaiting death. She didn't know where she stood with Ryan, how it would affect their working relationship, their friendship. And what did she do about the fact that she was in love with him? How long could she hold that in for? And then there was Salvatore.

Salvatore De Luca.

She pulled away from Pax and from the thought of Salvatore, pushing him from her mind.

'I'm okay, I guess. It's good to be back here.'

'It's good to have you back,' said Pax. 'Safe.'

She nodded. But she wondered just how safe she really was.

CHAPTER 3

RYAN OPENED ONE eye, then the other. His head felt a little fuzzy, but that was nothing compared to the pain stemming from his shoulder. 'Bloody hell,' he grumbled as he tried to sit up.

'Stings a bit, hey,' said Tilly with a chuckle.

Ryan would have given him a mouthful of swear words but the man stood by his bed holding a glass of water and some good pain medication.

'Oh, yes please,' Ryan swung his legs over the side of the bed and reached for the drugs. Once he'd swallowed them, he glanced at the patch on his shoulder. 'How long have I been out?'

'All yesterday and a bit of this morning.'

Ryan looked at his clock. It was eleven-thirty. 'Goddamn, I'm starving.'

'Thought you'd say that. Come on, I've made up mac and cheese for lunch, should be warm enough by now. Doesn't look like you want to wait any longer.'

Tilly was still wearing his torn black jeans from yesterday and Ryan knew he would have slept in the spare room down the hallway. Tilly had crashed here on a few occasions, usually when his medical expertise was needed.

'You right?' Tilly asked as he helped him get up.

'Yep, am now.' Ryan didn't bother with a shirt; too hard to get one on with one arm out of action. Instead he headed to the kitchen where the smell of coffee called to him.

'Is Jaz …' he said glancing around his house.

'No, I sent her home. Said I'll let her know when you woke up.'

Ryan nodded. It was probably a good thing. Now he could talk to Tilly with ease.

They took their full bowls to the table, Tilly carrying Ryan's strong coffee as he tried to get comfortable. Unsuccessfully. Ryan found that all the muscles affected by the bullet hole stretched across his chest to places he never thought possible. Everything ached, but the painkillers would help. Until then, he scoffed down his meal.

'So,' said Tilly, clearing his throat after he cleared his bowl. Ryan had finished his second lot already and was enjoying his coffee.

'So, I guess you want to know how it's going with the Sesha Serpents?' Jameson was the man they believed to run the Serpents, a group that were holding Taylor's dad to ransom for information from the Police to head off any drug raids. Only they just had to prove it and for that to happen Ryan was having to work his way in to his inner circle.

'Yup. Got in good with the daughter?'

Ryan nodded. 'Yes, seems all good and solid for the moment. But I need something to happen to get her father's attention. Jameson is who I need to get into bed with.' Sleeping with Annaliese was just a part of his cover, his mission. It helped that she was a looker, but it was still just a job. Jaz flashed into his mind: her hair swept across his body, her nakedness pressed against his. Quickly he picked up his coffee and took a gulp, only to choke on it. Served him right for letting his thoughts wander where they shouldn't.

What had they been talking about? The mission, right.

Ryan's mission was to infiltrate the Sesha Serpents, an organised-crime gang that Jaz had helped link to Jameson. They were working on a hunch that Jameson was behind the gang, plus a prostitution ring, drug running and other sordid things happening in their city.

'So, as far as we know, Salvatore isn't involved with the SS?' asked Tilly.

'No, can't find anything to link them as yet. Maybe they work separately, maybe they don't even talk. They are possibly each other's competition. Salvatore seems to only be in the drug trade, so my focus has shifted to Jameson and the SS. Especially after they manipulated Taylor's father.'

'Getting to someone that high up in the police force isn't uncommon,' added Tilly.

'Yeah, but usually they just offer a bribe. They resorted to blackmail and even harmed Taylor to get his dad onside. Just shows that they won't let anything stop them getting what they want.'

Tilly scratched the dark stubble along his chin. 'That makes Jameson a very dangerous man. What are you planning?'

'I might need your help. I need to force a situation that makes me look good in her father's eyes.'

'I'm sure we can do that,' Tilly said with a conniving smile. 'I've also gathered some more information. I've been following each of the bodyguards you marked. It seems they all like to hang out at a bar on Charles street, not far from Jameson's place. Some of them even live together at a nearby flat, all ready for when Jameson needs them.'

'I've noticed when he's at home he has his house protection, and when he goes out he has another couple. He seems to stick with this, but on occasion I have noticed a few changes.'

'Gotta factor in sick days,' said Tilly with a laugh.

But it wasn't really a joke, it was very much the truth.

'Tell me more about this bar they hang at?'

Ryan listened and took on everything Tilly said, because his life could very well depend on it. Luckily the pills were starting to work; without the pain it was easier to concentrate.

'So, what's up with you and Jaz?' said Tilly ten minutes later and right out of left field.

Ryan shook his head, trying to keep up with Tilly's train of thought. 'Say, what?'

'The lovely sweet Jaz,' Tilly said with a lick of his lips, and waggled his eyebrows.

Ryan frowned. He was instantly annoyed.

Tilly smiled and pointed at him. 'Yeah, that.'

He'd been snookered. Tilly was too good at reading people, that's why he was still alive in this game after so long. Ryan shrugged. The alternative was to lie, but he wouldn't get away with that. Not with Tilly.

'I honestly don't know what it is, or how to explain it,' said Ryan eventually.

'Well, I have no words of advice, mate. My missus left me 'cause she thought I was too secretive and having affairs. Kinda hit the nail on the head, didn't she? Anyway, that's different to this. Jaz knows what we do, she's one of us now. It could work or it could be a major fuck-up and the Agency could rip you a new one.'

Ryan knew what he meant. He and Jaz were both at high risk of early death. Plus, the distraction of the attraction alone could be enough to get them killed. This was why the Agency had strict rules prohibiting personal relationships between agents. Sure, there was a bit of interagency 'blow off steam' sex, but that was never talked about. It was all okay if it was just that, sex. Nothing love related. Not that Ryan thought this was love. But what they did in that hippy Wicked van hadn't been just sex either. He'd been wanting it as much as he tried to push Jaz away, and even now he was thinking about it again. Wanting more. Not more sex, just more of Jaz. Warning sirens were going off, and so was his phone.

'Hey, sis,' he said after eventually finding it in the bathroom. He shot Tilly an eye roll.

Tilly picked up their plates and gave him some space.

'Don't "Hey sis" me, big brother. Didn't you get my messages? The wedding is in two weeks! Please tell me you will make it and that you're bringing Jaz? I need you there.'

'Calm down, Steph. I'll be there, I promise.' He hoped like hell he could keep this promise. If he ended up with a chance to go deep undercover he could very well miss his own sister's wedding. 'Do you need me to do anything?' He regretted asking when he realised he would be useless for a while in his state.

'Just turn up, Ryan, that's all I want. Just please be there.'

'I will. You sound a little stressed. Is everything going okay?'

'Oh, just the usual wedding crap. My dress still hasn't come back from the seamstress and there's a gastro bug going around. I don't wanna be sick on my wedding day, Ry.'

'Sounds to me like you need a day at the beach,' he said trying not to chuckle. It was nice to hear everyday problems; for the moment he could picture a simpler life, a life that being with his family brought. Except he'd chosen this life of danger, secrets and alienation for the greater good. He just hoped his family hung in there with him through all his absences.

'Wanna join me for a coffee one day?' she asked. 'You always make me feel better.'

'Sure, I'll give you a call when I'm free in a few days. How's that?' It was the best he could offer. He had to give enough time for his shoulder to improve and for a gap in his mission detail.

'Sounds great. All right, thanks bro. I'll talk to you then.'

'Love you, Steph.'

The phone went quiet. Maybe Steph was unsure of what she'd heard.

'Yeah, I love you too, Ryan.'

He could hear her smile through her words. Good. One lady made happy today. Now he just had to figure out what to do with Jaz. They had things to discuss, and he didn't mean their lovemaking.

For a moment he wondered if he should tell Tilly about Jaz's medallion that now was in the hands of Salvatore, but the more he thought about it the more he decided to keep it quiet. He needed to find out more first before any guesses were made. This was not something to chat lightly about.

'So, how are you going to explain the shoulder to Annaliese?' Tilly sat back at the table.

'I don't know. I have to try to keep my clothes on around her, or say I had a cancer cut out.'

'A big bastard at that.' Tilly glanced at the large white bandage. It was stained with blood and would need changing soon. 'It's probably the best explanation.'

Neither of them could think of anything else that would fit. Everything had to be plausible.

Since starting this mission, Pax had given Ryan a whole new identity. He had a flat in another suburb, which he spent time at in case anyone came looking. His name was Reece Lancaster, and Pax had created an online profile for him, one case of assault at a bar and jobs that all linked back to James, who could cover for him. And he had a fake sister, so he had cover texting-out coded messages if needed. Should anyone chase this sister up they would find Sandy, who was also an MTG agent. It could get complicated and you needed your brain switched on at all times. But Ryan had plenty of practice and he found the best way to cope was to pretend he was an actor and really get into the role of the character he was playing, almost to the point he had to believe this was who he was. Especially if he managed to get in with Jameson, then he'd need to go hardcore. Cut off all ties to his real life. One mission kept him undercover for nearly a year. His cover story for his family had nearly worn thin, but Tilly and Pax would send them the odd postcard from his 'travelling adventures'.

'So, do you want me to tell Jaz you're up and about? Or you wanna wait until we've cleaned you up a bit?'

Ryan wanted to see Jaz, but didn't think he should. He didn't want to encourage her, but it was just so damn hard. What he needed was to talk to James. 'Yeah, you can, but tell her not to come around. We need to wait for the dust to clear. Tell her to go on as normal for now and I'll be in touch when I can.'

Tilly raised his eyebrows but nodded.

'And I wanna see James. Have you heard if he's back in WA this week?'

'Yeah, should be in sometime soon. He has a meeting with the WA government about funding, so I hear. You wanna set up a meet?'

'Yep.'

He needed to ask him a few questions. With a bit of luck, James could shed some light on this whole Salvatore shemozzle.

CHAPTER 4

Jaz sat on the steps dusted in white sand, her knees pulled up so she could lean on them, and stared out at the ocean. The cars passed behind her on the road, mixing with the sound of the crashing waves but she didn't really hear either. Her eyes were glued on the horizon where the water seemed almost black, but what she was searching for couldn't be found out there.

This spot did bring her some peace, it felt familiar and comforting. She'd come here with Marcus a few times. He'd been her pretend boyfriend, a way to get inside his family home and seek out information on his criminal dad. But in the process, Jaz had grown to care for Marcus, a lot. She missed his company. But not even Marcus could give her the answers she'd been searching for, yet avoiding at the same time.

It had been nearly a week since Jaz and Ryan had escaped with their lives. And in that week she'd neither seen nor heard from Ryan. Sure, Tilly had told her he was fine and back at work but it didn't ease the hurt. Was he avoiding her because of what happened in the Wicked van? Was it more than that? Was Jaz just being oversensitive because she'd admitted to herself that she was in love with him? Had she overanalysed this much before they had sex? Was Ryan back-peddling, regretting being with Jaz?

She had so many questions, they were driving her insane.

Anna and Tay had noticed her mood and tried to be there for her, but Jaz felt like she was closed off in a tiny box. Not even sitting by the wide empty beach and endless ocean made her feel any freer. She couldn't seem to escape the confines of her own mind. It didn't help that they had mock exams coming up and she really needed to study.

'I thought I'd find you here,' said Anna as she sat beside her and held out a takeaway coffee cup.

Jaz blinked before turning to her friend. She was out of her school uniform and in jeans, thongs and a T-shirt that read $E=mc2$. Her hair was in a long plait over her shoulder.

The smell of the coffee wafted towards Jaz as she took the cup with a smile. 'Thanks, this is just what I need.' It tasted as good as it smelled.

They sat in unaccustomed silence for a while longer, waiting for the coffee to work its magic on Jaz. She was halfway through when her friend finally spoke.

'Do you want to start from the beginning?'

What would be the beginning, Jaz thought?

She exhaled slowly. 'We were camped in the sand dunes, set up like backpackers and I'd just gone to the beach to scout, but I was spotted by one of the men patrolling the beach waiting for the drums to wash up. So, I ran back to Ryan and … improvised.'

Anna's eyebrows shot up. 'Improvised?'

Jaz couldn't help the smile that grew as she remembered the shock on Ryan's face as she pulled off her shirt and began to kiss him. 'I figured if we were too busy getting "busy",' Jaz quoted the air, 'then the drug dealer wouldn't see us as a threat. He'd just put us down as some backpackers getting it off by the ocean. It was all I could come up with in that moment.'

'Good thinking. I wouldn't want to disturb someone going at it.' Anna cleared her throat. 'So … how far did you go?'

Jaz tried to keep the goofy grin from her lips but it was hard. Anna's eyes grew wider with each second of silence.

'No way,' she drawled out slowly.

'Yes, way. We kissed for a while but the guy was still watching us, Ryan could see the light from his cigarette. So, I figured we'd have to keep playing along. I undressed, and pretty soon we both forgot about that guy. He left at some point but neither of us knew when.'

'Oh my God. What was it like? Tell me, tell me!' Anna was gripping her arm in eagerness.

'Let's just say it was amazing, even though we were on a stakeout and quite possibly could have been killed by that man and buried in the sand dunes.'

'I know, who would miss backpackers, hey? You're so lucky.'

'To be alive or to be with Ryan?'

'Both,' Anna replied with a grin. 'So, it was amazing? Nice.'

'It was, but now I'm afraid he has my heart and it's going to get torn in two.' Speaking her fear was hard but a weight off her shoulders at the same time.

'Oh honey, I know Ryan cares for you.'

'But he doesn't love me. His work comes first and I'm afraid he regrets what we did. I don't want it to be awkward, he's still a friend.'

'Has he still not made contact?'

Jaz shook her head.

'Pax and I have been going over Ryan's papers. Pax has been showing me how to create a record, and all this other cool stuff. He gave Ryan a rap sheet, has him convicted of a few charges so he looks tough. His undercover name is Reece Lancaster.' Anna shrugged. 'It's crazy, isn't it? Knowing just what goes on. I feel like we've been living like zombies, programmed to live out the perfect life, but now it seems as if we're actually in an episode of *Alias* crossed with James Bond, just without the British accent and suits.'

Jaz laughed. Anna sure had a way with words. 'I know. But I'm so glad you guys are on this journey with me. Where is Tay, by the way? You two are joined at the hip lately.' She'd noticed at school that Taylor wasn't spending as much time with his cool mates; instead he walked with Anna to classes, which was new.

'Tay's at the gym, training. I think he's on a mission to get abs like Ryan's. Imagine that,' she said with a swoon. 'I think since we both started with the Agency, he's feeling a bit out of the loop at school and seems happy to hang with us. I'm not complaining, I love spending time with Tay. Even if it is just studying.'

'Studying what ... his body? You don't need to study,' Jaz said with a chuckle.

'Hey.' Anna sounded like she was going to protest but then changed her mind. 'Yeah, you're right. He *is* pretty fit.'

Jaz felt much better already. Why hadn't she opened up to Anna sooner? Maybe it was time to see Pax about her other issue. Jaz stood up, determined. 'I've gotta go see Pax, you wanna come catch up with Tay?' she said, wiggling her eyebrows.

'Sure, why not. Can I catch a lift? Mum dropped me off.'

As Jaz drove them to the gym in her Jeep Wrangler, Anna didn't stop talking about the catastrophe of having to rely on her parents to ferry her around. 'I wish they'd just let me get a car already. At this rate I'll end up with an army tank.'

Anna suffered from a bad case of protective parents syndrome. Jaz could only imagine what they'd do if they found out she'd started working with a secret government agency infiltrating and destroying bad guys. There weren't enough days left in Anna's life for the grounding she'd get.

At the gym, Jaz parked out the front and went inside in search of Pax. Tay was with Cody, another recruit who was a year older and looked like a surfie with a deep tan and bleached blond hair. They were fighting on the matt, red welts over both their bodies as they swapped blows. The rest of the gym was empty. Not even Bags was in the boxing ring teaching lessons. There were only the grunts and slaps of skin against skin as Tay and Cody sparred.

It was rather cool watching two good-looking guys fight. Jaz glanced at Anna, who was spellbound. 'You right here?'

Anna nodded without taking her eyes off the guys. 'Yep, good as gold.' She grinned.

Jaz headed off to the office, then into Pax's house until she found him in his 'special' room sorting out stuff.

'Hey Pax,' she said entering. It still felt funny finally being in this room, when her whole life it had been locked up.

He looked over the rim of his glasses and put down the plastic sleeve he was holding for someone's ID. He was sweating but it was warm in this small room with all the computers and fancy printers.

'Am I interrupting work?' she asked.

'No, no this can wait. What's up? You look serious. Is everything okay?' said Pax as he rubbed his arm.

Jaz shut the door behind her and sat on the spare computer chair, which was now Anna's. 'Yeah, I have a few questions actually.' Jaz felt her heart begin to race. No wonder she'd put this off all week. She was scared, so scared her hands were shaking.

Pax slid his chair closer and took her hands. 'What happened? Is it Ryan? The mission?'

Jaz took a deep breath to try and settle her nerves, she could see Pax was now just as agitated, sweat beaded along his brow and his face seemed pale.

'No, as far as I've heard Ryan is fine and back at work.' Jaz managed to suppress the shiver that threatened when she thought of Ryan 'at work' with Annaliese. 'He's healing well, so Tilly reckons. This is more to do with the operation towards the end, when we followed the drugs to Salvatore De Luca's airplane hangar.' Jaz watched Pax carefully. The corner of his eye was twitching and his hands let go of hers as he sat back. His eyes darted across the room. Anywhere but at Jaz.

'Oh. What happened then?' he said softly.

She knew Anna would have already given him the rundown of events, but not even Anna knew about the necklace. 'We were made to kneel on the plastic. We were about to be shot point blank. Then my medallion swung free. Salvatore reached for it and asked me if I believed in God.'

Pax's bottom lip quivered as a drop of sweat ran down the side of his face. Jaz didn't like where this was going but she couldn't stop now. Like a detective, she needed to know more, even if it was life shattering. Even if it was her worst nightmare come true. Even if she could never go back to the way it was. She needed answers.

'Then something strange happened, Pax. He read the engraved name on the back. *Salvatore*. My father's name and his medallion. I thought maybe he'd laugh at having the same name, but instead he demanded to know where I got it from. Then it went a little crazy with gunfire as we made our move but I recall Salvatore saying that it was his medallion. *His medallion.*'

Jaz could remember the tone of his words, almost disbelief and shock, and how his brow creased as he stared at her medallion in his hand. It had only been seconds but she knew his reaction was not faked. He truly believed it was his. And if it was … Jaz shivered and continued with her painful question. 'Pax, there is no possible way that my biological father is the same Salvatore De Luca, is there?'

Pax had gone paler and looked like he was holding his breath, which just made Jaz feel even worse. But she needed to hear it from Pax, so she kept going. 'Because, as we were running from the hangar, his men had an opportunity to shoot us but Salvatore stopped them. Why would he do that? Unless that medallion really was his and it had him rattled. Pax, you know all about Mum, you helped her hide, you know her story and I'm betting you know who my real father is, don't you?' Jaz was just about out of breath when she finished. She'd also realised over this past week that Pax had overreacted when she first mentioned she'd run into Salvatore at the casino on a mission. Was that because he knew she'd just met her real father? It made sense Pax would know all her mum's secrets.

Her heart was in her throat and she felt as shitty as Pax looked. Only, now she realised Pax was pulling a funny expression, then a gasp escaped his lips right as he slid sideways to the floor.

'Pax,' Jaz yelped and dived down for him, and just managed to catch some of his weight before his head smacked the floor. 'Pax, are you okay?' His eyes were wide and she could tell he was in pain. She thought about the sweating, rubbing his arm, being so pale. Maybe it wasn't from her questions. 'Are you having another heart attack?'

He didn't reply but Jaz was already reaching for her phone while opening the door and screaming out for Anna. 'Hurry, it's Pax!'

Anna came running in seconds later, with Tay and Cody on her heels.

'What's happened ...' Her words died away as she saw Pax on the floor. 'Oh my God, Pax.' It came out as a squeal.

'Make him comfortable, I'm calling triple zero,' said Jaz, just as the operator came on the line. 'Yes, I need an ambulance,' said Jaz and answered all the questions as best she could and then did as instructed while they waited for the ambulance.

'This is déjà vu,' mumbled Jaz. Pax. Heart attack. In this same room.

Tears rolled down Anna's cheeks. Last time it had just been Jaz; Anna had been spared the horror of watching someone she loved struggle for life, but now they were all here. Anna stayed by his side, holding his hand and talking to him.

'It's okay, Pax. They're coming, you'll be fine.' Anna lifted her gaze to Jaz and her green eyes pleaded with her. *He will be fine, won't he?*

'Pax is tough as old boot leather, he'll be all right,' she said, but Jaz wasn't sure who she was trying to convince. 'I can hear the ambulance. I'll go show them in.'

The ambulance crew were methodical and before long had Pax on the stretcher, wheeling him out to the bus. Cody put his hand on Jaz's shoulder; it was comforting, so she allowed it. He called out, 'Hang in there, Pax.'

'Can I go with him?' Anna asked the female officer who was about to shut the doors.

'Um, are you family—'

She didn't get to finish her reply as the other officer who sat in the back with Pax yelled out: 'Cassy, need help here!'

'Oh my God,' cried Anna, her hand shooting to her mouth as she watched the man start compressions on Pax's chest.

Tay put his arms around her and she leaned into his chest, trying to shield her view but still watching from the corner of her eyes.

The ambulance officers worked together before Cassy undid Pax's shirt and they used the defibrillator on him.

'Oh shit,' mumbled Cody.

His grip on Jaz intensified but it didn't hurt. Right now she couldn't feel anything, just numbness mixed with disbelief. The ambulance lights were flashing while they worked on Pax. Jaz felt like time had stood still as they watched. Her heart was in her mouth and she wasn't sure when she'd last taken a breath.

'Okay, we've got him,' said the male officer as he leaned back. 'Let's go,' he said to Cassy.

Cassy nodded and her short blonde hair fell into her eyes before she moved to the back of the ambulance. Jaz finally took a breath, and realised she was almost gasping and felt faint. She also realised that Cody was holding her up, his arms tightly around her waist. When did that happen? She wanted to step out of his embrace, but would she be able to stand without him?

Cassy told them which hospital she was taking Pax to and then drove off with the sirens blaring. Anna hadn't asked to ride in the back again. Seeing Pax brought back to life had been a shock for all of them.

Jaz glanced at Anna now. Taylor was holding her tightly as silent tears trailed down her face. Taylor's head was tucked close to Anna's and he looked just as gutted. Neither of them had any answers, or words of support. It was all just shock.

Jaz stepped away from Cody and breathed deeply. Someone had to take the lead.

'What are we waiting for? Let's follow that ambulance.'

CHAPTER 5

RYAN SUPPRESSED HIS grimace as Annaliese tugged on his arm, not enough to damage the wound but enough to pull at the sore area.

'Come on Reecie, Daddy doesn't like to be kept waiting,' said Annaliese as she shot him a bright red lipstick-covered smile.

She was a very pretty woman, shapely, long legs, extra cleavage if you were into the fake kind and always was made up to perfection. Maybe a little too much. High-maintenance, with expensive taste in clothing and accessories. Probably why her daddy was in the crime business, to keep his daughter happy and fund her lavish lifestyle.

How Annaliese could walk so fast in her amazingly high black heels he didn't know, but she pulled him into the restaurant on Seventh Street. Deorro's was an upmarket place with designer meals. It was one of her favourites and she often had dinner here with her father. But this was the first time Ryan, aka Reece, had ever been invited. This was big.

Sure, he'd met her father, Jameson, a few times but only in passing as Annaliese introduced him as her boyfriend. This time was different. Ryan had told Annaliese he was looking for work, and just as he hoped she suggested her dad might have something for him. At the moment he had Annaliese hooked around his finger. He just needed to keep her interested enough to keep him around.

'Oh, there he is,' she said, waving to a man sitting alone by the back wall in a dark grey suit with white accents.

But he wasn't alone. Ryan counted two bodyguards, maybe three. Two guys sat at a nearby table and another man sat alone at another. They were in suits but looked the bodyguard type, with extra muscle, thick necks and darting eyes. Ryan also checked for exits, escape routes plus anything else that might help in case something came up.

'Hi Daddy,' said Annaliese, giving her father a hug and kiss. 'You remember Reece?'

'Mr Figlomeni,' said Ryan, shaking his hand firmly. He had to make an impression, and what better way than that.

'Reece, nice to meet you again. Sit. I've already ordered a bottle of wine,' said Jameson.

He was a tall, lean man whose chunky silver jewellery only added to the superior impression. He was a man who thrived on power, his head always held high, as if he looked down his nose at all those under him, and his dark eyes seemed to take everything in, just like Ryan had when he first walked in. This was a fierce opponent, one many had tried to catch out for years. He was cunning, clever and not to be outwitted. Ryan had to tread very carefully here and come across as real as possibility. He had to match strength for strength.

Ryan played it cool, ordering and then letting Annaliese take the stage with her ramblings of her life of parties, friends and social moves. Much to his credit, Jameson listened intently to her chatter, a besotted father indeed. Good to know. Ryan had learned that when Annaliese's mother died when she was six, Annaliese became his life – outside his crime business, and Ryan had yet to discover exactly how much she knew about that. All this would come out in time. Some undercover missions could be years in the planning. Ryan was lucky Jameson had a daughter who was easy to please.

'So Reece, Annaliese tells me you're out of work?' said Jameson halfway through their mains.

Ryan dabbed at his lips with the napkin, taking a moment to gather himself. It was batter up. 'Yes, I'm trying to get a job as a bouncer in the meantime until something better comes up.'

Pax had worked hard on making sure his past jobs, past employers, all matched up and all numbers worked should anyone ever check up. Ryan guessed that Jameson would have done a background check on Ryan the moment he started dating his daughter. So, it had been imperative that the details were right from the very start.

'What work are you looking for?'

'At the moment, something to pay the bills, but I'm after a well-paying job in security, preferably, as that's where I've worked before. I have a keen eye for trouble, so I'd like to stick with that. I know something will come up. In the meantime I'm not adverse to doing the small jobs. But I'd like to find something good soon because my lovely lady here deserves to be spoilt, and this is her favourite restaurant,' said Ryan. He hoped he'd played his cards right. Not too desperate, yet keen.

Jameson raised a bushy eyebrow. 'My Annaliese does have good taste and she does deserve the best.' He gave her a wink.

'Daddy, do you have anything for Reece? Anything to keep him going until work comes up?' Annaliese tilted her head and smiled, as if curling him around her little finger.

Jameson nodded. 'I'll have a look around, I might be able to find something to keep you out of trouble.'

Or put me into trouble, thought Ryan. 'Thanks, Mr Figlomeni, I'd appreciate that.' Ryan wasn't going to beg, or sound to desperate or overly keen. Play it cool, he reminded himself.

Jameson dipped his head in acknowledgement. He appreciated the formal way Ryan addressed him. Which was no fluke: Ryan had heard his bodyguards and workers call him the same when he first started gathering intel, no nicknames or informal names were used. Jameson obviously liked the respect.

They continued on with their dessert, and it was after their plates were scraped clean that Jameson pulled out his phone. 'Yes, Mr Tyson, bring the car around please.'

His bodyguards moved the moment Jameson got up. Not suddenly, but slowly and protectively yet still looking like they were going about their own business.

'Do you have to go already?' said Annaliese, standing up and reaching for her father.

'I'm sorry, honey. I still have some work to tend to. But it was lovely to see you. I'll go fix up the bill and then you can walk me out.'

'Thank you for dinner, Mr Figlomeni. Next time it'll be my shout,' said Ryan. He hoped to imply a few things: one, that he didn't want to be a freeloader and two, that he was man enough to pay for his girlfriend's dinner.

Jameson studied Ryan and then nodded. 'You look like a man of your word. I'd like that.'

They waited while Jameson paid and then they headed for the door.

Outside it was dark, the streetlights illuminated the road verge, along with the fairy lights around the restaurant's front windows. The bodyguards stationed themselves around Jameson, but at a few metres distance as they waited for the car to arrive.

'Can we do this again soon, Daddy?' asked Annaliese.

'Hey sexy lady, I'll do it with you,' came a shady voice behind them. A scrawny man wobbled closer smoking a cigarette.

Annaliese ignored him. The bodyguards tensed, but none of them moved.

'Bugger off, mate,' said Ryan, stepping closer to Annaliese, trying to shield her.

The drunk pulled a face. 'What, can't I talk to the pretty lady? She might prefer to come home with me,' he said, and shot out a hand, grabbing Annaliese's wrist.

Annaliese squealed, and before anyone else could blink Ryan elbowed the drunk, splitting his lip, and yanked his hand away from Annaliese, jerking it up hard behind the drunk's back and steering him down the road as the drunk tried to stop the blood running from his face while he cursed.

Ryan didn't risk a glance at Jameson, he just hoped he was watching.

'Time for you to head home.' Ryan gave him a big shove. Then he stepped back to Annaliese's side, reaching for her arm to caress it. 'You okay, baby?'

Her father had stepped closer to her, his brow creased and his body rigid as if on alert.

Annaliese hugged his side. 'I am now.'

Jameson's car arrived, a black Jaguar in the latest model, and the driver got out. 'Sorry, Mr Figlomeni, the traffic,' he stammered as he opened the back door.

Jameson glanced up the quiet road before turning to Ryan. 'How does being my driver sound? You're on call and get paid well. It would be handy having your expertise as well,' he said.

Ryan could see the current driver tilt his head in confusion, not sure what all this meant. Ryan lifted his head and squared his shoulders. 'I'd be honoured, Mr Figlomeni.'

'Oh Daddy, thank you,' said Annaliese hugging him. 'It's just until Reece can find something more permanent. Maybe you could work your way up in Daddy's business?' she added while squeezing Ryan's arm.

Jameson turned to his driver. 'Consider this your notice and last day.' He swung around to the nearest bodyguard. 'Mr Randall, please see to it that Mr Lancaster is ready for work tomorrow and that this dipshit moves on.'

Mr Randall nodded his large head, which sat on his thick tree-stump neck. 'Yes, sir.'

'Bye sweetheart.' Jameson kissed her and then shook Ryan's hand again. 'I'll see you tomorrow.' With a nod, he got into his car, a bodyguard each side, while Mr Randall stayed behind.

'Can I get your details, Mr Lancaster? I'll get Miss Naree to load you up on the payment system early tomorrow morning and ring you with all the details about work. Mr Figlomeni requires you wear a black suit at all times.'

'That won't be a problem.'

Mr Randall nodded again as he entered Ryan's number into his phone. 'I'll be in touch shortly.' Then he got into a black Commodore that had just pulled into the space Jameson's car had vacated.

'Bye, Randy,' said Annaliese with a wave. 'Wow, what a night,' she said, turning to hug Ryan. 'I knew Daddy would help with a job. I know it's just a driving job, but Daddy takes all the positions seriously. If you want to, babe, I know he'd make you head of security eventually, or at least second under Randy. Randy's been with him for a long time.'

Ryan brushed a strand of her hair back and tried to ignore the swell of cleavage that was pressed against his chest and threatened to burst from her blue dress. 'Yes, you were right. I know I can work my way up. I'll show your father how loyal I am.'

'He will love you like I do soon enough,' she purred into his ear. 'Let's go clubbing.'

'I'd love to, babe, but I want an early night. I start with your father tomorrow, remember. Got to be at my best.'

Annaliese pouted her lips. 'But the girls are going and I said I'd meet them.'

'You can still go, baby.' Ryan kissed her lips softly.

'Hmm, you tempt me so. Can we catch up tomorrow night?'

'Of course,' he said, tucking her into his side as they walked to his car. It was a Holden Statesman, black with all the paperwork leading to Reece Lancaster.

Ryan dropped Annaliese at her friend's place and then he headed back to his little flat. As he got out of his car, he walked to the bottle shop just down the street and browsed the aisles. When he saw Tilly enter the shop, he headed into the back fridge for a carton of beer. Tilly approached soon after.

He was in different clothes to earlier but nothing could hide the strips holding his bottom lip together. 'Shit, Tilly, sorry about that,' said Ryan out the corner of his mouth as he pretended to search through the beer selection.

'Na, mate, you did good. Better to make it real. Did it work?'

'A treat. Got the driver gig. Start tomorrow.' Ryan glanced at him and couldn't help feel a little bad about Tilly's lip, but it had to be done and it had to be convincing. But that wasn't the only thing about Tilly's face that worried him. There was something unusual in his eyes he hadn't seen before. 'What's up?'

'I hate to tell you like this, but … Pax is dead.' Tilly picked up a carton of beer, keeping up appearances. 'I'll get more info to you when I can. Sorry, mate.' Then he walked out.

Their exchange happened quickly and anyone who'd been watching would have thought nothing of it. Even though there was no one in the back beer fridge with them, they still played it safe. Ryan had his carton of beer and walked out, but it took every effort not to stumble as Tilly's words rattled through his head.

Pax is dead.

Surely not. Ryan's mind whirled, spinning forth arguments that proved Tilly must be mistaken, must have it wrong.

Like a robot, he had to walk out calmly and pay for his beer then walk to his flat, but inside he was a mess.

He made it back to his second-storey flat. It was a nice two-bedroom place with a grey-and-white theme throughout with red accents. Ryan put the beer on the table, opened it and stored two six-packs in the fridge, then turned on the TV before closing the black blinds on the windows. He undressed and went for a shower, and it was only then that he let the emotion come. Only then that he let in the thoughts of how this news would affect them all, at the Agency, at the gym. His heart ached as he thought about Jaz. He knew how much Pax meant to her and her friends. And the worst thing was Ryan started his new job tomorrow, which meant he'd be under more scrutiny. No more going to his real home, no more going to the gym, no more seeing Jaz.

He was now deep undercover.

It was killing him already.

CHAPTER 6

Jaz sat in the waiting room, staring at the wall with posters telling her to check her poo and to feel her breast and other helpful things, but where was the one about how to cope after a death? The one that kicked her in the stomach was the one that read, 'How to tell if you're having a heart attack'. She'd read it five times now, and each time that sinking feeling grew worse as she realised the signs were right in front of her but she'd been so worried about her own problems, her own scary thoughts, that she didn't see Pax struggling right in front of her.

It wasn't the only thing rolling around in her mind, though. Had she caused this heart attack? Was it her fault Pax was dead?

'Jaz, are you okay?' Cody touched her shoulder. 'You've been rocking like that for a while.'

The concern in his voice made her take note, realising she was indeed rocking back and forth on the white plastic chair. She sat still and then felt weird, as if she needed the movement to keep her mind busy and off the real problem.

Pax was dead.

After seeing the ambulance officers revive him, they all headed to the hospital with hope, only pausing long enough for Cody and Taylor to throw on their shirts. They all expected to see him in the bed draped in white sheets and hooked up to all sorts of monitors, much like last time. Expect this time they were greeted with a nurse, who immediately went to fetch the doctor.

Anyone who says, 'I'll just get the doctor,' and can't tell you themselves or lead you to the patient's room, sets off alarms. All four friends had looked at each other nervously.

The doctor came before their parents did. 'Are you family?' he'd asked.

'I'm his granddaughter. Is he okay?' Anna had said, bottom lip quivering.

He'd cleared his throat and clasped his hands together. 'Mr Johnson's heart stopped again in transit. The ambulance officers did their best and we continued to work on him when he arrived, but I'm so sorry to say we couldn't get him back.'

Anna had let out a sob then, and that had ripped through Jaz's heart more than the doctor's words had. As if it was more final because Anna believed it.

'He's gone?' Taylor had asked. Needing that clarification. Needing longer for it to all sink in.

Even now, as they sat waiting for their parents to arrive, Jaz still was struggling with the notion.

Pax is dead. Pax is gone. Pax will no longer greet her at the gym. Coffee and pastry will never be the same. The Ring will never be the same.

Anna was still crying, quieter now as she was wearing out, but her sobs and jerky breaths still remained. Taylor hadn't let her go and tears lined his face also. He too was staring at the wall with all its pamphlets. Cody had been pacing the length of the room; occasionally he'd come and sit beside Jaz before pacing again. He'd notified James but none of them had the heart to tell their family what had happened since arriving at the hospital. It wasn't something you texted or told over the phone.

She realised Cody was sitting there now, still waiting for an answer to his question. What had he asked? Was she okay?

No.

No, she wasn't. Her mouth wouldn't open, it seemed her whole body didn't want to function properly. She forced her head to move from side to side.

No, she wasn't okay.

Cody reached up and wiped at her face with a tissue before holding it out for her. Had she been crying?

Jaz took the tissue and found her face was wet and her nose was running, and with a few swipes the tissue was a wet ball in her hand.

'Girls, girls, how is he?' said Anna's mum as she rushed into the waiting room.

'Oh Mum,' said Anna, leaving Taylor's arms and launching against her mum's tall lean body.

Fresh tears and sobs started again. Lenore hugged her daughter fiercely but her green eyes shot to Jaz. Probing for answers no one wanted to give.

Jaz yet again could only shake her head.

'Oh my God. Oh my God,' said Lenore.

While Lenore and Anna wept fresh noisy tears, Jaz went back to rocking on her seat and studied the poo chart again. That was until her mum and Paul came in. Tash still in her office clothes, blonde hair in a high bun and blue eyes bright. Paul was in his work clothes too; he hated suits and much preferred a knitted jumper with his shirt and tie.

They rushed to her and sat either side. Cody went back to pacing to give them some space and Jaz was relieved when Lenore broke the news to them.

'He didn't make it this time, Tash. They couldn't save him. Pax is gone.' Lenore's green eyes were half-red, bloodshot and glossy.

'No. I can't believe it.' Tasha shot up from the chair.

'Love, what are you doing,' said Paul, who, Jaz suddenly realised, was holding her hand and rubbing gentle circles against her skin. When had he started that?

'I need to see him. I need to see him for myself.'

Jaz's mum stood strong, and for the first time Jaz could see the agent she used to be. The strength that radiated through her was unlike anything she'd ever seen from her before. Even if she was in a grey pants suit and black high heels. Spinning on said heels, she strutted out on a mission.

Everyone gaped at each other. Did they too feel as if there was some hope that Pax was really alive? If Tasha didn't believe it, then maybe it wasn't true.

They hadn't seen his body. What if there was a mix-up?

Jaz heard raised voices down the corridor and Paul stood up. 'Oh no.'

'I demand to see him.'

Yes, it was her mother's voice.

'We better go get her,' said Paul, pulling her up off the chair.

Jaz followed him along the corridor towards where they'd heard Tasha's demands.

They found her in Pax's room, her body flung over his. Jaz found herself studying Pax's face. It was as if he were simply sleeping. She itched to go and shake him awake. Except if her mum's body weight and crying didn't wake him, nothing would.

Tasha got up and kissed Pax's forehead. 'Thank you, Pax. Thank you for everything. I owe you my life,' she whispered as she wiped back tears.

But Jaz heard her mother's words and she knew exactly what Tasha meant, even if Paul didn't. Jaz stepped closer as her mum joined Paul. Jaz studied Pax's face, so at ease even his wrinkles seemed less defined. Jaz wanted to go and hold him but she was scared. Scared of how he would feel without a heartbeat, without the flow of blood in his veins. Would he be cold?

She couldn't do it. Instead she backed out of the room after her parents. 'I'm so sorry, Pax. I'm so sorry.'

They had all gone back to Jaz's place for a strong coffee. Anna and her family only lived a few houses down, so it was going to be one house or the other. Seeing as Anna's dad was still stuck at work for another hour, they came to Tasha's.

Paul was working their coffee machine, Simon was topping the coffee with lots of chocolate, Tasha was pulling out chocolate biscuits, slices and whatever else she had in the fridge until the table was full. Everyone sat around the long jarrah table, staring at the food, but no one reached out. Instead they sat there, eyes glazed over in silence.

Jaz stood between the table and the kitchen bench in limbo.

'Jaz, I'm gonna go check the gym is locked up properly and then I'm off home,' said Cody. 'But call if you need anything at all, hey?' His mop of blond saltwater-rinsed hair was knotted at the top of his head; it contrasted against his deep tan and black singlet. He wrapped his arms around her, pulling her tightly against his chest.

Jaz hadn't had this much contact with Cody ever, and the last time he tried to hit on her she'd dropped him to the ground. But now she found his hug comforting and realised that Cody had become a great friend to them all and had managed to join their little circle; or, more to the point, they had joined his. The Agency had brought them all together.

'You're not alone, okay,' he whispered.

Her body sagged against him, her arms went around his strong back as her head rested on his shoulder. In her mind it wasn't Cody who was comforting her, it was Ryan. Ryan's strong body holding her up. Ryan whispering soft words. But would Ryan even know? Could someone get a message to him? Would he be able to come to the funeral? She knew that the chances of her seeing Ryan would grow less likely the deeper undercover his mission took him. He'd be under closer scrutiny, and attending Pax's funeral would be too risky. Even trying to see Jaz would be risky, but in her mind she was dreaming of that moment when he'd come for her. But for now, Cody was as good as it got.

'You call me anytime, Jaz.' His lips were by her ear and his voice was tender.

'Thanks Cody. Thanks for checking out the gym. I can't ...' Her words fell away as she let him go.

'I know. I'll be around,' he said squeezing her shoulder, before heading out the door with a last goodbye to everyone else.

'Lenore, your coffee,' said Paul, as he placed a mug down in front of her while Simon brought Anna's and Tay's.

'Thanks Paul. I rang Jeffery, I forgot what time it was in America but this news couldn't wait,' said Lenore. 'He's going to book a flight home the moment we know the date for the funeral. It will be nice to have both my babies by my side again.' Lenore smiled at Anna.

Everyone nodded around the table. Jaz felt as if a bomb had just exploded and everyone was still shell-shocked and numb with pain. She didn't want to sit around the table and tell stories of Pax, and cry and laugh. Instead she turned and walked off to the stairs, up to her bedroom.

She grabbed the small photo album from the bottom drawer in her desk and went to her window, drawing back the dark curtains and unlatching the glass. Jaz climbed outside and sat just outside her window on the roof. It was night, most of the street was tucked up in bed, only the streetlights left up. Making herself comfortable, Jaz opened the album; the light from her bedroom was plenty to see by.

Two photos in and she found what she was looking for: a picture of herself in a white singlet, and resting around her neck was the medallion. Her father's medallion. She ran her finger over the photo. She knew every line, scratch and curve of that metal circle. It was all she had of her biological father and she'd clung to it like a queen to her crown. It would have killed her back then if she'd lost it.

Except now she had lost it but her gut twisted at the thought of getting it back. Did she want it back? Was it too tarnished? How could it hold the same value now?

Jaz flicked through a few more photos until she found one of Pax at the gym. He was down on all fours scrubbing the mats. A job that Jaz had taken on because she didn't like seeing him working so hard, especially at his age. This photo proved that Pax was a man who worked hard, had no airs or graces even though he came from a very wealthy family and had an inheritance that could see him living in a mansion, not a rundown house attached to a rundown gym. He'd been her grandfather figure, her inspiration, and her centre.

Jaz pressed her lips together as hot tears filled her eyes and spilled down her cheeks. She couldn't stop them now, even as she tried hard to control her breathing, but the more she looked at the photos of Pax at the gym the more she realised what she'd lost. She felt the big hole well up inside her like an abyss threatening to suck all the life from her.

If she hadn't have asked him about Salvatore and the medallion, would he still be alive? Pax hadn't had time to say anything, to answer her burning questions, and now he never would. Jaz was still no closer to knowing the full truth.

Deep down she knew that everything was too much of a coincidence. Yet it was like a war raging inside her mind; until she knew the truth, part of her would refuse to believe it was possible. It wasn't something she could go to her mum about without spilling the beans on the Agency. Her mum had fought so hard to give Jaz a safe, normal life, and she couldn't ruin that by telling Tasha she'd joined the same Agency. Maybe when she was older, but not now. Until then, Jaz would have to keep this secret. Maybe the only person she could talk to about it was Salvatore himself? Jaz shivered and drew her knees up. Was she mad?

The night was settling around her and the air was feeling crisper. How long had she been sitting out here?

Her album was closed but she could see Pax clearly in her mind. His smile, his soft eyes, his laugh a deep throaty chuckle. How long until those memories faded? How long until she'd be grasping at wispy threads of images? How long until life moved on without him?

CHAPTER 7

RYAN LEFT HIS flat, TV going and lights on, and went down to the secured parking below. The private parking meant only those with a card could get in – this way, he could leave a beat-up hatchback inside to drive out and hopefully not be followed or noticed if he was being watched. Now was one of those times he needed to escape the flat.

With his hat and sunglasses on, he sunk low into the driver's seat to give the illusion he was a very short person, and drove the yellow hatchback outside once the roller door opened. He drove around for a bit, doubled back, and checked he hadn't been followed, before making his way into the city to meet up with James.

He parked under the building then made his way to the office where Janice buzzed him in.

When Ryan entered James's office he found the Agency's Director sitting at his desk, his shirt sleeves rolled up to his elbows as he waded through paperwork. A lone chair sat opposite the large desk. The room was simple, with just one print on the wall. It looked like any normal office, except the paperwork James was looking through was a collection of information on suspects, drug shipments, trafficking of young girls and more. Not many people got to set eyes on what James saw, not even the Commissioner of Police, and only then if it was necessary.

'Ryan, grab a seat.' James sat back in his chair and stretched. 'Tilly said he told you about Pax?'

All hope that the news had been wrong vanished like a popped balloon. 'What happened, have you heard?' Ryan needed to know the full story.

'Jaz was with him when he had another heart attack,' said James.

Ryan drew in a shaky breath. Poor Jaz.

'He flatlined at the gym and the ambos brought him back, but by the time they got to the hospital he'd gone again and couldn't be revived.' James sighed heavily and rubbed his face slowly. 'I feel for those kids, they were all there, they all loved him, had grown up with him. It's devastating. Pax was here from nearly the beginning, he's been the glue that held this agency together. He'll be bloody missed.' James swallowed hard. 'I hate to say it, but it's lucky we brought Anna in when we did. Pax's expertise and knowledge is something that would have been hard to replace.'

Ryan nodded, trying to stay focused when his heart was racing. His mind was taken up with images of Jaz watching Pax suffer a heart attack.

'Looks like the funeral will be next week. I know you'd like to go but it's not going to be possible,' said James, holding up a hand as if he knew Ryan was about to protest. 'We're already taking a big risk to get you to your sister's wedding this weekend. Besides, we can't have all our people linked. Those of us who go will be undercover.'

'I know.' Ryan knew only too well but it didn't make it any easier. And James had pulled a lot of strings to get him out for Steph's wedding. He only had one sibling and if he didn't go to her wedding he'd regret it for the rest of his life – that, and Steph would probably kill him.

'So, it's all go with Jameson?' asked James.

He leaned forward, his blue eyes bright, and Ryan found himself lost in their resemblance to Jaz's for a moment. God, he missed her. He was so used to working with her, running into her at the gym, seeing her smile and the strength she radiated. She was a breath of fresh air in a musty stale room. She'd become someone special; he knew that, he'd been fighting it, but that night in the Wicked van had just about been his undoing. Jaz was even more delectable than he could have imagined. Even now he could still feel the soft mounds in his hands, the dip of her back down to the gentle curve of her backside, and that G-string! She'd surprised him.

James cleared his throat, waiting for an answer. Ryan shook the sweet memories from his mind.

He knew he had to distance himself from her. It had been hard, but jumping into this mission had helped. 'Um, yes. I've got my foot in the door thanks to Tilly. Now I've just got to do a good job and wait for my next chance to step up.' Ryan was aiming to get to bodyguard status. Driving

Jameson around was one thing, but being a guard would put him closer to the action and information. He had to be patient; it could take years and he had to prove he was loyal, which meant doing anything that was asked. Even kill. He hoped he didn't have to, but they were all prepared to do what was necessary to infiltrate Jameson's business and network.

'Um, James?' Ryan cleared his throat. 'While I'm here, I have a few questions about Salvatore.' Ryan didn't need to mention his last name, Sal was a well-known target.

'Sure, shoot.'

'What info do you have on him, like, before he came to WA? Who was working the De Luca case back then?'

James glanced at the photo on his desk. 'My sister, actually.' He kept looking at it as he spoke. 'Natasha was to get into the family home, and she did that by getting Salvatore's attention. He was young then, and from what Natty told me she believed him to be innocent. Tried telling me on many occasions, actually, that Sal didn't want to be like his father, nor did he want to join his business and even then I could tell that Natty cared for Sal. They say not to get involved, but when you're with someone for a long time during an op things can get a little blurry.'

'Yeah, we all know that too well.'

'You know, the main reason I came to Perth is because Sal did. After my sister went missing I just had a feeling it was because of Sal, and that Natty was hurt or that her cover was blown. I wasn't sure if it was Sal's dad, or whether Sal had been involved. So, when he suddenly moved, I followed. I watched him for a whole year, between my sister's disappearance and his move to WA. I saw a man suffering as I was, and I believed then that he truly loved my sister. At this stage I'd set up the WA agency and made a base so I could come and go and keep an eye on Sal, just in case Natty turned up. I half-wondered if Sal moved because he feared his own father may have done something, but I scratched that idea a few years later when intel started to come in that Sal had finally moved into the family business. He wouldn't have done that if he suspected his father of interfering with his relationship.'

'Right,' said Ryan as he tried to take all this in. 'Did Sal ever have any children? Any other women?'

James shook his head. 'No children that we know of, and the women have never been anything serious. I almost felt sorry for the man. Watching him grieve the loss of my sister was weird, and it was nice to know I wasn't the only one struggling. Maybe it was having Natty tell me about him and confide in me that made me feel for the guy; well, for a bit, until he started up business. If our parents had known about her affections for Sal they would have taken her out of that operation in an instant. Sometimes I wonder: if I'd told them, would she still be alive today?'

Ryan squirmed in his seat. The secret he kept was like an anvil in his lower intestines. His tongue burned with the desire to spill the beans and tell James his sister was alive and well. But it was not his secret to tell. Instead, he pushed on with another question.

'When did your sister go missing?'

James gave him the dates, and Ryan did a quick calculation. It fitted with Jaz's birthday, giving room for a few months that Tasha may not have realised she was pregnant or was deciding what to do. The more he learned of Tasha and Sal's involvement, the more it cemented the idea that Sal was, quite possibly, Jaz's father.

The room closed in on him as this finally sunk in. The man he hated, had been trying to take down since the killing of his mate Chris, was Jaz's biological father. It didn't sit right in his mind. But it explained Jaz's olive skin and dark hair, the same as Salvatore's. Ryan knew Jaz couldn't help who her father was, and he was sure she would be upset to learn the truth. Who would be happy to find out you had a drug lord as a father? Especially one you'd been trying to take down.

What a mess. Ryan's brain felt like it was going to explode. Especially as James was now talking him through the plan for his escape to his sister's wedding and who was in place to help.

For the first time in ages, Ryan felt like he was treading water and he feared that if he stopped he'd sink to the bottom like a bound body weighed with an anchor.

Somehow Ryan got through the next few days by focusing on the job at hand, which was being glued to Jameson's car and being where he was requested promptly. Jameson hadn't been anywhere new, just from his house to his warehouses and to meetings with clients and managers. Jameson was not one for idle chitchat, nor did he speak of his daughter during the work day, and Ryan remained quiet and professional unless Jameson spoke to him and required an answer. Friday night, when he dropped him home, Jameson shook his hand.

'Good job, Reece.'

'Thank you, sir.'

After Jameson walked to his house, Ryan doubled over clutching his stomach.

'You okay?' asked Jameson's bodyguard.

'I'm not sure, Mr Randall,' said Ryan, taking sharp breaths. 'I may have got gastro from my sister. I'm not feeling well at all.'

Mr Randall, whose first name Ryan was yet to learn, screwed up his face and took a step back. 'Will you be right for work tomorrow?'

Ryan shook his head. 'I don't know. Can someone fill in, just in case?'

'I'll get it sorted. Are you right to head home?' Mr Randall had inadvertently taken a few more steps back. To see the big man afraid was something new.

No one like a gastro bug. Not even a hard-hitting bodyguard.

'I think so.' Ryan stood up and breathed heavily. 'I'll make it.'

'Right. Let me know how you get on, Mr Lancaster,' he said before he walked off to check the perimeter of Jameson's house, which was his usual routine.

Ryan got back to his flat and called Annaliese to give her the same gastro story.

'I'm sorry, babe, I feel so sick. I've got it from both ends,' he said.

'Aw, honey. Do you need me to come over and look after you?' she offered, but he could tell from her tone she wasn't keen on the idea.

'No. I don't want to ruin your night out. I'll be fine. My sister's gastro only lasted a day or two, so I should be good by Sunday. Maybe we can catch up then if I'm better. I don't want to give this to you, Annaliese.'

'Are you sure?'

He could hear the relief in her voice. 'Yeah. I'll call you tomorrow and let you know how I'm going. I've gotta go, next wave,' he said with a groan.

'Bye baby, rest up.' Her tone was sincere.

Now the plans were all played out. He just had to wait until tomorrow.

In the morning he rang Mr Randall and informed him he was no better.

'You just stay there, Reece, and rest up. We've got Luke filling in for you today. Don't worry about a thing. Let me know Sunday if you'll be right for Monday.'

It was the first time Mr Randall had used his first name. 'Thank you, Mr Randall. I appreciate it.'

Next he called Annaliese, told her he was still violently sick and then let her tell him about her night and her plans for the day. He took note of what she was doing, just to make sure their paths wouldn't cross.

Then he put on his usual disguise and went down to the yellow hatch. He drove around until he was certain he wasn't followed, and then made his way to one of the safe houses. It was a simple brick and tile house that had seen better days. He wasn't at this safe house for long, instead he went right through it, out the back door. The yard was compact with a tiny garden shed along the back fence. Ryan entered this, shut the door behind him before moving the panel that allowed him to walk into the backyard of the house opposite. On his way through the small unkempt garden, he removed the hidden key from under the rock by the back door and entered.

It was another three-by-two red brick house, but it served the Agency's purpose. Ryan, out of habit, searched out the whole house before heading back to the main bedroom. Here, spread out on the double bed, he found the dark grey suit, black shirt and white tie for the wedding, a change of clothes, money, sunglasses, a card for his sister and his shoes. The bathroom was already kitted out with simple supplies, towels, toiletries. The other bathroom was filled with female supplies for the female agents. Each agency safe house was the same.

Ryan checked his watch. He had a few hours to himself and then he'd take all his stuff by taxi to his parents' place, where they would all get ready together.

There was a lot of double-checking, backtracking, watching the rear-view mirrors, and even then Ryan still was taking a risk he would be noticed, followed. But even if it seemed like overkill, he took every precaution. He found keeping his mind focused stopped it wandering to Jaz and the fact he would see her soon. Should he tell her about Salvatore? Had she already figured it out? How was she coping with Pax's death?

Ryan grunted at his own mental weakness and pushed the questions aside. He couldn't waste time wondering. Right now he needed to write down all the intel he'd gathered in the last few days. Soon enough he'd see Jaz.

CHAPTER 8

'JAZ, YOU LOOK absolutely beautiful,' said Tasha as she popped her head into her room. 'You just need a smile. Come on, Pax wouldn't want you to wallow.'

Her mum was right. Yet her smile was still absent.

Jaz stood by her full-length mirror, her silver halter-neck dress catching the light from the window and reflecting like shiny chrome on a car. Jaz had kept her hair down and her jewellery to a simple elegant silver necklace and hoop earrings. Her eyes were made up in a dark smoky look, lots of black and silver, eyeliner and mascara. She liked them like that, it seemed to fit her sullen mood. It seemed weird to be going to a wedding, enjoying new beginnings and happiness, when she was still dealing with Pax's death. His funeral wasn't until Wednesday.

Jaz didn't feel like going but she didn't want to disappoint Steph, and she also knew it might be her only chance to see Ryan. She had a gut feeling he'd chop off his right leg to make his sister's wedding.

'Do you need a lift, honey?' asked her mum, entering her room and putting her hand on her shoulder.

'No, I'm fine. Don't think I feel like drinking, but if I do I'll take a taxi home.'

Jaz leaned into her mum's shoulder and sighed like a vice had just pressed her lungs together.

'I know, Jasmine. I miss him too.'

Jaz headed to Crawley and pulled up outside the Matilda Bay Restaurant, the site for the wedding and reception. She climbed out of her black Jeep Wrangler and locked it. She felt a little out of place as she followed the blackboard signs pointing the way to the wedding. She didn't really know Ryan's sister especially well, and besides Steph, Steph's future husband, and Ryan and his parents, Jaz wouldn't know anyone at the wedding. She'd be the one standing awkwardly in the corner. For this reason she arrived just before Steph was due to appear. Already people were down by the Swan River, where views of the city skyline, Kings Park and all the boats and yachts on the river made for a stunning backdrop. Instead of a red carpet aisle, Steph had a white one over the lawn, with white fold-out chairs at either side now occupied by guests. Two large gumtrees, one either side of the aisle, framed the river view and blended with a few smaller trees at the back filled with round white paper lanterns. All the white echoed the white boats floating on the glassy water. Blue and white flower bouquets were tied to the chairs along the aisle, just enough blue to add some colour.

In the middle, waiting patiently, was Gazza, whose shaggy hair had been tamed and his dimples were like big craters with his nervous smile. He was chatting to his best man. Their soft grey suits, white shirts and blue ties were in keeping with the overall colours.

Jaz then remembered the blue dress Steph's friend and bridesmaid, Suze, had found when they'd gone shopping together. Suze, that would be another person Jaz almost knew.

She stepped closer to the crowd, her heels sinking into the lawn. She'd thought about flats, but she wanted something nice for when she saw Ryan. To be able to look into his eyes and see for herself if he was doing okay. Jaz was glad the crowd were all facing the river, but most kept looking back to see if Steph had arrived, and that's when she saw Ryan.

Her chest contracted and she almost gasped as her body was overcome with longing. His dark eyes met hers across the sea of heads and he stood up suddenly. He looked amazing in his fitted suit, but it was his face she couldn't look away from. They must have stood watching each other for what seemed like ages before his mum reached up, slapping his arm and saying something that sent Ryan striding down the aisle towards her.

Jaz could only watch as he came closer. She was so in love with him it hurt. Dark mysterious eyes that displayed his soul; she would never tire of them.

'Hey, Jaz. Was starting to think you weren't going to make it,' said Ryan, his voice husky and sexy. His eyes dropped down over her body, from the plunging V-line, fitted waist and split that opened up down the length of her left leg to her high silver heels, and then back up again.

She revelled in his appraisal and couldn't help but reach out to adjust his white tie, needing to touch him. 'Sorry, I didn't want to get here too early considering I don't know anyone.' She let go of his tie and flicked her lashes up towards him. Those dark eyes were swimming with emotions, with flicks of red and gold she tried to decipher. Did his shoulder still hurt? Was his mission going okay?

'How are *you* going?' she asked as she breathed him in. Her mouth began to water at the thought of kissing his neck and drinking in his scent. It was sharp and sensual.

Ryan looked over her shoulder and then reached for her elbow. 'Come, we've kept you a spot up with us.'

He led her past all the guests down the middle of the aisle, which was a little nerve-racking as people gawked at her wondering who she was. Music started up as they made the front row and Ryan's mum Kathy welcomed her. Gazza was too nervous to talk, he just shot her a wonky smile.

'Glad you could make it, Jaz,' said Kathy in a bright green mother-of-the-bride outfit that had maybe a little too much lacework on it.

Ryan sat on the empty seat on her right, sandwiching her in as if she were a part of their immediate family. Seeing as she was the only girl Ryan had ever brought home, maybe they thought she almost was. Ryan had set them straight, saying they were just friends, but had any of them really believed that? Jaz glanced at Ryan and found he'd been watching her. Could he tell? Was it all over her face? She felt her face glowing with the smile that was instinctual whenever he was near.

The crowd started 'oohing' and 'ahhing' as Suze made her way down the aisle in the afternoon warmth. The air was fresh and, for Jaz, saturated with Ryan. She was sure the gentle breeze was wafting his cologne purposely under her nose. Jaz turned to see Suze in a full-length pale blue strapless dress that fell in soft folds from under her breasts. Behind Suze came Steph, with her father Frank guiding her. He wore a smile from ear to ear as he watched his daughter with pride.

Steph wore a lace headpiece with a small beaded veil that draped over her curled hair. Her dress was a strapless beaded bodice with a soft falling skirt.

She looked radiant and was dabbing at her eyes with a tissue the moment she saw Gazza waiting for her.

Jaz sat through the ceremony and wondered if she would ever get married. With her life working for the Agency, would she be happy to marry and settle down? Maybe at some stage, but at eighteen it wasn't something she'd thought a lot about. However, as she glanced across to stare at Ryan's hands resting on his thighs, she couldn't help thinking she could easily spend the rest of her life with Ryan. His hands were strong and manly. She remembered them over her skin, holding her breasts, buried in her hair, holding her as he kissed her hungrily. Jaz swallowed as she tried to keep those memories at bay. Lifting her eyes, she found him watching her again. Her breath caught in her throat as those dark circles drew her in and exposed her. Did he know exactly what she'd been thinking? Had he been remembering it too? There was heat in his eyes, a desire she'd seen before and she so desperately wanted to kiss him, or even just hold his hand.

Ryan cleared his throat and shifted in his seat so he was almost facing away from her and watched the rest of the ceremony. Jaz felt the loss of his attention and shivered.

Frank gave away his daughter and came to sit with his family. Kathy moved up to the edge of the aisle with her camera clicking away, and Frank settled into the vacated seat next to Jaz.

'Don't you look lovely,' he said, leaning across to kiss her cheek.

In another ten minutes, Steph and Gazza (who was Gavin during his vows) were married, and everyone clapped and cheered.

Jaz stood back as everyone went to congratulate them, and in the end it was Steph who came to her with a hug.

'So glad you're here,' she said. 'I'll catch up with you later,' she added with a wink before they departed for photos.

Frank yelled over the crowd that drinks would be in the courtyard before the reception, and slowly everyone mingled across to the large building that had many windows to take full advantage of the river. The courtyard had been decorated with more round lanterns hanging from overhead lines, and tall cocktail tables were scattered about, with some extravagant white lounges off to one side giving people a choice of seating. Waiters brought around glasses of wine and beer, others with plates of finger food. Jaz reached for a glass, mainly because she felt like the red jelly bean in a bag of green ones.

Ryan was caught up chatting to a couple of pretty girls – Jaz hoped they were cousins – and Kathy and Frank were busy mingling with family and friends. So, against her previous statement, Jaz took a big sip of the wine and went for a stroll by the river.

She stopped not far from the water's edge and watched the way it lapped at the sand so gently. The water and the view had kept her entertained for the whole glass of wine; in truth, Jaz hadn't really seen any of it, just staring off into space. Lately she'd felt more like an outsider not really partaking in life. It all seemed too hard with Pax, Sal and Ryan all mixing up her emotions.

'Are you Ryan's girlfriend?' came a female voice.

Jaz turned to find not a woman but a girl, maybe around twelve. She had wavy blonde hair and wore a short blue dress.

'No, I'm just a friend. Why? Do you like him?' she asked teasingly.

The girl giggled. 'No, he's my cousin,' she said screwing up her face. 'Why are you standing out here all by yourself?'

'Well, because I don't really know anyone besides Ryan and Steph, and they're both busy.'

'You know me now. I'm Juliet. And that's my big sister Alison who's with Ryan.'

Ryan saw them glance across to where he stood with the girls. 'She's sixteen and my other sister Sam is eighteen. I'm the youngest.'

'Wow, lots of sisters. And you are all very pretty.' Jaz held out her hand. 'Hi Juliet, I'm Jaz. I only have a brother who's nearly fifteen. And thank you for coming to talk to me.'

Juliet smiled and shook her hand. 'Jaz, that's a cool name.'

'It's short for Jasmine,' came Ryan's voice behind them.

Instantly her body pulsed with adrenaline.

'What do you think of my friend, Juliet? Do you think she'll survive the night with our family?' Ryan put his arm around Juliet, giving her a gentle squeeze.

'I think so. She has me as her new friend. I'll make sure she's not left alone.'

Jaz smiled, she liked Juliet a lot already.

'All right kiddo, can you take this back to the table for me, I need to talk to Jaz if that's okay. I'll bring her back soon,' said Ryan, and he took her empty wine glass and gave it to Juliet. 'Thanks, squirt,' he added as she walked back to the courtyard.

'She's lovely,' said Jaz, watching her go.

'I think you have a new best friend. Sorry for leaving you alone. I've been trying to get away but my family haven't seen me in ages. You know, the same old story,' he said lightheartedly. 'Come for a walk?'

Jaz nodded and they headed away from the wedding party.

They walked in silence until they found a vacant bench by the river, not far from the boat ramp. After they sat Ryan turned to her, reaching for her hand, and Jaz begun to smile until she heard his words.

'I'm so sorry about Pax, Jaz. I can't imagine how hard it's been for you,' he said tenderly.

Jaz turned away and focused on a boat moving with the small waves. She couldn't afford to tear up now, not with all the eye make-up she had on. Closing her eyes, she revelled in the feel of his hand holding hers, the warmth it brought, almost electric. It gave her strength.

'I feel as though I killed Pax,' she whispered. It just came out; her innermost thoughts, which she'd kept buried from everyone else, just gushed from her when Ryan was near. He was the only one she could share this with and until she'd spoken the words she didn't realise how much they'd been weighing her down.

'What are you talking about, Jaz? James said it was a heart attack.' He tugged at her hand, making her look at him. 'Tell me.'

'I,' Jaz paused. If she said the rest out loud, did it make it true to some degree, and what would Ryan think about her when she told him about Sal? Would it change their relationship? Would he see her differently? Should she risk it?

'Spit it out, Jaz. I want to help.'

How could she argue with that? But still she couldn't help feel that this conversation would change things. 'I asked Pax about Salvatore. I told him how he took my medallion and how Sal thought it was his.' Jaz thought she'd just better blurt out the whole lot at once and rip that band aid off. 'I then asked him if it was possible that Sal was my father. I don't know if it was talking about Sal that set off Pax's heart attack or maybe he was already having one when I got there, but the thing is I didn't realise he was struggling. I was so caught up in my own problems, my own stupid thoughts about where Salvatore, the medallion and I fitted in, that I didn't see the signs. I should have, Ryan, maybe I could have saved him.' Jaz struggled with the last sentence, felt the big beach ball working its way up her throat, turned away and blinked rapidly.

'No, don't think like that, Jaz. You know it won't bring him back. Damn.'

She turned back to him when he swore. It confused her, but he looked even more confused; actually, he seemed torn. But she wasn't sure over what. Maybe he did want to hug her, just not in public? He took his hand away and all of a sudden she felt a chill spread over her skin.

'Jaz, I went and saw James the other day. Mainly for work but while I was there I asked him about Salvatore.'

Her eyebrows shot up. This she wasn't expecting. Why would Ryan do that? 'Why? What did you say?'

'After what Salvatore said about your medallion I couldn't get it out of my head, so I asked James about your mum.'

Jaz squirmed on the seat. Just talking about this made her so uncomfortable, especially knowing it had been bothering Ryan also. 'And?' she prompted.

'He told me that your mum's last mission had been to get inside the De Luca family and she did this through Salvatore. He said that your mum ended up caring for him and that she believed he was a good guy stuck in a bad family. Then she went missing. Jaz, from the time she went missing and you were born is about nine months.'

His words hung in the air like storm clouds about to hail. Eventually she spoke. 'So, you also think Sal is my real dad too.'

'You do have similarities, and it all fits. Why else would your mum run away to give you a better life? She didn't want anyone to know about you, not Sal in case his family controlled you, nor her own family for what they'd think. Maybe she was worried they'd make her terminate the pregnancy? If what James thinks is true, then she did love him, but not enough to leave the Agency.'

'So, instead she left them all.'

'All for you,' he added.

'So, the guy everyone has been trying to catch, the Agency's work, the man who killed your best friend, could very well be my father.' Her words were spat out a little harshly but she was feeling angry. Angry that something so major was kept from her. Angry that this could change her life and angry that it would change the way Ryan felt about her. 'How can you stand to even look at me knowing that?' She tried not to bite her lip too hard.

'Jaz.' He said her name as he ran his hand over his head. 'Don't be like that. You are nothing like him. You can't take on his errors just because you might be related. It doesn't work like that. You are still the amazing you.'

'Then how come you've been avoiding me,' she whispered as she felt her anger drain away and her fears come crawling into its place.

'I haven't,' he said unconvincingly. 'I've been busy.' He glanced around for any close-by ears but they were alone. 'I was lucky to make it here today, Jaz. I'm deep undercover now, Jameson has given me a job as his driver and the next step is to continue to work my way in. I'll be off the grid for ages, months, maybe even years, however long it takes. You know that.'

Yeah, she did and it sucked rotten eggs. She felt like a two year old, a tantrum wanted to erupt from her but she held it in along with her frustrated tears.

'I won't even be able to communicate with you, let alone anyone else. I was actually hoping you could help cover with my family, especially Steph. I've told them all I've got a job on a cruise ship in security and that will get me to Peru where I'll trek up to Machu Picchu. I figured it's somewhere off the beaten track where I'm unreachable. I've written a few postcards, they're in my house. Can you post them off every few months?'

She couldn't very well say no, could she? Here he was, trusting her with his family and his secret. Surely that wasn't all just work related? But she could feel him slipping away. Already his mind was on his job and she knew what he was implying.

I'm going to be away for a while, I may not come back, there is nothing for us. Well, she added the bit at the end but she was sure that's what he meant. The wall he was building between them was getting higher and higher, as if he'd become a skilled brickie overnight. The space beside her was feeling cold and empty and she craved for his warm hands but they stayed by his side.

Taking in the strong line of his jaw, his full lips and up to his eyes, she tried to memorise it all. She knew the risk he was undertaking and that tonight could be the last time she ever saw him. It made her want to throw herself at him, sob uncontrollably and refuse to let him go. But she didn't.

'Of course I'll do that.' And her heart was breaking with every word. 'Please be careful.'

CHAPTER 9

RYAN WAS MESMERISED by Jaz's eyes – always had been and always would be – but today with the dark make-up she was looking hauntingly beautiful. The pain of losing Pax was still fresh in her eyes, the sadness pulled at his chest, as well as a mingling of other emotions. He could tell she'd been battling with the thought of Salvatore as a father. He still didn't have his head around it and he wasn't personally affected like Jaz.

Seeing her turn up at the wedding, he thought he'd be prepared, he thought he was right in his mind, but he was nowhere close to control. She'd stolen his breath, his mind, his body. No woman had ever done that to him. Even now, sitting beside her was hard. He felt like a raging teenager as he battled to keep it on lockdown.

He'd just told her that he was going deep undercover, he could be away for ages and she knew the risk, knew it could well be the last time they saw each other, and her reaction had floored him. He truly saw the strength she wielded. A beautiful person who seemed so slight but was a tower of muscle and intelligence, maybe a little headstrong and seemed to find trouble easily, but it was a heady mix. One he seemed incapable of resisting.

'Are you sure you're okay with that?' Did part of him want a bigger reaction? A hug? Kisses? Her clinging to him in a goodbye embrace? Even though it would just make things harder. He was torn but he knew the right thing to do was to walk away and not lead her on. What happened in the Wicked van was a one-off, it didn't come with commitment ties and they both knew that. Their line of work made it impossible. The Agency's work had always come first in his life, almost before his family even.

'Yes. If there's anything I can do to help with Jameson, you know where to find me. Okay?'

She fluttered those thick eyelashes and her words drifted away into nothing as he lost himself in her eyes again.

'Um, so what are you going to do about Salvatore?' asked Ryan as he forced himself to look at the river instead. He might have half a chance of focusing if she didn't smell so divine. Like a field of flowers in the spring sunshine, his head was swimming in it.

Jaz sighed heavily. 'I don't know, Ryan. Can I do anything? I don't want to go to Mum about it. I can't have her finding out that I'm working for the Agency, not after everything she did to go into hiding from those she loved. I want her to have that dream for as long as possible. And I don't want to have anything to do with Salvatore. Paul is my father.'

'So, you don't want to find out for certain? Do a DNA test? It would be easy to get a sample from Salvatore.' Ryan would do it himself if it was what Jaz wanted.

'Do I really need one? It all fits. My skin, dark hair, his being Mum's boyfriend and the dates. I'd just rather leave it be. As long as he doesn't try to find me it's all good. Everything can go back to the way it was.'

Ryan studied her face. He didn't think she believed anything could go back to the way it was. No Pax. A drug lord for a father. Being with Ryan in the Wicked van. He was sure it all had changed her. Jaz had changed him, he knew that. She'd made his life fuller, along with her crazy dedicated friends, and yet at the same time she made it more difficult.

'If you're sure?'

Jaz shrugged her slim, muscled shoulders. She could hit like a boxer yet she wasn't built like Rambo. She was a secret weapon in her own right. He loved that combination of femininity and power.

'Come on then, let's go get something to eat. The finger food's yum.' He stood up. 'I'll introduce you to my family. I'm sure they're all dying to know who you are.' He'd seen the sidelong glances, his aunties whispering about the new girl and asking if anyone know who she was. He'd bet his right arm that most of them assumed she was his girlfriend.

It would be nice to let them all think that.

Together they walked back to the party and Jaz ate the finger food while

Ryan chatted to people. He made sure she was always by his side and introduced her to aunties and uncles, old friends and cousins.

His cousin on his mother's side sauntered up to them. He was a few years
younger than Ryan and used too much hair gel and cologne. He held out
his hand to Jaz, his eyes starstruck. Jaz did have that effect on people even
though she had no idea. 'Hi, I'm Brent, Ryan's cousin.'

Ryan pushed Brent away. 'Goodbye Brent.'

'Hey,' he said, but he stayed away when Ryan shot him a cold stare.

'That wasn't very nice,' said Jaz. 'You even gave him your killer glare.'

'Believe me, I've just saved you.' Ryan took a sip of his beer before he
spoke again. 'Killer glare, what do you mean?'

She raised her brow at him. 'You can be a very scary man, Ryan. When
I first met you I had a feeling you were dangerous. I've seen that look and I
know it kills,' she whispered. 'Literally,' she added.

He knew she was thinking of Pakistan. He wished that hadn't happened;
it had been traumatic for Jaz and he never wanted to see her go through
that again, yet in this line of work he knew it wasn't the last time. 'You were
scared of me?'

'I did think you were stalking me, remember.'

Jaz smiled and he could feel his own face break out in a goofy grin.
'Gosh, those were the days, weren't they?' It seemed as if that was years ago
when she was just an innocent young girl who kept popping up on his radar.
'You didn't seem to stay away.'

'Bit hard when you were everywhere I was,' she teased. 'But to answer
your question, I don't think I was ever scared of you, I just had a feeling you
could be very scary if you wanted to be. Yet the man I was getting to know
had a big heart. I could tell you were a good person, even with that killer
glare and those mysterious dark eyes.'

He chuckled at her description of him.

At this moment he felt like he was flying, he was with his family and this
time with Jaz was amazing and all seemed so great and happy. But he knew
tomorrow would be a different story and it stabbed him in the guts every
time he reminded himself. Time could be so fleeting.

'Hello darling, sorry I haven't got back to say a proper hello.' Kathy
came up and draped herself in his arms. He narrowly avoided the bright red
lipstick kiss to his cheek.

'Hey Mum. Steph be back soon?'

'Yes, I'm rounding everyone up now to head inside. Jaz, you'll be sitting with us right next to Ryan,' said Kathy.

'Thanks Mrs Fletcher, it's been a beautiful day,' said Jaz, fazed by her blatant matchmaking.

'It's Kathy,' she growled warm-heartedly before talking about the wedding with Jaz.

Ryan stood watching the exchange. His mum was so taken with Jaz and it was weird merging his two lives together. To have Jaz share his family and his agent life was surreal. It made his life seem not so disjointed.

Before long they were ushered inside the building to a special function room that his mother and Steph had spent hours preparing. Fancy white coverings with blue sashes were over each chair, situated at round tables with homemade blue name tags and bright centrepieces of white bouquets up in high glass vases and blue beads that draped from them. The bridal table had two white chairs with the extra high backs, like thrones for a king and queen. There were more balloons near the dance floor, which was at one end of the room.

It didn't take long for his family to all find time to chat to Jaz. Curiosity must have got the better of them. As long as he could keep Brent away, it was all good. But she looked like she was enjoying herself and he caught her laughing and smiling a lot and he was glad. He wasn't sure how much longer he could have handled that sadness haunting her eyes, and scooping her up in his arms would only make matters worse.

They made their way through the meal and dessert, watched Steph and Gazza cut the cake, and then came the speeches. Damn, he'd been dreading this bit all day.

'Ryan, if you could come up here,' said his dad after giving a moving speech. 'I believe you have a few words for your sister.'

He clamped down on his jaw and at the same time felt a hand clutch his arm.

'You'll be great,' said Jaz beside him. 'Relax.' Her lips curled up into a smile just for him.

How did she know him so well? He thought he was so good at keeping his emotions hidden, in many situations it was his strength, but Jaz had always been able to see right through him. How did she do that?

She drew her hand away, and he got up to join his dad by the bridal table where he held the microphone.

Ryan had left his jacket draped over his chair and automatically rolled up his shirtsleeves. It felt hot in the room all of a sudden.

He took the microphone and glanced at his sister and Gazza instead of the eighty people in the room. 'Well, Gaz, you're a gutsy man to take on our Steph but we're so glad you've taken her off our hands,' he said teasingly, which drew a few chuckles from the crowd. 'But in all seriousness, welcome to the family. You are lucky to have found each other and I know you'll both be happy together. She's an amazing sister and if you can show her how to cook and clean, I'm sure she'll make a great wife.' Steph shook her head and he laughed. 'You're the best sister a brother could ask for, and I know I'm not around much these days but it doesn't mean I love you any less. I wish you both the best as you start your new life together. To Steph and Gazza,' he finished as everyone raised their glass to toast them.

Ryan then went and hugged his sister.

'Thanks bro, I love you too,' she said, dabbing at tears. 'I'm just glad you could be here. And Jaz as well. Gosh, she's a stunner. Are you two dating yet?'

Ryan had just squatted down by her chair but he was tempted to get back up and walk away. 'I wouldn't miss your wedding for the world, Steph.' If she only knew the lengths he'd gone to, to be here. 'And you know Jaz and I are just friends.'

Steph gripped his arm, probably because she noticed how much he was ready to flee. Her face set hard, maybe it was all that wedding make-up but he recognised her serious face. 'Ry, I'm not stupid.' She brushed her hair back from her face, she was a bit flushed but that was a lot of wedding dress she was wearing. 'I've seen the way you are together.'

'We're really good friends,' he said with a shrug. 'I do care about her.'

'And she does too. Everyone's talking about how you gawked at her when she turned up.'

'I didn't gawk,' he scoffed.

Shit, had he been that bad? She had knocked his socks off. If his mum hadn't snapped him out of his Jaz trance, he could have ended up embarrassing himself more. 'I hadn't seen her in a while. She *is* gorgeous, who wouldn't look.' Which was true, it wasn't just Brent he was having to fend off.

Steph's eyebrows nearly met as her forehead creased. 'Whatever you wanna keep telling yourself, big bro, but for the record I don't believe it one bit. I think you're just lying to yourself but who am I to say, I'm just the sister you hardly spend any time with.'

'Ouch, low blow.' But he knew it was the truth. His job made him absent a lot and the rest of the time he just found it too hard to see them. All the questions and the probing about what he was doing, did he have a girl-friend, where was he working. Sometimes it was easier just being the absent brother and son – until Jaz made him realise that family was important and some things were worth it even if it made life hard. And since then he'd had more contact with his family and it had been nice. Steph even came around to the gym and had met Jaz's friends.

'I'm sorry, but it's true. Come and dance with me,' she said jumping up.

'Aren't you supposed to do that with Gaz?'

Steph made a point of looking for him. 'I think he went to the bar. Come on. Let's start a trend.'

She took his hand and dragged him through the tables to the dance floor. The music had been put back on after the speeches and Steph's favou-rite band Birds of Tokyo's song 'Lanterns' was on.

'Remember when you had to chaperone me to the Big Day Out just so I could see the Birds play,' said Steph as he spun her around. 'And the sound was awesome by those big speakers. Best band ever.'

Ryan had protested about having to take his sister who was underage at the time, but in the end they'd had a great time together and both enjoyed similar taste in music. It was moments like that he knew he should cherish, especially now that his little sister was married. Shit, soon she'd probably be having kids.

'What? What's wrong?' Steph asked as she stopped dancing.

'I was just thinking that soon you'll be having your own family. I'll be an uncle. How crazy is that.'

Steph smiled as guests joined them on the dance floor. 'It's strange, for sure. What would be stranger is if it were *you* having the family,' she teased.

'Yahoo.' Their father danced past having the time of his life. His dance partner was Jaz and she was laughing again. It was a sound Ryan never wanted to forget.

'Daddy,' yelled Steph and lunged for him. 'Sorry Jaz, you're stuck with him.' She gestured to Ryan.

Ryan smelled a rat but held out his hands to Jaz and smiled. 'Shall we?'

'You better be as good as your dad,' she said taking his hands.

He drew her to his chest and waltzed around the room – well, more like slow circles. Dancing wasn't his strong point, finding the exits and shooting out targets at the same time was more his style. Glancing at Jaz, he bet it was more hers too.

'Having a good time?' he asked her as they decelerated with the change of the song. It was a slow Katy Perry number, not that he would ever own up to knowing that.

'Yes, I am actually. I wasn't sure if I would. I've had lots on my mind lately but I think this was the break I needed.' Her eyes sparkled and the lights bounced off her dress. 'You have a great family.'

He nodded as she leant in and rested her head on his shoulder for a moment. Her hand was on his arm, the other he held in his hand tightly. This close he could smell the frangipani scent of her hair and feel the warmth of her body. Ryan tried to step without treading on her toes but his mind seemed stuck on the skin of Jaz's lower back where his other hand was resting. He was sure she wore the backless dress on purpose, just to torment him.

'Jaz, you know today is just … you know it's the wedding and my family is here … and tomorrow it will all go back.' Shit, he didn't know how to say what he felt he needed to say. He didn't want to give her false hope or lead her on. He knew Steph was right when she said that Jaz cared about him. He could see it in the way she looked at him.

Jaz stopped dancing. 'It's okay, Ryan. I get it. I know a goodbye when I hear it.'

Her words were like a steel rod through his heart. He didn't mean for it to be cruel or painful, just realistic. Yet she had a set, determined expression on her face. One that seemed far too grown-up and understanding. And it was killing him.

'If you don't mind, it's been a long day, so I'm going to go home. Goodbye Ryan.' She stood on tippy toes and kissed his cheek. He itched to shift those lips towards his. 'I hope I see you again. Be careful.'

She pulled out of his embrace and walked off through the dancing partners. Her shoulders were back, her walk strong. Yet he felt like a slinky, ready to bend over and flop, preferably down stairs. He'd been so worried about hurting her that he didn't factor how much it would shake him. He wasn't prepared for such a quick goodbye, even though he knew it was for the best.

Damn, she'd disappeared from the room. Shoving his hands into his pants, he made his way to the bar and wondered how he was going to keep a cheerful disposition now the light had left the room.

CHAPTER 10

JAZ MADE IT all the way to her Jeep and drove home without a single tear. But only because she knew that when she started she might never stop and driving was hard enough in the city, let alone if you couldn't see. And then she still had to get past her mum, who would want to know all about the wedding. Tears, snot and crying like a baby were not what she needed her mum to witness right now. She didn't want the questions, well, the interrogation more like it. So, Jaz sucked it up and even managed a few words to her mum and Paul about the wedding.

'I got a few photos,' she said. 'But I'll show you tomorrow. Right now I wanna have a hot shower and scrub this make-up off.'

'Yeah you do look a bit freakish,' said Simon with a cheeky grin. He'd just walked into the kitchen in his striped pyjamas and blond hair.

'Says the walking banana.' Jaz hugged him because she felt the need, leaving poor Simon a little confused to her sudden affection. 'I need sleep. I'll see you all in the morning.'

'You sure you're okay, Jaz?' said Tash, pulling her in for a hug on her way towards the stairs.

Paul was at the table with a cuppa and a big book, but he looked over the top of it with concern.

'I'm fine, guys. Just tired. Was hard to smile lots when you don't feel like it,' she said, her voice wavering just a tad. If she didn't go soon she wasn't sure how much longer she'd last, especially when her mum was hugging her so tightly. It was if she knew she was cracking, like an egg held too tightly. Soon she'd burst apart into a gooey sobbing mess. 'Night. Love you.'

Pulling away she headed up the stairs, taking her shoes off as she went.

Inside her room she let the shoes fall to the floor, about the same time the first tears dripped from her chin, and flopped onto her bed in an unlady-like manner.

The barrage of emotions she'd managed to contain since that moment on the bench seat with Ryan when he more or less said goodbye overtook her. And then again on the dance floor, where he made her heart feel like a bashed-in piñata. It had taken every bone in her body, every ounce of strength she had to keep it together but now she let it go. At this rate she wouldn't need a shower as she'd cry all her make-up off. But after half an hour or more of wallowing in sobs she managed to get into the shower, scrub her face raw, then climb into her worn pyjamas and crawl back into bed.

The worst thing was, tomorrow wouldn't be better because now there was no Pax and no Ryan. All she had to look forward to was a funeral and exams. Jaz clutched at her pillow as more tears welled, until sleep finally put her out of her misery.

The days before the funeral Jaz walked through life as a visitor. She got up, ate, went to school, tried to focus, tried to listen to what her friends were saying and then went home. Because they were both upset about Pax they understood, but Jaz noticed they could still share a joke and a smile. Jaz couldn't. Not with Ryan gone too.

Come Wednesday they all met at the gym, it was the first time Jaz had gone back and nothing felt more like coming home than the moment she stepped through the door. It all turned pear shaped when she found herself looking for Pax. Waiting for him to come out of the office with a cuppa in his hand. But he never did and never would again.

'This is wrong,' said Anna, who turned to Jaz.

She'd said exactly what Jaz was feeling and in seconds both of them had tears rolling down their cheeks, which had their mums diving for the tissues in their handbags.

They were here to set up for the wake, yet they couldn't even get past the front door without crumbling.

'We'll never get anything done at this rate,' said Tasha dabbing at her eyes.

Lenore smiled through her own glassy eyes. 'I know. Where shall we start?'

Jaz took over then, needing something to grip onto. She took them to the storage room to take out the fold-out tables. Paul was off hiring chairs with Anna's dad, while Tay was here to clean, but it hadn't been necessary because Bags, Niles and Tick had scrubbed the place spotless before they arrived. They'd left a note in the office offering to help if there was anything else that needed doing. She loved those guys, they had all made a weird family, The Ring family.

Jaz put the note down and stood in the office, looking at the door that led into Pax's house. It would always be Pax's house. No matter what happened next. She wondered who was going to clean out his house. What about all his Agency gear? Surely Pax had made a contingency plan. She didn't think he'd let them sell it and had hoped he'd left it to Anna's family for safekeeping. But what would they want with a rustic gym? They'd probably sell it. Then she really would have lost a huge part of her life. This gym was everything, even though it didn't seem like much to others.

Anna's mum had been made executer of Pax's will. She told them the night of his death. She said he'd made a new will after his first heart attack and that after the funeral she would read the will out to them all, but not until they had said their goodbyes. Jaz had walked away, didn't want to hear anything about it, still too stunned with his death.

Tasha walked past and opened the door with Jaz's keys. They would need the kitchen to set up the urn and fridge.

Jaz hated the fact that the world continued on. Life wasn't feeling very fair at the moment.

'Hey, chicken.' Anna slipped her arm around Jaz's waist and rested her head on her shoulder.

Anna was wearing a black dress with pearls around her neck and a pair hanging from her ears, her hair swept up into a bun, making her look very Audrey Hepburn. Jaz had gone for a bright dress, mainly red with green leaves and yellow frangipani flowers, much like Pax's Hawaiian-inspired shirts he always wore. She hoped it would bring a smile to his face if he was watching, and to the people who knew him well. Her mother, on the other hand, was in black and had a fascinator in her hair with a black spotted veil that covered most of her face. She looked very elegant but had Jaz wondering if it was more to do with hiding herself in case any Agency people turned up at the funeral. After all these years she was still careful, which reminded Jaz how much she needed to keep her Agency involvement a secret.

'Lucky we have keys and I can still get back in,' whispered Anna. 'Yesterday after school I got a message from James. He wanted to meet me.'

Jaz guided Anna back out the office and down towards the change room, away from prying ears. 'Why didn't you tell me this?'

'I am now.'

'Did you meet up?'

'Yep. Tay went with me.'

Jaz felt suddenly a bit out of the loop.

Anna continued. 'James just wanted to check I could still access all the computers. He needed an ID made up for one of the operatives. He's also going to get their guy back in Vic to visit and continue with my training. Mind you, Pax had most of it covered. It's just some of the government database stuff and records that we haven't covered. I've got passports down pat,' she said with a sad smile.

Anna, without any prior experience, had made Ryan's fake passport when Pax had his first heart attack. It had been an emergency to get Ryan's passport done and Anna had worked it out on her own. But she was clever like that. Computer genius ran in the family. Her dad didn't own one of the biggest computer companies for no reason.

They didn't get to talk anymore about her meeting with James because it was time to go to the funeral.

Taylor took her hand as they walked into the crematorium; he held Anna's in the other and walked them to the front of the room just behind their parents. Tay looked so grown-up in black slacks and a black shirt with a tie. He was trying to be there for both of them but Jaz knew it was Anna who had his heart. Only Anna hadn't yet realised how Tay felt.

As they sat he kept hold of their hands, but with Anna's his thumb was working gentle circles across it and he kept glancing at her as if checking she was okay. It wasn't hard to miss the love shining from Tay's eyes. Jaz was glad Anna had Tay because right now Jaz hadn't been as good a friend as she should be. She was lost in her own suffering, too afraid to share it with Anna yet because she didn't want it to be real. She didn't want to believe Ryan was gone from her life. Plus Anna was the one person who would understand just how much it was killing Jaz and she didn't want to burden Anna with more sorrow.

Jaz looked around the room, trying to see who was here. Mainly Anna's family and their friends. She'd seen Tilly on the way in, dressed as one of the funeral assistants. She wondered if they knew they had an extra, or maybe this was one of Tilly's day jobs? It wouldn't surprise her. Not much did these days. Tilly acknowledged her with the smallest of nods.

Jaz twisted in her seat; she was searching for Ryan, just in case, even though he said he wouldn't make it. She still looked.

'Do you think Ryan will come?' asked Anna. She'd been watching her search the faces.

Jaz shook her head. 'No, he said he wouldn't but … you know.' Hope did funny things to people.

With one last look around the room, Jaz caught the eye of a man at the very back and recognised James.

The full reality of this situation made her heart race. What if James ran into her mum? Would he recognise her from a distance? Would her mum spot James? Jaz glanced to her mum who sat at the end of the chairs with Paul and Simon. They were chatting quietly among themselves. What were the chances they would bump into each other? Would her mum be expecting something like this? She probably didn't even know her brother worked the Perth office from time to time, unless Pax had mentioned it. Jaz was dying to know and wished Pax was around to ask.

With a bit of luck, James wouldn't hang around or come to the wake for fear of being recognised or connected back to Pax or anyone else in the Agency. James lifted his hand and scratched his chin and then made the sign that the Agency used to say, 'I see you.'

Coming from James she knew he meant a lot more than those three words. Jaz turned around to face the front as the service started.

Jaz tried to read from the little booklet, it had Pax's photo on the front and listed the order of events. Anna had done a great job and even listed his fake certificates at the back. A little inside joke that made her smile. Pax would have got a good chuckle from that.

After the service they all made their way to his coffin to say goodbye and put a frangipani flower on his casket. His favourite flower. It was a nice sentiment that Anna's mum had organised, picking all the flowers herself from her garden and from the ones growing around Pax's house. Jaz had picked her own one from the pink tree he had out by his front window. She breathed in its scent one last time before placing it down. She couldn't speak, her voice would crack if she tried, instead she said a silent goodbye as her eyes watered and tears escaped. It still didn't seem real and every time she thought of his body inside the shiny brown casket she just about lost the plot. The only way to get through was to not think about it, just as did with her Agency work. Push it to the back of your mind and continue on.

Wiping her eyes with a tissue she followed the rest of their families out of the building, not even glancing at the faces who watched them leave. Jaz did look for James when they reached the back of the room but he wasn't where she'd last seen him. Please God let him have left already.

'Did you see him up the back?' whispered Anna. 'Do you think your mum—' Anna mouthed the rest of her sentence. *Saw him?*

'I don't think so,' she whispered back.

'Imagine if they did. Wonder how she would have reacted.'

'I kinda wished she had seen him and vice versa, it would bring all this out into the open,' said Jaz.

'And cause a shitload of chaos,' added Tay as he worked his way between them. 'Come on, I'll drive us back to the gym once everyone's finished with the hugging.'

Tay was right. It would have turned all their lives upside down, and Jaz didn't need that kind of chaos. She needed her mum to be at home with Paul and Simon, things as normal as possible. How would things go down once James found out his sister really was alive?

Outside, people were hugging and smiling with tears in their eyes. Bags, Tick and Niles stood to one side together, all dressed up. Tick looked quite respectable and stylish with all his tattoos hidden; you'd never guess he'd been a dangerous gang member once upon a time. Bags still looked a bit like Vin Diesel, large due to his boxing and love of protein shakes but no one here would know that he loved to write and spent a lot of time at the computer, his goal to one day be published.

'Come on, let's see the guys,' said Jaz. She hated that they stood back as if outsiders when in fact Pax thought of these guys as family and had more to do with them than his own family besides Anna.

'Thanks for cleaning up the gym,' said Jaz as she hugged each one.

All three wore dark sunglasses and Bags reached under his to flick away a stray tear.

Jaz would often come to the gym to find Pax with the guys, having a cuppa and listening to their troubles. Most people came to Pax's gym to let out some frustrations, to stay fit and to seek Pax's listening ear. Jaz doubted his family truly understood just how much Pax did for people. They knew nothing about his Agency work.

'It was all we could think of but you let us know if there's anything else. Jimbo couldn't make it, he's over east but sends you all hugs. Do we have to give our keys back?' asked Niles. He was so tall his black pants were near his ankles, Michael Jackson style.

'We'll know more this afternoon when Anna's mum reads out his will. We'll let you know when we can. We're heading back now,' said Jaz as Tick put his arm around her shoulders. They sure made a funny mix and lots of people glanced their way, probably wondering who these three guys were. None of Pax's family really knew him. It was sad, but in a way that's how Pax liked it. He wasn't a fan of his wealthy family and had inadvertently made his own at the gym and within the Agency.

'Righto. We'll follow you back too,' said Bags, his voice croaky.

'We've put on a banquet of Pax's favourite pastries,' said Tay. 'He'll be spewing he's not here to help us eat it.'

'Don't worry, Tay, I'm sure he's living it up wherever he is now. Coffee and apricot danishes galore,' said Anna as they made their way to the car park.

It didn't take long for all the food to disappear and most of the guests departed soon after. Jaz was happy about that, she didn't like all these strange, uppity folks in Pax's gym. She saw their judgemental looks and the screwed-up noses at the smell she loved. Including Anna's family.

'God, I'm glad they're gone. I really think I was born into the wrong family, just like Pax,' she said.

'Your folks aren't that bad,' said Jaz.

'They're okay, but all my aunties and uncles are so snobbish. It irks me.' Anna's face grew red the more she seemed to stew over the idea.

'Ladies, you are wanted in the kitchen,' said Tay. 'I'll finish cleaning up here with the guys.'

Tay stopped Anna, his hands caressed her arms. 'You okay?'

'She's fine, just pissed off with her family.' Jaz took Anna's hand and pulled her from Tay's grasp. 'Come on, Annabanana, let's get this over with.'

At the table sat Lenore, Tasha, Paul and Anna's father Eric. They looked far too serious.

The chairs scraped against the floor as they pulled them out and sat down.

'What's up,' said Jaz. Everyone was looking at them.

Anna's mum wasted no time getting to the point.

'Pax has left his house to both of you, equal shares,' said Lenore. She didn't sound too pleased with this. 'Now, you don't have to keep it, we can sell—'

'*No!*' said Jaz and Anna together. They looked at each other and smiled, really smiled. Jaz saw in Anna's expression what was probably on her face. Things could stay the same, nothing would have to change, Anna and Jaz could still work from the gym.

'Jaz, he's left the gym to you and also has left you both a ridiculous amount of money, which,' Lenore turned to the other adults at the table and grimaced, 'we are not sure about you having just yet. I totally disagreed with this part but Pax insisted. He let me put an age stipulation on a big chunk of it but he still wanted you to have some money to help with the running costs of his house and the gym.' Lenore's shoulders slumped and her mouth turned down. 'It's still too much but I guess you are classed as adults now.'

Jaz turned back to Anna. 'This is amazing. Did you know?' she asked Anna.

'No. We can stay here whenever we want.' Anna's freckles were bright as if glowing from the excitement. 'Maybe we could move in?'

'No!' said her parents. They had high hopes for Anna, and slumming it in an old gym wasn't one of them.

'Nothing needs to be decided now,' said Tasha, trying to calm the confrontation she knew was probably coming between kids and parents. 'Let's just keep everything as normal, there is still a big process to go through and you won't have the money straightaway. We would prefer it if you went through us, so we can help you be responsible with the money and not waste it.'

Jaz pulled a face. 'Mum, we're not silly kids. There is nothing I want the money for except for keeping this place running.'

'I wouldn't mind buying a car,' said Anna carefully, as she waited for her parents' explosion. 'And that's it, I swear. Please,' she begged.

'We'll discuss it at home,' said Lenore.

Jaz could tell she was pissed at Pax. They no longer had control over the girls; if Anna wanted a new car she could now buy one, well, when the money was released. She knew it was this that freaked the parents out the most. They were scared of losing their girls, scared that they were no longer needed.

'It's okay, Mum. School finishes soon and we'd be on our own anyway. You have to let us be in control of our own lives and be responsible for our own actions. No doubt we'll probably stuff up but we know we can come to you. We're not little girls anymore.'

Tasha pouted and glanced at Paul. 'How do I answer that? She's right.'

Paul held her hand and smiled. 'This doesn't have to be a bad thing, nor change anything,' he said. 'We have smart, capable girls. It will be fine.' His words were for Lenore and Tasha, the worried mothers. 'We just need to take baby steps, it's a bit hard for us parents to let you go.'

As they continued to discuss the money, all Jaz could think was that the gym was hers. Anna could still run her Agency work from the special room and Jaz could keep the gym running and use it as her alibi. She had visions of running classes for young women, self-defence, how to fight off attackers, and also ways that other Agency members like Cody could come and train. Pax had no doubt thought all this through. He was proud of them, joining the Agency and continuing his work even though it had worried him. This was the news that was going to help get her over missing Ryan. She could throw all her energy into The Ring. Maybe life wouldn't be so bad after all.

CHAPTER 11

IT HAD BEEN three weeks since Pax's funeral and it crossed Ryan's mind often. How had it been? How were Jaz and her friends? What was happening with the gym? These were the thoughts that came.

He got ready for his day as usual, putting on his suit and making sure it was perfect. Last night he'd written out notes from the places he'd taken Jameson yesterday, including a new destination. His notes went into a Coke can, then into his recycling bag, which he tied in a knot so it was recognisable, then on his way to work he dropped it at the edge of the flats where the rubbish bins were kept. He knew an operative wouldn't be far away to collect it, because it was checked every morning at this time. His notes then made their way back to James or the commander.

From there the other agents would check out these stops that Jameson made, keeping eyes on the places to see who came and went. Everything was documented, as they never knew when some important piece of information might pop up.

Ryan made it to Jameson's compound with ten minutes to spare. He always arrived early, was checked in through the big gates then would park in the staff area behind the big shed that housed Jameson's cars. His private residence was further up a rise to make the most of the ocean views. Ryan had learned that Jameson had two houses he moved between, this one in the city and a much larger acreage block near his farming land.

Ryan would take the car out of the shed and wash and clean it ready for the day's work. Mr Randall would always notify him of times the car was needed but he had to be ready to go in an instant. It was Ryan's job to make sure it was always fuelled up too. He'd done that last night after dropping

Jameson home so this morning he was just going to give it a quick wet and shammy. Not that the shiny black sleek-looking Jaguar needed it.

His phone rang when he was almost done. Leaving the cloth to dry on a nearby tree branch, he answered it.

'Hey, baby, you shouldn't ring me when I'm at work,' he said straightaway.

'I know,' said Annaliese, 'but Dad won't mind. It's me,' she said, matter-of-factly. 'Are you picking me up tonight? Remember we have that dinner with Sophie?'

Ryan groaned inwardly. He could handle Annaliese, play the doting boyfriend, but it was hard work when they met up with her friends. He disliked them even more. At least now he excused himself from the drugs they took, saying he didn't want to jeopardise his job with her father, and Annaliese took that as a good sign. Still, it made it difficult at times.

'Yes, I'll be waiting at your door at seven, babe. I'll let you know if your dad has any late errands but we should be good to go.' From the corner of his eye Ryan could see movement at the house, bodyguards looking more lively and doing a double-check of the area. 'Look, I've gotta get back to work. I'll talk to you soon.'

'See you then, Reece. Tell Daddy I love him,' she said before hanging up.

Ryan got the nod from Mr Randall to bring the car over, so he quickly jumped in and drove it up the paved driveway to the front door. The turning circle was tight out the front of the house, made harder because of the overgrown bushes and shrubs that were overdue to be hedged. Maybe Jameson liked the privacy they provided?

Jumping out, he opened the back door and waited for Jameson to exit his large oak doors. They were on heavy black hinges and no doubt thick and bulletproof.

Jameson walked out, his dark blue suit clean, his black leather boots shining and his walk slow and commanding. Jameson didn't rush for anyone, everything was done in his time and every move he made seemed so precise and deliberate, which just made him come across as calm, controlled and important.

'Good morning, Mr Figlomeni,' said Ryan as he held the car door open.

'Morning, Mr Lancaster.' Jameson climbed into the back of the car.

Ryan never spoke to Jameson unless spoken to, and Jameson was always polite. Old-school values and attention to detail seemed to be his thing.

Ryan shut the door and slipped into the driver's seat. Mr Randall rode in the back with Jameson, and a spare guard sometimes took the front seat. It was usually Mr Wilkins who rode shotgun on their visits to the warehouses, and occasionally to different meetings that Ryan was yet to infiltrate. Being made to stay with the car was limiting, he really needed to find a way to step up. Maybe Mr Wilkins needed to disappear or get sick. It could be arranged but would have to be done carefully. A man like Jameson didn't like changes. A man like Jameson was always double-checking his back.

Ryan drove Jameson to his first meeting, at a bank in the CBD. Even after a month or more working as a driver, Ryan never let his guard slip, was always trying to take in his surroundings, people coming and going just in case there was a clandestine meeting in the works.

The second stop was at a restaurant for lunch, which meant Ryan had time to grab a meal from the nearby Subway, which he ate outside by the car. His job involved a lot of waiting, but this was a prerequisite to being an agent. Patience was the key, waiting for that one slip-up.

Next Ryan drove Jameson out of the city centre and towards his market garden, no doubt to check on the books and everyday running of his businesses. The scenery of tightly packed houses changed to bigger spaces and rows of growing vegetables. Ryan had been here before, so he knew Jameson like to be driven straight to the warehouse or large shed-like structure in the middle of the farm. The house was to the left and closer to the road. It looked Italian in style with white walls, pillars, terracotta tiles and garden statues.

The shed was cream in colour and had crates of all sizes stacked around one side, and rolls of black plastic. He knew the plastic was probably for the strawberries and not burying poorly performing workers, but still his mind connected it to Jaz and their experience in the hanger together with Salvatore. He didn't want to think about her, but she often crept into his mind without warning. Her smile, her silky dark hair and those contrasting blue eyes, so bright and intimidating. His lips twitched with a need to smile but he fought it off.

Ryan stopped the Jaguar outside the shed, and Jameson exited with both bodyguards, leaving Ryan to wait without a time limit. Workers came and went, some on small tractors, others on motorbikes. He didn't know what was inside the shed, except for what he saw when the sliding door opened so the tractor could drive in its trailerloads of lettuce and other vegies. More workers were inside, sorting and packaging, and down the back of the shed looked like an office area. Ryan sighed; there was no way he could get near them without being seen. He still tried, by walking around the shed, with his phone to his ear pretending to take a call, but he couldn't hear anything, nor were there any windows within reach, just a door that was solid and locked. All he could do was stand by the car.

While he was waiting he did notice a small man hovering around the shed. He was dressed like all the other workers – blue uniform that looked like it had been passed down from worker to worker, and boots covered in soil. Ryan took a stab at his nationality, maybe from South East Asia, Philippines, but it was his anxious manner that brought him to Ryan's attention. Why was he nervous? Had he just stolen something? Maybe he'd been hiding drugs? A list of possibilities rattled through Ryan's brain until he noticed the door to the shed open and Mr Randall came out, followed by Jameson.

Ryan opened the car door in readiness.

The nervous-looking worker came closer and called out. 'Mr Figlomeni, sir. You find my daughter?' he asked.

'Excuse me,' said Jameson, stopping reluctantly. The look in his eyes gave away the fact he knew exactly what this man was after.

The small man took a step closer, and that's when Ryan realised he had a large knife in the back of his pants. The worn handle was just visible. No one else had noticed this, only Ryan had the advantage to spot it.

'I work free so my daughter, Yanna, come to Australia, you say you bring her. It's been long time. Where is she?'

The little guy was desperate and angry. Ryan glanced to Mr Randall but he just stood there with his arms crossed, and the other bodyguard had continued to walk to the car, not seeing this man as a threat. But Ryan knew that any man who has something to fight for, to die for, should never be underestimated, no matter their size or shape.

'Mr Randall, where are we on this Yanna situation?' said Jameson, turning to Randall. He was calm, not at all ruffled.

'The girl is still working off her debt, sir. Another month or two, I believe.'

'No. I pay her debt, not Yanna. You said.'

Randall eyed him off. 'You knew it came with a price—'

But before Randall had even finished his sentence, Ryan was running for the little man. He'd seen his arm move to his back, going for the knife, and in a split second Ryan knew he had to take action.

'Knife!' he yelled as he tackled the man to the ground, grabbing his arm. In the scuffle the sharp knife cut Ryan's hand and he felt the blood release. It looked like a knife used for the farm work; Ryan hoped it was clean.

'Reece ... what?'

Jameson called him by his fake first name in the shock of his sudden movements. Ryan looked up as the man wriggled underneath him. Randall had taken up position in front of Jameson but it was a little too late. Jameson would have taken a knife to the belly and he knew it. His eyes were large as comprehension set in.

Twisting the man's arm, forcing him to release the knife, Ryan then bent it back in a hold while he removed the weapon from him. With a flick he sent it sliding through the dirt at Randall's feet. Randall bent to collect it while Ryan got up, bringing the man with him and holding him tightly.

'Sorry Mr Figlomeni, but I only just saw the knife,' said Ryan.

'No, no need to apologise. That was mighty impressive. Thank you.' Jameson glanced at his other two bodyguards as if to say, *What the heck do I pay you for?*

'Sorry, Mr Figlomeni, I didn't see it from this angle,' said Randall solemnly.

'What shall I do with this one, sir?' asked Ryan. He felt sorry for the man he held. He was now crying and mumbling about his daughter. Ryan knew that he was the innocent man in all this. He guessed his daughter was being used in prostitution under the pretence of paying her way to Australia. But he doubted that poor girl would ever be released now. It sickened him knowing this man's daughter could die if she didn't comply, and he should have let him attack Jameson but the man would have only paid for it with his life, Jameson would have lived and nothing would have stopped. At least this way Ryan was hoping for a leg up into Jameson's world. He might even eventually find these girls, put Jameson away and shut his business down. The Agency wanted all the links from overseas found and severed. It would need more than just cutting off the head of the snake.

'Mr Randall, will you please deal with this?'

Randall nodded and took the man from Ryan. He was no longer resisting; he probably knew his fate. Death? A holding cell?

As Randall took the man into the shed, Ryan pulled up his jacket sleeve so his cut hand didn't bleed all over it. He dug a tissue out of his pocket and used it to help stop the bleeding.

'Are you okay, Reece?' said Jameson.

Ryan took that as a good sign. Was there a little trust growing?

'Fine, sir. Is there somewhere I can get cleaned up before I drive you home?'

Jameson's brow rose. Ryan was dying to know what he was thinking.

'Yes. Mr Wilkes, will you please drive us up to the house. My house-keeper Mrs Latina will help you. Will it need stitches?'

'No, sir. This will be fine. I just need to stop the blood and then I'll be right to go.'

Jameson nodded and went to the car. Ryan still managed to shut the door for him before getting into the front passenger seat.

At the house Jameson led him inside and called out to his housekeeper.

'Yes, Mr Figlomeni,' said a large lady in a white uniform. She had sweat along her brow as if she'd been vacuuming or doing something vigorous. It made her dark curly hair, streaked with grey, cling to her head like a wet mop.

'Can you help Mr Lancaster get cleaned up, please. I'll just be in the drawing room having a quick scotch. I'll have one waiting for you,' he said with a nod to Ryan.

Mrs Latina took him to the laundry and used a flannel to clean his wound. She rattled off words in another language but Ryan got the gist from the tone of her voice that she was unimpressed with the deepness of his cut. 'Stay,' she said before ducking off and returning with a first-aid kit. She bathed it in antiseptic before putting little sticky strips on it to hold it together then bandaged it up to keep it clean.

When she guided him back to the drawing room, Jameson thanked her.

'Is very deep, sir. Will need stitches.'

'Thank you, Mrs Latina,' said Ryan bidding her farewell. 'This will be fine.'

She shook her head, frowning at Ryan and walked out, clearly unimpressed that he wasn't rushing off to hospital.

'I think you've earned this,' said Jameson holding out a glass containing a nip of scotch.

Not to offend, Ryan took it. 'Thank you, sir. I'm ready to go when you are.'

He could tell Jameson had been trying to work him out this whole time. Probably wondering what Ryan thought about the man he'd apprehended, about his missing daughter, about if he'd go to the hospital with his wound, and hopefully he was wondering if Ryan was trustworthy enough.

'Annaliese did tell me you were a great bodyguard, but I thought her affection for you perhaps made her prone to exaggeration.'

'I understand, sir.'

'But you've clearly shown me twice now that you are more than capable of handling any situation.'

'And with the utmost discretion and protection, sir. I take my work very seriously. I don't plan on letting you down, nor any future employers. I'm very grateful for this job but I do hope to move to a position I'm more qualified for. I don't want my weapons training to go to waste.' He hoped he wasn't pushing his luck. 'Sorry to speak out of turn, but I am keen to secure a position in the league of Mr Randall's position. Eventually I'd like to run my own business.'

Jameson took a sip of his scotch and let it wash over his tongue before swallowing it. 'You are a man who wants to get to the top. I see that. You have more dedication than most of my staff. They're happy where they are, yet I see that you are over-qualified for this position, even though you do it well. I have a feeling you would do any job well.'

'Yes, sir. I've been trained by some of the best. I will not let situations like today happen again. I'm set to take you home if you are ready?' he said, quickly finishing his drink. He wasn't really in a rush to head off – every moment in this house Ryan was trying to take notes, commit what he'd seen to memory; any little detail could help – but he wanted to come across as an eager-to-please employee.

'Let's go.'

They walked to the door and Ryan quickly opened it for him and checked the area outside. 'It's clear, Mr Figlomeni.'

Jameson paused by the door. 'Reece, how would you like Mr Wilkins' position as my bodyguard?'

'Sir?' Ryan held his breath. He didn't want to blow this. Everything was riding on this next step.

'I do not feel safe around Mr Wilkins, I do with you. I would prefer it from now on if you took over his position and he became the driver. Would that suit you?'

'Very much, sir. Thank you.'

'Great,' he said, shaking Ryan's hand. 'I'll inform Mr Randall.' He glanced across and saw Wilkins leaning against the car. 'Mr Wilkins, you can drive us home please. Mr Lancaster is unfit to drive.'

'Yes, sir,' said Wilkins, quickly moving to open the back door.

On the outside Ryan was walking to the passenger side door, on the inside he was doing a victory dance. He was now one step closer.

Into the den of the lion he went.

CHAPTER 12

Jaz walked to the gym from school, as she had nearly every second day this past month. She didn't bother driving; she needed the exercise and the weather was nice. Her schoolbag was heavy with books, study for exams was nightmarish but Anna was helping. The gym was theirs now, so meeting there after school felt right, their own place where no one could kick them out. Jaz picked up her pace as she saw The Ring come into view. She had thought about giving it a new paint job, but why? It still worked fine on the inside. A new coat of paint would probably just make it a target for the local thugs. Mind you, Jaz would be quite happy to have someone to challenge right now. She had so much pent-up frustration that sparring with Tick or Cody just wasn't cutting the mustard. She wanted a raw, adrenaline-filled fight.

Some days when she walked back from school she almost wished that gang that had attacked her before she was recruited would come upon her again. This time she'd be ready for them. She was older, wiser, stronger and capable of playing dirty to survive. This time she wouldn't need Ryan to save her. This time she knew she had what it took to win no matter the odds.

The gym door was open, letting in the warm afternoon air. Jaz stepped inside and smiled. Nothing had changed. Muhammad Ali's pictures still hung from the raw brick walls, everything was in its normal position, as Pax wanted it.

'Hi ya, Bags,' Jaz yelled out to her mate, who was down in the corner leading a group boxing lesson.

He raised his padded hand and gave her a wave while still instructing the group.

Jaz headed into the kitchen and found Anna and Tay.

'You took your time,' said Anna as she looked up from their pile of books, papers, pens and highlighters. Her iPad was off to one side, with a plate of Tim Tams and coffee cups.

'Yeah, hard slog with these buggers,' she said thumping her bag down onto the table.

'Pull up a chair, Anna is going over some boring stuff,' said Tay as he got up. 'I'll make you a cuppa.'

'Thanks Tay.'

'Hey,' said Anna. 'It's not "boring stuff", it's physics.'

'Same thing.' Tay shot her a teasing smile.

Jaz sat down and got her books out, along with her iPad and notebook. She liked her afternoons studying with these guys. It was a nice routine to have. They would study, then Anna would go into Pax's computer room while Tay and Jaz sparred. Sometimes Cody came by too.

It had been a month since Pax's funeral and longer since Ryan's goodbye but still she couldn't help but look up every time someone entered the gym. How did she stop her heart from hoping? Would this feeling ever go? Or was she doomed to wait for Ryan her whole lifetime?

'Cody said he was coming by this arvo with some news from Tilly.'

This made Jaz sit up. She stared at Tay, waiting for more.

'That's all I know,' he said. 'I'm hoping it's a mission. I need a break from all this study and I'm ready to do some serious stuff.'

Jaz sighed heavily. 'Yeah, me too. My brain is just not taking any of this shit in.'

Tay put the coffee in front of her and the smell immediately improved her mood.

They got a good hour of study in, Anna made sure of it. By the time they packed away their things, Cody had arrived. He was in surf shorts and a white Rip Curl singlet. He always looked as if he'd just come from the beach; it was only when they were training or went on missions that he dressed differently. Cody waited until Bags and the group of clients had left and they had the place to themselves before he mentioned his news.

'So, I got a few words from Tilly.'

'Yeah, and?' said Jaz impatiently.

'Ryan has moved up a position to Jameson's bodyguard. He's in dangerous territory now. The chances of him walking through that door are zilch now, until it's all over, and you know it—'

'Yeah, I know,' said Jaz, cutting Cody off. 'It could be years.' Or forever, her mind whispered, causing her skin to pucker with goose bumps.

'But ...' Cody drew out the word for ages. He watched her carefully, knowing it was killing her. She could have throttled him by the time he eventually smiled.

'Cody!'

'Okay, okay. Tilly said if you could meet him tomorrow on the corner of Hutton and Miner Street at four he'll pick you up. He has a side mission for you if you want it.'

'What about us?' said Tay.

'Don't worry, you and I are on protection detail when Anna meets up with Ray, the other Agency computer geek, over the weekend.'

'Not nice,' said Anna.

'When I said computer geek I meant techno superstar,' corrected Cody as he tugged on Anna's side plait that draped over her shoulder.

She grinned and Tay frowned.

But Jaz had stopped listening to their banter. All she had on her mind was meeting with Tilly, a few streets across from the gym, tomorrow. What did he have? Was it more news on Ryan? Did Ryan need their help?

How was she going to function until four tomorrow?

Somehow Jaz managed to get through a long dinner with her family and then a full day at school where she tried really hard on her last lot of mock exams, ready for next week's finals. Her parents kept asking how she was going, was she prepared for her exams, but Jaz really had no answers besides 'okay'. She already had her future path picked out and it didn't involve university or top grades. In her line of work she needed a better shooting average than high marks in her exams.

After school Jaz drove straight home in her Jeep. She didn't want to waste a moment. She changed out of her uniform into her canvas hi-tops, black skinny jeans and dark blue singlet. With no clue what Tilly wanted, she tried to be prepared in dark, comfortable clothes.

'Simon, I'm off to the gym to study with the guys. I'll text Mum later and let her know when I'll be back. Call me if you need anything,' she said sticking her head around his bedroom door.

He was still in his uniform and had started on his homework. He blinked behind his glasses and nodded. 'Yeah, righto, sis.'

Their parents both worked until late anyway, so Jaz and Simon had always looked after themselves. 'See ya.'

Jaz left her car at the gym and walked to Tilly's designated meeting place. She didn't have to wait long on the corner before a red Ford Falcon pulled over.

'Hey,' said Tilly as she got in. He suited the older car, with his long skinny body dressed in jeans and a black T-shirt. A cigarette hung from his mouth, burning slowly. Thankfully his window was down.

'Hey back,' she said as she put on her seatbelt and Tilly took off down the road.

The silence was hard to take when she had so many questions. In the end she ran out of patience waiting for Tilly to speak. 'So, what's going on?'

Tilly smiled as if knowing he'd won some secret bet. 'You lasted longer than I thought,' he said after pulling his smoke from his mouth.

'Is this about Ryan? Is he okay?'

'Yeah, so far he's still reporting in like clockwork. He's had some luck come up that enabled him to get closer to Jameson. It gets riskier for him now, though. More chance of being caught.'

'Yep. So, what do you want me for?' The glint in Tilly's eye told Jaz he had a plan brewing.

'Jameson's staff all like to hang out at a pub not far from where the staff flats are. He keeps his bodyguards quite close, his top man stays in his house for extra protection, some in the flat out by the car shed and the rest at a flat a few blocks away. But this bar is frequented often by some of them. I've only been in once and found it's not the sort of place you can just stop by, it has a very local crowd. The best way in is for you to get a job behind the bar. As a girl you could easily get among the guys while they're drinking, they'd like a young girl like you hanging around and wouldn't be suspicious of a ditzy barmaid. No offence.'

'None taken.' And there wasn't. Jaz understood full well what she could bring to this party that other operatives couldn't.

'And it could also be a way for you to keep an eye on Ryan; he might start to join the lads at the bar. But you'd have to remain calm, level-headed and not give anything away. Even the slightest look could be interpreted.'

Her heart began to race. Tilly was offering her a job that would bring her into contact with Ryan, it was both risky and daring. But she wanted to do it, not just to see Ryan but to help gather intel, but she was keen to do anything that might help Ryan be done with this mission quicker.

Tilly pulled his car over and stared at her. He'd stopped in someone's driveway, cars whizzed past behind them. 'I'm very serious here. I need you to know what's at stake. I'm a bit dubious about using you, but on previous form and due to your assets,' his eyes dropped to her chest, 'we believe you're the best person for the job.'

'I *am* the best person for the job, Tilly. I can do it.'

'Are you sure? I know you two have a connection, I'm not blind and neither are others. Do you understand you could risk his life if you do anything stupid?'

Jaz wondered what he meant by that. What did Tilly class as stupid? Smiling at Ryan? A glancing touch? A secret kiss? Now her mind was just getting carried away. She would love to do all the above but not if it meant jeopardising Ryan.

'Yes. I know what's at stake. What do I need to do?'

Tilly backed the car out and continued to his destination. 'We'll give you a false name and ID, I'll get Anna onto that asap. You need to work on who you will be, backstory, etcetera, and get it down pat. Then you need to find a way to get a job at that bar. There isn't one going, so you'd better think of a way to get in there. And there will be a lot of night shifts. Can you handle that?'

She knew he was thinking about her home life.

'Yes, I've been thinking about moving into Pax's house. I need to put some distance between me and my family. If I shift, then I can come and go as I please.' Now she had more reason than ever to move. Her parents weren't going to like it but she was eighteen, so legally they couldn't do a thing about it. She would figure out a way to make them understand, this mission depended on it. Maybe they'd let her stay every second night, or whatever nights she could get work at the bar. *If* she could get work at the bar.

'That would work. Your friends would cover for you.' Tilly parked on the side of the road and pointed up the street. 'See that oldish brick building mid street? That's The Duke. It has a main bar with a small dining area – you might have luck getting a job there first. Around to one side is the sports bar, where the guys hang out. There is FOX on the big TV, darts, pool table, and whatnot. This is where you want to try to be.'

'Okay, got it. When do you want me to go for the job?'

'How about now?'

'*Now?*' Hell, Tilly did like throwing her in the deep end. Shit, she had no experience pulling beers or any other sort of bar work, she'd only just turned eighteen! She'd used her fake ID to get into nightclubs, not to work behind a bar.

'Why not? You look great. Just go and make them an offer they can't refuse.'

She wasn't taking kindly to Tilly's flippant tone. Sure it was easy for him, he was the trained one, he'd probably done stuff like this on the fly all the time. But then Jaz realised that this was how things got done. This was how the Agency trained their operatives: throw them in the deep end and see if they float; if they do, they will be brilliant operatives. Well, one would hope. Better than the other option of sinking.

'Sure,' she said, a little uncertainly.

Tilly was watching her intently. She could read the What-the-fuck-are-you-waiting-for expression on his face.

'Wish me luck, then,' she said, opening the door.

CHAPTER 13

THE STEPS TO the pub were never going to give her enough time to figure out what she was going to say. She might have had half a chance if her brain wasn't too busy panicking.

The pub had a veranda with poles onto the street, decorated with metal lacework in flaking cream paint. The door was solid, painted in faded heritage green with a brass knob and brass panel to push on. The middle of the door was used as an advertising board with fliers for counter meals, sports games, the TAB and local bands. Just standing at the door she could smell the alcohol and hot chips.

Pushing it open, she followed the dark green patterned carpet that held the smell of beer like a sponge. It was quiet inside, just a couple sitting at one of the six tables eating. Remembering Tilly's description, she went left to the bar area where the carpet gave way to jarrah floorboards. A heavy wooden bar ran the length of the room with black worn stools underneath. There were some simple and well-used dark wood round tables, dotted with The Duke beer coasters, and matching chairs. The green carpet reappeared along the back wall where a pool table, dartboard and juke box sat. A big screen TV hung opposite the bar, looking new and out of place.

Jaz hadn't been in many pubs but she did like the feel of this one. There were two guys sitting at the bar watching the soccer on TV, their hands gripped around large glasses of beer. Another man was behind the bar, resting his elbows there as he too watched the game. They glanced her way and she smiled.

'Hiya lads.'

She flicked her hair back over her shoulder and walked towards them with her chest out and a little swing to her hips. All three watched her as she came and stood beside them.

'So, Mr Barman, do you run this joint?' she asked, keeping her smile in place.

The barman looked to be in his late forties, short dark hair with lines on his face, a tattoo showing from under his black T-shirt and a beer belly out of place on his otherwise lean body.

'At the moment I do,' he said slowly. 'Why?'

'Well, today is your lucky day, 'cause I'm looking for a job and I think your wonderful establishment would be perfect.' She crossed her arms as she leaned back on the bar, fully aware it pushed up her breasts, making her singlet stretch.

The bartender frowned. 'We ain't looking for anyone.'

'Aw, come on. I could liven this place up. Don't you guys reckon? Wouldn't you like to see me pour your next beer?' Jaz slid closer to the two old guys, one who now gulped down the yellow liquid in his glass.

Both looked like they were in their fifties, maybe sixties.

'I certainly would, Ted,' said the one with stained teeth. 'You were just saying last week that this place needed something new, besides the TV.'

'Craig, you should just finish your beer,' said the barman, Ted. He frowned and looked at Jaz. 'How old are you, anyway?'

'Legal. I'm eighteen. Finished school and looking for a job to pay my bills.' Well, a little lie; she was very close to finishing. 'What do you reckon? Willing to give me a go?'

'We don't need anyone,' said Ted.

Craig and his mate made noises of distress. 'Bert and I would be happy to see this bright flower when we come. Ten times better than your ugly mug, Ted,' said Craig.

'Well, what if I worked a few free shifts and see if I can't liven this place up a bit. Then, if I'm all right, would you think about hiring me? I'm a hard worker. I'll do whatever you say and I won't have my head stuck on my phone like other kids these days.'

'She makes a valid point,' said Bert.

'Who asked you two gits for your opinions, hey?' said Ted to the old blokes.

'Want us to take our money elsewhere?' Craig offered. That shut Ted up. 'Give the girl a go, what have you got to lose?'

'You bastards are more hassle than you're worth,' Ted teased. He glanced at Jaz again, looking her up and down. 'All right, I'll give you a go. Come back at six tomorrow night, things get busy then.' He smiled as if he really was going to throw her into the fire.

'I'll be here with bells on. You won't regret it, Ted. Thanks, Bert and Craig, I owe you a beer, after I start earning wages, mind you,' she said giving them a wink.

'I like her, Ted,' said Bert with a grin.

Ted's face cracked into a smile. Maybe he was a big softie after all. If Jaz could make it so he couldn't do without her, then she just might have her foot in the door.

'Thanks, I'll see you tomorrow!' Jaz turned around and bounded off towards the door.

'Hang on a minute,' yelled Ted.

Jaz paused and glanced back.

'What's your name?' he asked.

Jaz smiled but then had to think quickly. She needed a new name but one that started with the same sound and close to her own name so she would turn if called it. Heaven forbid she forgot she had a fake name, but this would at least help. 'Jeni,' she said eventually. 'See you later.' She winked and skipped to the door.

She already had a good feeling about this job.

Tilly was waiting for her, reading a paper and smoking.

'You know you could light yourself up doing that. Fire, paper, whoosh,' she said as she climbed in.

Tilly gave her a stupid look before folding up the paper and driving off before pulling the smoke from his mouth.

'How'd it go?'

'Yeah, all right.' Jaz watched the houses flash past as they made their way back to the drop-off point near the gym.

'Go on, spill,' said Tilly giving up impatiently.

That'll teach you for doing it to me to begin with, she thought, trying not to smile as she relayed what happened. 'So,' she finished, 'do you want me to get Anna to do up a new ID ready for tomorrow?'

'Yep, make it a driver's licence and tell her to make the address the safe house closest to the pub. So, he's really going to give you a trial?'

'Yeah. Initially he wasn't interested, but luckily the two old blokes were there. I think they helped win him over. Now I just have to do the rest tomorrow.'

'You'll be fine. You're a quick learner, Jaz, and quick on your feet.'

Wow, a compliment from Tilly. Jaz locked that away in the special-moments compartment in her brain.

'Leave your car at the safe house and take the bus to the pub,' he added as he pulled up by the road verge.

'Thanks Tilly. I appreciate this chance.'

'Just don't screw it up. Stay in contact and I can advise you as you go. But for now we'll work on you getting the job first and settling in. It could take a few weeks or months before we even want to make the next move.' He nodded for her to get out of the car. Their chat was over.

She didn't even get a goodbye, just the roar of the car as she shut the door.

Back at the gym Jaz found it locked. She let herself into Pax's house to find her two best friends watching a movie together in the lounge room. It had a great old leather button couch that he'd picked up from an antique shop, along with the coffee table, old record player and a cabinet full of other random things he'd collected. The carpet was a thick brown, almost shag-pile length, and heavy mustard curtains hung over the only window. The room felt antique and different, just like Pax.

Even though it was a long couch, her friends were sitting together up one end, Anna leaning into Tay for warmth. This room was always cold because the fireplace on the side wall didn't work; it was just there to look pretty now. Pax had been meaning for years to buy a gas heater to stick in the gap, one that looked like logs burning. Maybe Jaz would do that with some of the money he'd left her?

'Hey guys, what are you watching?' But she didn't have to ask as she saw their favourite movie *The Goonies* at the part where the boys find the pirate ship.

Tay reached for the remote and paused the movie. 'Hey you, how did it go? What did Tilly want?'

Jaz joined them on the couch and told them the plan. 'And so I go back tomorrow to try to win Ted over.'

'Gosh, Tilly doesn't waste time, does he?' said Anna, frowning.

'I guess we can't afford to.' Jaz shrugged. 'And I have to ask Mum; no, actually I'm going to *tell* her that I want to move in here.'

'What? At Pax's?' Anna sounded shocked.

'It's the perfect solution. I can come and go as I please and keep an eye on the gym. I'll tell Mum I want to run this place after school's finished, so why not move in now. Do you think she'll go for it?'

'Shit, I wish my mum would. She'd kill me for even asking. But maybe she'd let me stay here on occasion if you are here.' Anna's eyes lit up. Green swirling seas. 'Oh, this could work.'

'Do you want Pax's room?' asked Jaz.

No one had touched anything of his, nor mentioned cleaning out the house. Despite the fact that the place now belonged to them, they hadn't even gone into Pax's room.

'No. You take it. You'll be the one who'll get to stay here and run the gym. Maybe when I'm twenty-five my parents will let me make my own decisions,' Anna said with a roll of her eyes.

'If you're sure?' Anna nodded. 'Will both of you help me clean it out over the weekend? It's not something I want to do alone.'

'Sure, of course. What are we going to do with all his clothes? We have to keep his favourite Hawaiian shirt,' said Anna.

'How about we get one framed to hang in the gym next to Ali?' said Tay.

'Oh Tay, that's brilliant.' Anna gave him a hug and he almost blushed.

He cleared his throat. 'How about we watch the rest of this movie and then make a start on the room before we all go home?'

'I like the sound of that,' said Jaz.

'Me too.'

'Oh, and Anna, I need a new driver's licence for a Jeni, for tomorrow, please?' Jaz said remembering.

'Jeni? Yeah, I guess it will do,' said Anna studying her. 'I'll whip one up while you guys start on the room.'

'It's a plan. Thanks.'

They all squished together on the couch and Tay pressed play.

Jaz pulled out her phone and sent her mum a message saying she would be late.

She didn't want to live her whole life at the gym. She had been thinking she would like her own nice house like Ryan; even better would be sharing his house. She sighed. That was a far-out pipedream. How could that ever become a reality? Thoughts like this did nothing but make life harder. So, with a forced effort she focused on the TV and watched as Mike stuffed his marble bag full of jewels from the pirate ship belonging to One Eyed Willy.

CHAPTER 14

Jaz arrived at The Duke at fifteen minutes to six. She wore a plain black V-neck T-shirt that was a little snug and denim shorts with her black hi-top Converse. Ted had been wearing black and she hoped it had been a uniform of sorts. She walked in and went straight to the bar. Ted was wiping down the bar top and almost groaned when he saw her.

'Hi Ted. I'm ready to start. What do you want me to do?' she asked brightly.

'First let me check your ID so I don't get caught with an underage kid.'

Jaz whipped out her new driver's licence and waited for him to hand it back. 'Righto, have you ever poured a beer before?'

'Nope, but I'm ready to learn.'

Ted had her filling glasses with the perfect head on them in no time and then it was onto using the till, where to wash the glasses, and then he showed her the kitchen and said she could help them out in here when things were slow, doing dishes and clearing tables. Jaz took it all in her stride and stayed in the kitchen to finish some dishes before popping back out to the bar to see how Ted was getting on.

In her absence it had got busier and she quickly ducked around picking up empty glasses, getting them washed and even took a few orders while Ted was busy at the other end of the bar.

'Craig, Bert, you boys made it back,' she said when she finally saw some faces she knew. 'What'll you have?'

'Hello, lass. We'll both have a middy, thanks.'

They sat at the two empty stools by the bar, their usual seats she guessed, and placed a twenty-dollar note each on the bar.

Jaz shot them a smile as she poured both glasses. 'Voilà, what do you think? Not bad, hey? Just the right amount of froth?' she said as she took their twenties and dumped their correct change back on the bar in front of them.

'Yeah, I'd say you done really good there,' said Bert, licking his lips.

'You guys are my special lads tonight. Just give me the nod and I'll be over to fix you up.' Jaz gave them a wink. 'Now if you'll excuse me, there is a lad over there who can't play pool properly.'

While everyone seemed happy with drinks, Jaz ducked over to the pool table where two guys in their late twenties, maybe early thirties, were playing a game. 'No drinks on the table, fellas. Who's winning?' she asked as she took the beer off and held it waiting for the responsible owner to fetch it. She plastered on a big smile so they wouldn't get upset.

'I am,' said the guy with longish blond hair. 'Thanks. You any good at pool?' he asked.

'Maybe.'

'Take my next shot?'

'Sure. If you keep your beers off the table, I'll give it a crack.' Jaz took the outstretched pool cue and indicated to the red ball. 'You smalls?' He nodded and Jaz took the shot, only just sinking it. She was a bit rusty. It might be something to work on if she wanted to keep doing this. 'There you go. You ready for another drink?' she asked, indicating to their low glasses.

'Why not. Can we get two of the same, thanks.' Blondie took out a fifty and handed it to her.

'Be right back,' she said.

She got their beers and their change and was about to head back when Ted gave her an appreciative nod. Well, that was a start.

But getting Blondie to drink more ended up with causing trouble when Jaz deemed him too drunk and cut off his beer.

'Ted? Do you think he's had enough?' she said, asking for clarification.

'Yep. Sorry, mate. Have a water on the house,' said Ted placing a bottle of water on the bar.

'I don't want a fucken water, this is a pub, for fuck's sake,' said Blondie, getting agitated.

His friend backed him up with some supportive words, which didn't help the situation at all. They were starting to cause a scene. Jaz went to the friend and told him to head outside for some fresh air.

'We will, but with a beer,' said Blondie, slapping his money down on the bar.

People turned to watch, waiting, the chatter died down in the otherwise noisy bar.

'Come on, mate. Why don't I walk you out,' said Jaz softly. She was hoping her charm would cool the situation.

'Piss off,' came his reply.

'Do you want to walk out here on your own steam or do you want me to drag your arse out and embarrass you in front of the whole pub? It's your call, mate,' she said harshly. She was using her serious voice. He was in trouble now.

'Who the fuck do you think you are?' He laughed.

'Ted, do you mind if I remove this man from your establishment?'

Ted's eyebrows were working overtime as he tried to figure out how the hell she intended on doing that. She could tell he was worried, more for her safety than anything. 'Um, I better do it.'

'It's cool. I've got it. Come on then, let's go.' She reached for his arm and he flicked her off.

'I ain't moving till I get my beer,' he growled.

Jaz was sure he was about to add 'bitch' on the end but stopped short. Maybe he was concerned with the look she was giving him. Actually, she was quite happy he needed to be escorted out. Ted couldn't say no to her if she could handle the drunks.

'Fine.' She reached for his arm again but before he could flick her off again she whipped it around behind his back and reefed it up to his shoulder blades.

'Hey, ouch.' Blondie tried to fight her but in his drunken state he was no match for Jaz's strength, and in the end she felt his defeat.

She guided him to the door, directing him with the tension on his arm. Ted followed and held out his money. 'No hard feelings, mate, but rules are rules.'

Blondie shot Jaz a funny look when she let him go. 'Who are you?' he mumbled before taking his money and walking away, with his mate following. He rolled his shoulder and stretched his arm as he went. A smile tugged on her lips. Getting physical was so much fun.

Jaz walked past Ted, back inside, dusting off her hands, and went back to collecting empty glasses.

Jaz didn't know how long Ted wanted her to work for that night, so she just kept going until they closed up. It was nearly eleven-thirty and her feet were killing her, and she was wondering if she was half-drunk on just the smell of grog alone. After she saw Bert and Craig out the door, the last hangers-on, she plonked herself down in a chair by the bar and looked at Ted. 'Are those two always the last to go?'

'Na, I think they stayed for you,' he said with a smile. 'You did good, Jeni. You must be stuffed, you didn't stop.'

'Told you I work hard,' she said, pushing her luck.

Ted just shook his head and poured them both a Coke. 'You know how to handle the drunks too. Had practise?' he probed.

'You could say that. My mate back home was a Mixed Martial Arts fighter and he taught me a few things. He loved all that stuff and it's rather cool once you get into it. Saved my arse a few times from creepy guys who couldn't handle "no".'

'Can't say I've had that problem,' said Ted with a chuckle. 'Well, you're full of surprises, Jeni. You'll be good for this place, I reckon. You seem to brighten up this bleak old room, and the guys like it. A lot of them will be back because you made their night enjoyable, maybe not Blondie but that's no great loss.' He let out a big sigh. 'I guess I better hire you.'

'Really?'

Ted nodded. 'Really. I'd be stupid not to.'

Jaz did little fist pumps. 'Thank you, Ted, you won't regret it.'

'So, tell me a bit about yourself, Jeni?'

Jaz told him as much as she dared. She'd planned her story out during school today, three pages of notes. More than she did for her study.

She told Ted how she lived with a friend in a flat, hence she needed a job. Her parents were from a country town.

'Ah, that explains the friendly nature,' he said. 'You seem very trustworthy.'

She took that as a good sign. They chatted for another ten minutes and he took her phone number so he could text her next shifts through. 'I'm after anything, Ted. If you need to be somewhere, I can come fill in during the week. Just let me know.' Jaz wasn't sure when Jameson's boys came in, so if she could get work at all different times then she might be able to piece together their routine. She had no clue if any of them were here tonight and it wasn't really her goal. Tonight had been all about impressing Ted so he wanted to hire her, and getting the hang of this job. Getting to know the regulars would come within the next few weeks and that's when she'd take note of Jameson's guys.

Tilly was also getting the intel for her to look at over the weekend so she could familiarise herself with Jameson's bodyguards. That way she would know them the moment they stepped into the bar.

'Thanks for the Coke, Ted. I better be getting home.'

'I'll get all the paperwork sorted for tomorrow night. You can come back tomorrow and do this all again?' Ted raised an eyebrow curiously. He could probably tell how beat she was, but he was testing her.

'Sure can. I'll be here. Same time?'

'Same bat channel,' he said with a smile and Jaz laughed. Pax had always said that too.

'Night Ted.'

Jaz walked outside into the cool night air. Music was beating away in the distance from a house party maybe. The streetlights lit the way as she walked towards her bus stop. This would be her new routine. She would also have to bring a backpack to put her things in, a jumper and maybe a knife for safety in case she was jumped this late at night waiting for the bus. But hopefully not tonight. Tonight she was too dead on her feet to fight. If she was attacked she'd make sure to tell them that.

Saturday morning Jaz made her parents breakfast. They gravitated towards the kitchen as the bacon started wafting.

'What's going on here?' said Paul as Jaz handed him a large mug of coffee. 'You hungry, Jaz?'

'Yes, and I thought you might be too. Pull up a chair. Eggs won't be a second.'

'Oh, thank you,' said Paul sitting at the table.

Tasha picked up her mug from the breakfast bar but she didn't move. She was in her weekend wear of Lorna Jane workout suit: black tights and a matching jumper. 'What's happened? Did you crash your car? Fail your exams?' Tash raised her eyebrows curiously.

Paul glanced up from the table, only now realising he'd been bribed.

'Nothing like that,' said Jaz as she put the eggs onto the toast next to the bacon. 'But I do want to talk to you both.' She handed Tasha her plate, then carried her own and Paul's to the table.

'It must be serious for this?' said Paul. He was still wearing his blue fluffy robe.

'Hey, where's mine?' said Simon as he walked into the room in his striped pyjamas.

'It's still there, everything's hot,' said Jaz. Simon rolled his eyes but went into the kitchen to start on his breakfast.

Jaz and Paul started eating but Tasha didn't move a muscle.

'What?' said Jaz with a mouthful of egg and toast.

'Sorry, I just can't eat until I know what this is about. I'm really nervous now. Are you pregnant?'

'Mum!'

'Ew, gross,' said Simon from the kitchen.

Jaz put down her fork. 'It's nothing like that. I want to move out.' There, she'd said it. She watched her parents, waiting for the explosion. When nothing happened she continued to put her case forward. 'It's just that I want to keep the gym running, you know what that place means to me and it would be so much easier if I lived there. And I don't mean full-time, I could still stay here every second night or less, whatever. But the gym is my life, after school's done I want to introduce some new classes and workouts. Like a self-defence one for girls. I could go to other gyms and offer this as well. I've been thinking about it a lot,' she finished in a rush.

'I can tell,' said Tasha. She glanced at Paul and he pulled a face that looked like defeat. 'We were wondering when this would happen.'

Jaz tilted her head to the side. Had she heard that correctly?

'You're eighteen, and who are we to keep you from your life? But I know we both like the idea of you still staying here. We were scared you'd move out full-time, but honey, please know you are welcome to come home any time. We still want you around, want to see you, and Simon will miss you too.'

'No I won't,' said Simon with a cheeky grin.

'Really, so I can sort of move into Pax's place?' She half-expected them to put up more of a fight, but her mum had always been realistic, unlike

Anna's mum who seemed to think Anna would never want to leave home, nor would she let her.

'It's not Pax's place anymore, Jaz. It's yours and Anna's. Pax came to me, telling me his wishes and hoped I'd be on board with what he wanted because he knew it's what you'd want. And he was right. You've always had a connection with that place, this is your life now. You're an adult.' Tash looked like she was at a funeral but it was clear she meant every word.

Jaz got up and hugged her. 'Thanks Mum. That means a lot. I'm gonna make a start on clearing out Pax's room today. Tay came up with the idea of framing one of his awful Hawaiian shirts.'

Both her parents laughed but agreed it was a fabulous idea.

After breakfast she went to the gym and made a start until Tay and Anna joined her. Pax had a plain room: cream walls, wood furniture, polished floorboards and a soft rug by the bed. Old antique cupboards were along one wall and his bed was newer but a solid wood frame. Jaz had already pulled down his brown curtains and was going to buy some in jade with a matching bedspread to lift the room, and maybe a new cream rug and some cream accent pillows. In no time the room would have her stamp on it but remain with a thread of Pax.

'Look at you go, Sadie,' said Anna when she arrived in denim overalls and a white shirt. A patterned bandana was wrapped around her head.

'Long way to go yet.' She'd only stripped the bed and curtains, dumping them outside, plus brought in some garbage bags to put all the clothes in.

Tay was right behind her. These two were seriously joined at the hip.

'I hope we don't find anything, you know, gross,' said Tay.

Jaz and Anna pulled a face and shook their heads. 'Eewww, Tay.' Anna pushed him away. 'You can do the stuff under the bed then,' she teased.

'Maybe you should,' he said grabbing her around the waist and carting her to the bed where he tipped her upside down. 'Can you see anything scary?'

'Tay,' Anna squealed. 'Tay, put me down.'

'Not until you tell me the coast is clear under there.' Tay held her tightly as Anna put her hands on the floor and glanced under the bed.

'Hey, it's actually clean under here, just some shoes.'

Tay let her down gently, taking his time letting her go. Jaz watched with fascination at her friends. What was holding them back? Maybe they were waiting for her to tell them it was okay if they wanted to be together. Maybe they were scared about ruining a friendship, a bit like what Jaz might have done with Ryan.

Without realising, she'd sunk down into an old leather chair in the corner of the room as she thought about Ryan. Her chest ached like nothing she'd experienced before.

'You okay, Jaz?' Anna was by her side, holding her hand. 'Tay, can you put the kettle on please?'

When it was just the two of them in the room, Anna tilted her head towards her so she could look in her eyes. 'I'm worried about you, my friend. What's going on?'

Jaz felt like she was on the edge of a cliff face, the wind pounding at her back inching her closer as she tried her best to keep herself together. Pax. Salvatore. Ryan. Jaz had to share something with Anna before she exploded.

'At Steph's wedding, Ryan more or less said goodbye.' Her voice was almost a whisper.

'Goodbye? What do you mean?'

'I guess that he didn't want me, and the fact he was going undercover and may never come back. He didn't want me to wait. I don't know, all of it. Do you think he knows how I feel? Do you think that's what's scared him off?'

'Oh honey.' Anna knelt down by the chair and held her hands. 'Did you ever think that maybe he's trying to spare you pain, or maybe even spare himself pain?'

Jaz frowned at her. Why would Ryan spare himself pain?

'I'm sure he cares about you, Jaz. I've seen the way he looks at you, and protects you. Maybe he was just scared? I'm sure it would have hurt him to walk away.'

Jaz smirked a little. 'Actually, it was me who did the walking away.'

'You did?'

'Yeah, we were dancing and I realised I didn't want to make things harder when I knew it was goodbye. So, I just walked away. It nearly killed me but I didn't want him to think I was weak. But I do feel weak, Anna. As if Ryan is my kryptonite. Like I'm only half a person when he's not around. It's so strange. Is this what love does to you?'

Anna smiled at her sadly. 'I guess. I'm yet to really experience a real love. But hey, you still have us, and the gym. I wish I could make you feel better.'

'You have. Just getting it off my chest helps.'

'I wish you'd come to me sooner.'

'I didn't want to admit it, that he was pushing me out of his life, you know?'

'I get it,' said Anna. 'Hey, so what's gonna happen if Ryan ends up at this pub with the other Sesha Serpent dudes and he sees you?'

'I don't know. That's the thing. No one knows what's happened, not even Tilly. I'm not sure how Ryan will react at all. I'm guessing he'll just carry on unaffected, as if I'm just like another operative and not someone he slept with.'

Anna pulled a sad face. 'Hey.'

'I know, it's my own fault. I talked him into it. I wanted it, no strings attached. Only my heart had other ideas. I didn't know it was going to change me.'

'Would you sleep with him if you could go back, knowing what you know now?' asked Anna.

Jaz thought for a moment. To go back and change the most amazing moment in her life or not? The thing is, it wouldn't really change a damn thing. She was already in love with him by that stage, she just hadn't realised how much. That night with Ryan was worth every bit of shit she was going through now.

'Yes, I'd do it all over again in a heartbeat.'

CHAPTER 15

RYAN STOOD OUTSIDE the door of the office building, where he was told to wait while Randall and Jameson went inside for a meeting. He'd been waiting here for an hour and a half, it was hot in the afternoon sun. At least Wilkins got to sit inside the car, which he left running so he had the air con. Sweat was beading along Ryan's forehead and he could feel his shirt sticking to his skin under his suit coat. But he didn't take it off because it hid his gun, in a holster given to him by Randall.

Randall was proving to be a tough nut to crack. Ryan made Randall look bad in front of Jameson, so in getting this job he had put the other workers offside. He'd been trying to make up ground ever since. Maybe Randall thought he was gunning for his job, which was true. And Wilkins was grumpy about being the driver but he knew it was that or nothing. He was probably just waiting around for Ryan to mess up so he could get his old job back.

Last night, as Ryan had done a perimeter check around Jameson's house he'd heard some of the staff talking near the quarters.

'He'll be gone the moment the boss's daughter dumps him,' said Wilkins.

He should have been polishing the car, but he was a slacker.

'Do you think he's after Randall's job? Randall says he's not worried but I think he is,' said Bud, another of the house guards. 'I heard Reece is over-qualified for this job.'

'Bud, you're an arse,' said Wilkins. 'No one can be more qualified than Randy. Stop spreading shit you don't know.'

Ryan had listened for as long as he dared, just in case anything else was mentioned about Jameson, but it was just staff whinging and then talk about going to the pub.

Ryan needed to get in with the boys, he needed them onside and already he was working on a plan to achieve that.

His phone rang, and with no sign of Jameson he quickly answered it. 'Annaliese?'

'Hi, baby. You free to talk?'

'At the moment yes, but when your dad comes out I gotta go.' She knew the routine. It meant he'd hang up on her. Luckily for Ryan, Annaliese thought it was endearing how professional he was for her father.

'I'll be quick. I'm just hoping we could do something tonight?'

'I'd love to babe, but I was hoping to do something with the boys tonight. They still aren't happy with me, you know, dating you. I'd like to try to win them over.' That and he liked to take a break from Annaliese whenever he could.

'How about I pop over for a bit just after work. I'll be quick, I promise?' she said with a purr.

The door opened behind him and he quickly ended the call. 'Okay, see you then. Bye.' Tucking the phone away he checked the area as Jameson emerged. He nodded to Randall to say the coast was clear and they walked Jameson to the car.

When Jameson was safely at home, Ryan just had to hang around outside until he was needed again. He got to knock off at five tonight, though if Jameson decided to go out late they would be called back.

'So, what's this pub I hear the guys talking about?' Ryan asked Randall as he met him by the house on one of his perimeter rounds.

Randall gave him a blank look. It had been two weeks since Ryan had scored Wilkie's job, you'd think Randall would cut him some slack.

'Look, I get the feeling everyone is pissed at me. I'm not after your job, or anyone else's, if that's what you're worried about. I'm just here until I can find a better job or start my own business.' Ryan turned away from Randall and gazed down the driveway. He could see Wilkie down the bottom, buffing the rims on the car.

Randall was quiet for a while. Ryan didn't pressure him, just left the ball in his court.

'It's called The Duke. Not a bad place, the beer's cold and the fellas like it.'

Ryan turned to thank him but Randall had already headed back inside. Was that his first welcome of sorts? At least Ryan had the name of the pub now, it was almost as good as an invite. Soon he'd show up and shout the boys beers and try to win them over that way. If he could work on Randall, get him to like him more, then the others would follow. They all looked up to Randall as the leader of the group.

When the day was over Ryan headed back to his flat. He'd decided to stay in and not pressure the guys at the pub just yet. Let what had happened with Randall simmer and work its way to the rest of the staff and then he'd see.

But staying in meant Annaliese.

She knocked on his door at six.

'Hello, Reece.'

Annaliese looked like she was ready for the club. Little strapless black dress, heels, hair cascading over her shoulder and the reddest lips. She was a head turner, yet to Ryan she was just his job. Annaliese lacked life, she wasn't interesting nor did she do anything that impressed him, much less amazed him. Some blokes probably like their trophy girlfriends, but Annaliese was not the kind of girl for him. He liked girls with spunk, like Jaz. She was never far from his thoughts.

'Don't you look amazing,' he said, pulling her into his arms and swinging the door shut.

'I brought wine,' she said with a smile as she waved the bottle in her hand.

'Later,' he said, taking it and putting it on the table. Annaliese groaned as he grabbed her backside.

She, in turn, pulled off the black shirt he'd put on after his shower. Her fingers ran over his chest, tracing the lumps of muscle with long red nails as her waist pressed against his.

Ryan bent and kissed her bare shoulder, then her neck, before kissing her ear lobe. He'd kiss her everywhere in the hope he didn't have to kiss her properly. It was the hardest part of all for him, to kiss her convincingly. He slapped his hands against her legs then ran them up towards her bum, dragging her fitted dress up with them. She had nothing on underneath. He went exploring, her breathing intensified as she pulled out the condom in his pocket before undoing his jeans, pulling them down, setting him free.

He waited as she slipped on the protective skin.

Ryan grabbed her butt and lifted her up. Annaliese put her arms around his neck and lifted her legs, wrapping them around him as he leaned her back against the door.

'Oh baby,' she purred.

Annaliese was kissing his shoulder in between her groans, no doubt leaving lipstick smeared all over his skin. But he couldn't focus on that. He closed his eyes, pushing her hard against the door as he found his rhythm. He closed off his ears to her noisy groans and words she liked to mumble. He sunk deep into his thoughts, picturing long raven hair that glided over his skin like a satin sheet. He thought of the tight, fit body that could take down a grown man, hell, it could take him down if he wasn't careful. That thought alone turned him on. He imagined her lips, the taste so sweet and innocent. He remembered what it was like to cup her perfect breasts in his hands and as he grew closer to release he let Annaliese kiss him, but in his mind it was someone completely different.

At work the next day Ryan found Randall easier to be around. He hoped the rest of the staff noticed.

'Get ready, the boss has a stop at the warehouse and we don't want another incident like at the farm,' said Randall. 'Just stay a metre or two from the boss at all times unless told otherwise.'

'Righto. I'll have my eyes peeled.'

'Morning, Mr Lancaster,' said Jameson as he came out to get in his car. He was in a deep velvet suit with a black shirt and tie. A matching fedora on his head.

'Morning, sir.' Ryan sat in the front with Wilkie and they were silent all the way out to the warehouse. Jameson wasn't the chatty sort.

Ryan thought they were going to the shed on his rural property but instead they were still in the city, heading towards the shipping area in Fremantle. He took note of every detail, because it was a new place. Wilkie pulled up outside a large corrugated-iron shed. Shipping containers were stacked outside, and judging by the size of the shed there were probably a few inside. It was next door to a fresh-seafood business, their boats and packing crates stacked outside too.

Randall ejected the clip on his gun and reloaded. Ryan did the same. His nerves started to tighten with excitement. This visit was something special. Ryan focused, taking in every detail, from the flaking black and white sign on the shed, 'Drake Industries', to the dimension of the shed. He was accustomed to searching for hidden rooms, false walls and missing space.

When he got out the smell of the ocean was strong; they must be just a stone's throw from the channel. The breeze was quite resilient, lifting the bottom of their suit jackets. Jameson's hand went to his fedora.

As per Randall's instructions, Ryan followed Jameson closely, his hand ready to reach for the gun. Randall keyed a number into the keypad and opened the door, checking inside before waving Jameson in.

That was interesting. Why would Randall need to check inside a locked place? Did they have workers inside they didn't trust? Ryan tucked those details away as they moved through the large building. It stunk of fuel, salt, wet wood, mould and another dirty smell he couldn't put his hand on. No one seemed to be working today, but there were a couple of forklifts, stacked crates and fridges and freezers that lined the back wall. None of their intel had brought them any connection to this side of Jameson's business. The seafood industry would give him access to the water, allowing him to bring things into and out of the country. Ryan wondered what ingenious ways he used to bring in the drugs or girls.

A half wall sectioned off an area that looked like a prep area for the fish. Then there were rooms beyond that, an office, kitchen area, and a room or bedroom area, which looked like it was used casually. Maybe by staff pulling long shifts? There was another room but the door was shut. Ryan checked the ceiling, walls and corners for cameras. There had been one over the main door they'd come through and another outside the office. If there were more he was yet to find them. He'd have to be careful. If he seemed untrustworthy, or was caught in areas he shouldn't be, he could blow everything. Each step had to be slow and meticulous. For now he would play the dutiful bodyguard.

They came to a stop at the end, at another door with a coded keypad. Randall entered this code as well. If Jameson trusted anyone it must only be Randall.

'Stay here, and keep watch. You can make yourself a cuppa,' said Randall. 'We won't be long,' he added, following Jameson.

Okay, so this was as far as he went. He was dying to know what was behind the door but he couldn't see a thing before they closed it.

Ryan tried to check again for cameras. When he was certain he had them all covered he casually walked back to the couple of rooms they'd passed. He went and got himself a coffee, just to keep it real. Then, with his foam cup, he went and tried the door that interested him. He found it opened. What if there was a camera inside?

Did he just take the chance? Just pretend he was having a stickybeak? Lots of people would want to see what was behind a closed door but body-guards were supposed to just do their job.

What to do?

You didn't get anything without risk, so Ryan took it. Slowly he opened the door enough to poke his head inside. It was just a normal square room, with a bed and wash sink, much like the other one. Except, on the second glance around the room, he spotted a lady's shoe poking out from under the bed and a very long strand of dark hair hanging from the basin. Did they have female staff with their own separate sleeping areas? Or was something else at play?

Ryan shut the door and went back to the kitchen. He wanted to look for any clues, even the fridge might hold something. Then he stood at the door to the office and could see the screen with one of the cameras' feed on it. He didn't dare go in, just leant against the doorjamb and searched the desks. It all looked like paperwork, pallet sheets and orders. Why was no one here? Did this place only run at certain times? Ryan would make sure the Agency got an operative to keep the place under surveillance.

Something flashed past on one of the camera screens and Ryan stepped inside the office to get a closer look. He now had a reason. Watching the screen he saw the person again and quickly pulled out his phone and took a photo of him. Randall would be interested to know who was moving around the building. While he was inside the office Ryan glanced around. No hidden cameras that he could see, but that didn't mean there weren't any. For all he knew this could be a test. Not wanting to push his luck he stepped out of the office slowly, while trying to take in papers on the desk. He doubted that anything of interest would be left about. What he needed was to get into that room Jameson was in now.

He was walking out of the room just as Randall came out the door. The squint of his eyes gave away his surprise at finding Ryan in the office.

'Mr Randall, I just captured someone out the front of the building on the camera. I got a photo. Do you recognise this person?' Quickly he stepped towards Randall and held out his phone.

Randall glanced at it then nodded. 'It's okay, that's just Pete. He keeps an eye on the place. He was probably just checking the outside while we were here, or chatting to Mr Wilkins.'

'Oh, yep. Good to know. Sorry.' He'd have to warn the operative that he wouldn't be alone in watching over the building. Hopefully this Pete was the only one.

'Don't apologise, I'd rather you come to us with any little detail,' said Jameson as he shut the door. 'Please, take me back home now.'

There was a weird smell that clung to both their clothes and Ryan tried hard to place it.

'Yes, sir.' Ryan turned to Randall. 'I thought I was best suited watching the cameras while I waited,' he said softly as they made their way out of the building. 'And I helped myself to a coffee too.' He wanted them to think he was honest.

It would take time to build up their confidence in him. Especially if Jameson was keeping this business secret from his daughter. But then again, if he liked Ryan enough he might just groom him to take over the family business one day. Ryan almost shuddered at the thought. How many years down the track was he thinking? Would he have to marry Annaliese before that happened? Did he want to go that far undercover? Maybe once upon a time he'd have been prepared to do that for the Agency and for the greater good, but now something lurked in his mind, changing his way of thinking, making him feel a little selfish. He just couldn't put his finger on what.

CHAPTER 16

Bang. Bang. Bang. Bang.

Jaz lowered her gun as she stared at the target. The smell from her gun was strangely comforting. And the kick it let off with each pull of the trigger filled her with an awesome energy, yet she felt calm and relaxed. It was like she could rest her mind as she thought about nothing else but the target.

'Holy shit, Jaz, you're getting bloody good,' said Cody as they both pulled off their ear muffs.

His mouth was open for a second before his smile spread across his tanned face. His eyes sparkled and Jaz couldn't help but smile too. The range was her second favourite place after the gym. Derik and Stew who managed the place were becoming fast friends like Bags and Tick. These were her kind of people. Cody, Taylor, Ryan, Tilly and Anna. They all felt the same when firing a weapon or fighting. They all understood what she felt and they all were on the same level. Jaz wasn't a loner anymore. She wasn't the odd one out, it was as if she'd finally found her crowd. It was an amazing thing to realise you had a big circle of friends you could call family.

'Yeah, well, I've been practising lots, and I'm so in love with my gun.' Jaz tilted her shiny Firestar handgun. The handgrip was black, but the barrel was steel and it was engraved with a phoenix. Ryan had brought her the 9-millimetre for her birthday. It wasn't new, but the Star Firestar was a compact pistol designed for concealment, and Jaz found it very stable when shooting and the recoil was offset by the weight of the gun. She'd researched everything on it; well, actually Tay told her all about it being a know-it-all on guns, and she'd been shooting with it every moment she could get. She wanted to feel like the gun was an extension of her arm, a part of her own body. She took out the magazine. Tay had also taught her how to pull it down to clean it. It had been the best lesson she'd ever had. If only her exams could have been on that she would have aced them!

'Hmm, I can tell,' said Cody.

He had a bruise on his cheek from their sparring yesterday. She'd got him good with her foot. It was her fault, she should have held back but sometimes she just wanted to go hard. She wanted a fight, a real fight, something she could sink her teeth into, someone who could push her to her best. At the moment she was taking on Cody and Tay at the same time to give her a workout. She loved that but didn't like hurting her friends. Cody had suggested entering her into a proper fight against other women. The idea had merit, not that she'd tell Cody that.

'So, how does it feel to have your last exam tomorrow?' he asked as they packed up their guns. Cody had to return his to Derik to lock up, but Jaz got to put hers in its case and take it home. Anna had made her a gun licence. It was weird that she could cart a gun around legally. No bullets, though.

'Like it couldn't come fast enough. I want the exams done, school finished so I can focus on my job at The Duke,' she said softly so Derik couldn't hear.

Cody nodded. 'I still think you should be studying with Tay and Anna. You only get one chance,' he added with a smirk.

Jaz groaned. 'I can't look at another bloody chemistry book, I have study overload. I swear, Cody, this has been better exam preparation than last-minute cramming.'

They said goodbye to Derik, signed out with Stew and jumped in Jaz's Jeep and headed back to the gym.

Jaz had been sleeping at the gym for nearly two weeks, on and off. She tried to go home as much as possible, leaving the nights she needed to be at work the nights she stayed at the gym. Anna was even allowed to stay on the odd night as well, under strict rules. She had to study, go to bed at a reasonable hour and could only stay when Jaz was there. Then Anna had text messages from her mum while she was there. Seriously, Anna couldn't wait to cut the apron strings but her mum kept tying on more.

'Hey, guys.' Jaz found her friends at the kitchen table, books out among empty coffee cups. She shut the door behind Cody as Tick was running a self-defence class for his sister's friends. Probably earning adoring fans the moment he took off his shirt. Teenage girls, they probably wouldn't take anything in besides how many muscles there were in a six-pack.

Mind you, Jaz was the same around Ryan. Very hard to concentrate with his awesome body so close she just wanted to touch it. It seemed like years ago when he first came to the gym and they sparred. Some days she wished they could go back to that.

'Hey, Jaz. How did you shoot them?' asked Tay.

'She's getting worse,' said Cody. Tay frowned. Cody rolled his eyes. 'She's too good. It's horrible.'

Anna laughed. 'How did you go?'

'Cody can hold his own. Don't let him fool you,' said Jaz. 'I'm gonna go have a shower and get ready for my shift. Are you staying the night?' she asked Anna.

'Yep. I think Mum's getting used to the idea. I think that fact that I'm still alive has reassured her I'm not going to die cos I'm away from home. Tay's going to come back after he's had dinner with his dad.' Sometimes Tay stayed the night in Jaz's old single bed. Anna hadn't changed their room at all, she liked it and it came in handy having the extra bed.

Anna found it a little bit scary being in Pax's house on her own, so Tay usually came and they watched TV until Jaz got home. They were onto the last season of *Game of Thrones* and had already got *Orange is the New Black* ready to go next.

'Can I watch too?' asked Cody. 'I got two episodes in when my mate wanted it back.'

'Sure,' said Anna.

Jaz left them to chat about the last episode he'd seen, so they could work out which one it was. In her room she grabbed her pub clothes, which consisted of either shorts or black leggings and a black T-shirt. Ted didn't care what was on it; as long as she wore mostly black it would look as if they had some sort of uniform.

Jaz tied her hair up into a loose bun on top of her head, chucked on her shirt, three-quarter leggings and Converse hi-tops. At the last minute she decided to put a little bit of make-up on, just enough to make her eyes pop without looking too made up. She knew she had to start making her move soon and had to look nice enough to attract attention from the Sesha Serpent boys.

'Righto, I'm off. See you guys at midnight.'

'I just hope you don't fall asleep during your exam tomorrow,' said Anna.

'I'll be all right, Mummy,' said Jaz as she gave her a hug.

Jaz drove to the safe house, put her Jeep in the garage so it was hidden and then caught the bus to the pub.

'Teddy, how's it going?' said Jaz as she walked into the bar and dropped her backpack in the back room.

Ted shook his head and frowned. 'You know I hate that,' he said.

'So you say,' she said, knowing that he actually liked his pet name. He was a great boss to have. Actually, Jaz was enjoying this job more than she ever imagined.

Thursday nights were usually quiet compared to Friday or Saturday, but it was good in that it gave her the freedom to chat to the patrons, and Ted let her play pool or darts with them. He saw the benefit of Jaz creating a fun atmosphere.

'Bud has been asking for you,' said Ted, nodding his head towards the pool table.

'Has he now.' Jaz glanced over at the guy in his mid-twenties. He was maybe her height, maybe a fraction shorter. He had a buzz cut and thick eyebrows and was a little stocky, but that could be from his muscles. It looked like he pumped weight. He wore T-shirts that seemed too small as they wrapped tightly around his biceps. It was nearly two weeks ago that she'd first got to learn his name and it was at this time, when shaking his hand, that she saw the ink circle from a tattoo partially hidden by his watch. Jaz didn't need a closer look. She knew that Sesha Serpent tattoo well. And with that information she only had to keep an eye on who he mixed with and she found some more tattoos connecting the rest of the gang members. There was one guy who was with them once but she couldn't find the mark, but she was sure it was somewhere on his body. So far she only knew Bud and Stevo, as they had introduced themselves and were here more than the others. Hopefully they all came again, not just Bud.

'Well, I'll go say hi, while it's quiet,' said Jaz. She reached for a basket and put some salted peanuts into it. A little thing Ted liked to do, give out free nuts. It was a winner. Jaz was finding she was having cravings for the salty nuts when she wasn't working, and not only that, she was feeling at home in the beer-smelling pub.

'Hiya, Bud. Want some nuts?' she placed the basket on the nearby table and picked up a pool cue. 'Quick game before it picks up?'

'You betcha,' he said with a smile.

As he set the balls up, Jaz chalked the end of her pool cue. 'So, my regular pub-goer, what do you do for a day job?' Jaz made sure not to pepper him with questions that would seem out of the ordinary for casual conversation. Seeing as they were alone this could be the best time to find out a little bit.

'I'm a bodyguard.'

'No way, that's cool. Can you fight and stuff?' she asked, feigning interest.

'Yeah, it comes with the territory.'

'So, do you have to protect someone famous? Am I allowed to ask?' Jaz took the first shot and the balls broke apart with a loud clink, followed by more clinks as they smacked each other.

'Na, he's not famous, just a rich guy who wants protection. It's quite common. Before this guy I was a bodyguard for a mining magnate.'

'Cool. It sounds like a fun job. Do you get to have a gun? Like the movies?' Jaz missed her shot and finally Bud got to take a turn. Jaz studied him as he moved for his shot.

'It's not that exciting. Actually, it can be quite boring. Some days I wish someone would attack him just so I had something to do,' he said with a wink. 'And I do get to carry a gun sometimes.'

'Really? Wow.'

Now that Jaz had puffed him up like a peacock she moved onto other questions. 'So, are you alone tonight or are you meeting friends here? Stevo, was it?'

It was Jaz's turn and as she bent over she was sure Bud was looking at her backside. That could come in handy.

'Um, yeah I think they're coming. Stevo said he was, maybe Wilkie will too.'

Wilkie, that was a new name. Jaz put that to her memory bank as she took another shot and sunk a ball before moving onto the next.

'My turn with the questions. So, how old are you?' asked Bud.

'Eighteen. Is that okay?' she teased as she sunk another ball, causing him to groan.

'Not if you keep beating me at pool. I'll have to come more often so I can sharpen my skills.' He tucked a hand into his jeans pocket.

'Maybe you should play me if you want some competition,' said a man who walked up to Bud and nudged him. His voice was penetrating, causing Jaz to shiver slightly.

Jaz took her shot, missing the ball and stood up. She'd seen this guy before and it wasn't Stevo. This tall skinny guy, whose jeans hung low off his narrow hips and were held there by a black studded belt, had eyes a cognac colour, the same as his trimmed hair. His cheekbones were defined like his jaw.

'Is that so?' she challenged.

'Jeni, meet Wilkie,' Bud said with a wave of his hand.

'Nice to meet you Wilkie,' she said, walking over to shake his hand. A few more had come into the bar and Ted would need her to work, but this moment was too good to waste. 'You work with Bud, hey?'

Wilkie shot Bud a glance and Jaz wondered if Bud was a talker. He'd be her target if he was. Wilkie might be one to avoid if he was worried about what Bud would say.

'He said he had workmates coming by,' she clarified. Wilkie seemed to relax then.

'Yeah. Why I need a drink,' he said, rolling his eyes at Bud.

'Any more of you coming? Shall I bring some more nuts? Get you a beer, Wilkie?'

'Just Stevo,' said Wilkie. 'I'll have what Bud's having,' he added.

'Sure. Here, you finish up this game, I've started it for you,' she winked, 'and I'll go get your beer. I'll be back later if it gets quiet.' Jaz took the money Wilkie held out. 'Thanks for the game, Bud.'

'Hey, you still need to finish a game with me. I won't be happy until I can beat you,' he said with a warm smile.

'I'm not going anywhere.'

She took Wilkie his beer but had to get back to the bar to serve a few others while Ted was dealing with an issue in the kitchen with Mateo, the chef. Something to do with the prawns. Jaz made a note to ask for chips for her dinner. When she finally got back to check on Bud and Wilkie's beer situation she found Stevo had joined them. He was short and a little wide, probably in the mid-forties. His hands were rough and his tooth chipped but he was nice and polite.

'Hello there, young Jeni.'

'Stevo, good to see you again. Can I get you the usual?'

He gave her a wink and a nod as he fished out his wallet from his jeans. 'Thanks, Jeni, that'd be great.'

Jaz walked back to the bar, feeling comfortable in her surrounds and smiled to herself. She had three Shesha Serpents, Bud being the best one for her to get close to as he was the youngest and seemed like a talker. The next step was to keep flirting and get Bud to talk, which would be much easier at the end of the night after a few beers. She just needed to do it without Ted getting upset because she wasn't doing her job.

If only Ted knew how important this was.

CHAPTER 17

RYAN HAD BEEN asked to hang around the house until Jameson's guest left, which was fine by him. It gave him an excuse not to catch up with Annaliese before she caught up with her friends for their Thursday night dinner. He tried to keep her at arm's length without making it noticeable. Hopefully it was working, maybe it was even keeping her keen with him playing hard to get.

'Thanks for helping out, Reece,' said Randall after they both saw off the guest.

Ryan couldn't find out much about him but his car number plate was locked away in his brain. He'd pass that on and Anna could find out who it belonged to.

'No problems, I don't mind. I was only going home to a takeaway dinner and TV,' said Ryan, hoping Randall would take the bait. He counted to five in his head.

'You know the guys are down at The Duke. You should drop in and say hi. I'm sure they'd appreciate a beer or two,' he said straight-faced. Randall had a strong, cemented facial expression that gave nothing away. Ever. He was a solid man, and his bulk may have you thinking there was nothing much between his ears but Ryan knew better than that. He'd seen Randall at work and knew he would be cunning and clever. He was not a man you wanted to slip up in front of and Ryan could tell Randall took his job seriously. To the point that it was all he lived for. He'd bet a hundred bucks that Randall was single, no family and no outside interests unless it was cleaning his gun.

'Thanks, Mr Randall, I might just do that.'

'Just call me Randall,' he said. 'The others do.'

Ryan had finally been accepted. He almost smiled at the win.

He nodded. 'I'll be off then. See you tomorrow.'

'Righto. Make sure Wilkie doesn't get out of hand. He gets fired up easily.' Randall turned and went back inside, leaving Ryan to ponder his words.

Hopefully Wilkie didn't get fired up over Ryan taking his job.

Ryan went home first; well, to the Agency flat, and had a shower, changing into jeans and a white V-neck T-shirt before driving to The Duke.

He pushed open the door, the familiar pub smell greeting him. Around the corner he saw the main bar area and it didn't take him long to find Bud, Stevo and Wilkie. Taking a deep breath, he headed their way. Stevo was the first to spot him as they sat around a table with beers and nuts while they talked.

'Hey guys, Randall said I'd find you here. Next round's on me,' he said quickly, trying to butter them up before they shut him out.

'Randall sent you?' said Wilkie. His voice was gruff and a little on the disbelieving side.

'Yeah, after we knocked off he suggested I come to The Duke and catch up with you guys. Not a bad pub. So, who's for a beer?' Ryan chose to ignore Wilkie's confusion and clear discomfort. For all he knew they were probably having a big bitch session about him before he walked in.

'I'd go another,' said Bud. He lifted his arm and waved towards the bar.

'Me too,' said Stevo.

'Jeni, over here,' said Bud, almost singsong.

'Hey Bud, what can I get you. Another round?'

That voice. Ryan's heart raced instantly, like a shot of adrenaline. He closed his eyes for a moment as the barmaid's voice triggered Jaz's image. He'd take any reminder of her at the moment, it had been so long. But when he opened his eyes and turned to say, 'I'll get the round,' his words just about fell from his lips.

It was Jaz.

He blinked a few times. Still Jaz.

He should know, those amazing electric blue eyes, that raven hair that haunted his sleep and that soft subtle skin that his fingers itched to touch. Oh my God, it was really her.

She was looking at him in less shock than he probably was. 'Got some money?' she asked.

Quickly he gathered his thoughts and pulled out his wallet. 'Yeah, sorry. Long day.' His hand almost shook as he held out the note. She lifted it from his fingers and floated away, a hint of frangipani all that remained. He couldn't help but turn to watch her walk away. But he knew he had to cover his tracks. 'Now I see why you guys come here.'

'I know, right? Jeni's great,' said Bud.

'You better not keep looking at her like that or Annaliese will have your balls on a platter, or Jameson will,' said Wilkie with a smirk.

Ryan laughed and pulled out a chair and sat. 'He'd bloody skin me alive, after Annaliese had dropped my balls in a blender.' He pulled a face and reached for some nuts as the guys laughed. Which was good because he needed a moment to gather his thoughts.

Jaz was here at the bar. Working. How? Why? His body was going mental on the inside while outside he tried to remain calm and relaxed. Every fibre of his body wanted to glance at her again but he knew he couldn't, he had to wait until she returned. He couldn't bring any more attention to her. The guys had started chatting again but Ryan kept munching on the peanuts so he had an excuse not to participate just yet. He was still in shock. When his eyes had found her it had blown him away. He hadn't realised just how much he'd missed Jaz and he ached with longing to reach for her, press her hard against his chest and hold her for eternity. Even now his heart was still racing, his body alive with electricity. He wasn't sure if he could even get it to function properly, because all it wanted was Jaz.

'Here you go, fellas.'

She was back. He got to look at her as she deposited the glasses full of cold beer on the table in front of them. Jaz came around to him to put his beer down, her hips brushing against his arm and it was such sweet, sweet pain. She was so close it was killing him. This was worse than any torture he'd ever endured. His teeth were crushed together, his jaw aching, his chest thumping, his skin on fire.

'Here you go, mister,' said Jaz.

Those blue eyes cut right through him. A hit like a bolt of lightning.

Jaz was his reason for getting through this mission, she was what he wanted to come back for, she was all he could think about and, he knew now, she was his life. He loved her. He loved her like he'd never loved anyone before. It was all-consuming. From his toes to his fingertips he knew she was the girl for him, for life. The more he'd tried to push her away the more she seemed to seep into his heart. How had he not known, not realised?

'His name is Reece,' said Stevo.

'And he has a girlfriend,' said Bud.

Ryan was shaken from his musings and those piercing eyes.

'Hi, Reece with a girlfriend. I'm Jeni. Here's your change.' Jaz waited for him to hold out his hand before dumping the coins into it.

Then she moved over to where Bud sat. 'I reckon I have time for a game soon. You think you're ready? Want to go practise some more?' she teased.

Ryan felt his chest tighten as he watched her flirt with Bud. He'd already figured when they called her Jeni that she was undercover too. Who had sent her in? He could guess why they got her to do it, already she was making headway with these boys. She knew all their names and seemed to be on good terms with them. Just how long had she been working here? It had been, what? Nearly two months or more since he'd last seen her? Was it three? Yet he knew she was the girl for the job, going on the performance she'd just given. She was as cool as a cucumber around him, but he was dying to know if she was jittery on the inside like he was. Did she still want him? Probably not after he'd pushed her away, but that was for her own good, he'd been protecting her. Or maybe was he protecting himself?

As he admired her backside – perfectly fit from all those high kicks she loved to dish out when they used to spar – he wondered if he had been in love with her all along and was just afraid to admit it. With the Agency and their undercover roles, how would it ever work?

But for the first time Ryan realised he didn't care. He loved Jaz, and having this time away from her had made him understand he never wanted to be apart from her again. He wanted her to be his girlfriend. His real one, just his alone.

'You play pool, Stevo, or darts? Wanna game?' he asked, trying to focus on his mission and not Jaz's gorgeous body taunting him. He needed a distraction, and pool or darts seemed like a good idea.

'Yeah, I don't mind darts. These buggers rather play pool but I used to play in a club back in the day,' he said rising from his chair.

'Cool. Best you take it easy on me then.'

'Take him to the cleaners,' said Wilkie.

Ryan didn't glance back to see Jaz, instead he put all his energy into playing with Stevo. He had to work hard to give the old guy some competition. 'I don't think you've got rusty at all, Stevo,' he said after their first game.

'You're doing all right, don't you worry. Give it a few more rounds and you'll get your eye in. You've got a good throw.'

'You think?'

Stevo nodded and finished his beer. 'Would you like another one?'

'Yeah, all right. Let's get this next game started first.'

'So, how long have you had this job?' Ryan asked as he threw his three darts.

'Working for Jameson? About fifteen years. I watched Annaliese grow up before my eyes.'

'I bet it was hard on her growing up without her mum,' said Ryan.

'Yeah, and with Jameson off doing his work. Sylvia, Mrs Latina, his housekeeper, practically raised her. She still works at his first home, where Annaliese grew up.'

'I meet Mrs Latina, she helped fix up my cut. She wasn't afraid to speak frankly to Jameson,' he said as he remembered her telling Jameson that his cut needed stitches.

'She's the only person who can get away with that, you know. Probably because she helped raise Annaliese. I wouldn't want to cross her.'

'That's how I feel with Randall,' said Ryan with a grimace.

'Nah, Randall's all right once you get to know him. He sometimes comes to the pub but it's not often he likes to leave Jameson's side. He *is* the job. But he seems to like you if he sent you down here.'

'Told me to call him Randall, too,' Ryan added.

Stevo's eyebrows shot up. 'Well, there you go. You'll fit in here okay. It's just different for the guys to work with someone who's dating the boss's daughter, you know?'

'Yeah, I get that. It's not easy for me either. Actually, Annaliese makes it hard to stay professional.'

Stevo chuckled. 'She's always loved the attention, that one. And Jameson gave it to her in spades when he could. Spoiled her more like it, but as a dad, we tend to do these things.'

Ryan put down the dart he was about to throw. 'You've got kids?'

He nodded. 'Yep, just a girl. She's all grown up now. Lives with her mother north of the city. But I tried to be there for her when I could. They change your life.'

Ryan finished off throwing his darts and wrote up his score with the chalk on the board. 'So, is Wilkie okay? Does he hate me for getting his job? It's not like I was after it.'

Stevo stepped closer, his darts in hand. 'Pay no mind to Wilkie, he's a slack bastard who complains far too much. This is probably just what he needed to get him moving. He'll get over it soon enough 'cause everyone will have stopped listening to him.' He gave Ryan a wink. 'And Bud you don't have to worry about. He likes everyone and loves to chat.'

'Chatting up the barmaid, more like it,' Ryan said with a chuckle.

They both turned towards the pool table where Jaz and Bud were playing a game while Wilkie watched on.

'He's not the only one. Wilkie will give it his best shot if he doesn't bore her to death. But she's a good sort, Jeni. She reminds me of my sister when she was younger. So free, full of life and friendly as. You don't get those sorts these days, that want to take the time for a chat.'

Ryan was trying to keep an eye on their pool game, hoping that when they finished Jaz would go back to the bar and he could go and get their beers at the same time. He just wanted to have a moment with Jaz, without the other guys. Luckily they went into another game as Stevo was enjoying himself, his empty glass forgotten. He pushed Jaz to the side so he could focus on asking Stevo more questions. This was the most he'd ever got out of Stevo besides the morning 'Hello'. This is where he could cement a better relationship, one where Stevo and the others would open up to him. Still, he knew that could take time before they shared anything of use.

A roar of laughter went up by the pool table. Jaz looked like she was having fun, she was so good at her job. But it did make his ten times harder.

The love of his life was across the room. His eyes feasted on her in the short time he was allowed, while his body remained in tune to her position always.

CHAPTER 18

JAZ LAUGHED LOUDLY, which wasn't normally her thing but she was still nervous and jittery from seeing Ryan. She was at the bar when he first walked in and joined the guys at the table. He hadn't seen her but by golly she'd seen him. It was hard not to. Tall, jeans hanging from his body like a magazine model's and that shirt clung to him perfectly. It didn't seem out of place like Bud's too-tight shirt.

Ryan had taken long strides, his dark eyes taking in his workmates. Jaz had all but melted into a pool of desire behind the bar. It felt like she had waited for this moment for ages, and yet here he was. Finally.

Her restraint was put to the test. This is where she had to act the part, pretend he was no one special. Which was hard when the guy she loved, and had missed like crazy, was just a stone's throw away. But Ryan wouldn't be impressed if she slipped up, or gave anything away. So, Jaz had steeled herself to be strong, just as she had been at the wedding. No matter what she felt on the inside, it was what she showed on the outside that counted. Then Bud had waved and she'd had to face Ryan for the first time.

His shock had been noticeable to her, she knew his dark chocolate eyes like the back of her hand. They'd almost flecked with gold when he looked upon her, setting a fire burning all over her body.

But she was sure she played it cool enough. Ryan took it all in his stride and his mates were none the wiser.

Now she chalked up the pool cue and took a moment to glance at Ryan while Bud and Wilkie were behind her. Gosh darn it, he was so hot she was having trouble functioning.

'Here you go, Wilkie. I'll play the winner out of you two. I better get back and serve some beer for a bit, okay? I'll be back.'

'We'll be here,' said Bud. 'Oh, hey.'

Jaz stopped and Bud reached for her hand, slipping some money into it. Then he gave her a smile.

'Two?' she asked.

'Yes, please. Thanks Jeni.' Bud let her hand go and Jaz made her way back to the bar.

She got their beers ready and then Ted took them to Bud while Jaz filled more glasses for the old guys sitting at the bar.

'Can I get two more, please?'

Her heart did skip a beat upon hearing Ryan's voice and she savoured the feeling. As she reached for two glasses to fill, she glanced his way. 'Sure thing.' Those eyes. Looking away was hard, thing and she found her hand was shaking as she tried to fill the glass.

'Here you go.' Jaz put the glasses in front of Ryan.

'Thank you, Jeni.' He said her name as if it was a question. 'What a surprise.'

'A good one I hope,' she said, taking his money slowly so she could drag out this interlude.

'Definitely.'

He smiled. It was just for her. She wanted to kiss him more than she wanted oxygen.

'You worked here long?' His question sounded normal amid the bar chatter, but Jaz knew he was after specifics.

'Nearly a month. It's a good job. I like it. Much better now though,' she said, dropping her voice for the last part. She gave him his change, the brief touch of his skin driving her mad with longing.

'I really like this pub. I think I'll be back quite a bit.' Another smile.

'Good.' She grinned back and hoped it wasn't too goofy. Ryan turned and left with the beers after pocketing his change.

Jaz wanted to watch him walk away, perve on his lovely backside, but she knew better. She served another bloke, checked they all had plenty of nuts left in their baskets before making her way back to Bud and Wilkie. She passed Ted on her way.

'Hey, boss. Okay if I keep playing some pool with the guys? Puleeese,' she begged.

Ted nodded his head. 'Ah, may as well,' he sighed. 'You won't get a chance tomorrow. Steak night, they'll need you in the kitchen I reckon.'

'Yeah, righto. No problems,' she said with a smile.

'You do that to me every time, twist me around your finger, don't you. Go on, get.' Ted walked off muttering something to himself.

Jaz skipped off to the pool table. 'So, who won?' she asked.

'Me,' said Wilkie. Bud was frowning.

'Only by one shot. Was a close game,' Bud added.

After they started their game Jaz tried her luck at some more questions, directed at Bud, the talker.

'So, is that other fella with the girlfriend another workmate?'

Wilkie laughed. 'Kind of. He's dating the boss's daughter, so we know how he got the job.'

'You don't like him?' Jaz asked.

Wilkie shook his head as Bud said, 'He's all right.' Wilkie frowned. 'Well, he is. It's not his fault the boss promoted him. He did happen to save his arse.'

'Jeez, didn't take you long to jump onto the Reece ship, did it. What? You think the boss'll notice you if you're Reece's best mate, is that it?' Wilkie was getting revved up, the pool forgotten.

Bud's face went a little pink but he didn't back down from Wilkie.

'Well, he's a lot nicer to talk to than you sometimes. Maybe if you gave the guy a break you'd see he's all right.'

'You think everyone's all right, Bud. You're like a sad puppy looking for friends.'

'Hey,' said Jaz.

Wilkie shrugged. 'Just saying it how I see it.'

'He wouldn't like to hear what I'd have to say if I said it how I saw it,' said Bud with a smirk.

'What are you implying, midget,' said Wilkie standing toe to toe with him.

'Now, now Wilkie. We have a game to finish.' Jaz tried to stand in between them and push Wilkie away. 'How about you have a break before you say something you'll regret.'

Wilkie looked at her, she could see his mind ticking over. He wasn't finished with Bud but he didn't want to do anything in front of Jaz. He must have thought he had a chance with her, or maybe he just wanted to beat Bud.

His lip twitched and then eventually he stepped back. He took his pool cue and went to find a ball to hit.

Jaz put her hand on Bud. 'Sorry, it's my job to deal with that,' she said softly. 'Tosser,' she added in a whisper.

Bud smiled. And over his shoulder she caught Ryan's gaze. He'd been watching but didn't interfere. Which was a good thing; he didn't need another reason for Wilkie to get on his high horse and cause a scene.

The rest of the night went well. No more problems with Wilkie. He left first, which was nice because the other two guys and Ryan seemed to get on really well. Jaz tried to catch snippets of the conversation as she passed. Sometimes she'd stop by with the next round and stay for a chat.

At one point she was out the back, sweeping the floor before they closed up for the night. As she took a bag of rubbish out to the bin, Ryan came down the narrow corridor for the toilet.

'Hey you,' he said with glossy eyes. He'd had a few beers but was still in total control.

'Hey yourself,' she said. 'Can you open the back door for me, please?'

No one was around but still, just to be safe they played their parts. Ryan nodded and pushed open the heavy door for her as she lugged out the big bag.

Outside it was dark and the only light Jaz had to work off was from the windows, as the back light had blown a few nights ago. Ted was supposed to have fixed it already.

Ryan followed her outside but held onto the door to help shed some light. Jas dumped the rubbish into the bin, which was a step away. She felt Ryan's hand on her arm as he let the door fully shut. He pulled her in for a hug and she didn't fight it one bit. To be leaning against his chest again was pure heaven. No words were spoken but Jaz had a funny feeling that he'd kissed the top of her head in that short moment.

Then he was gone, back inside, and Jaz was left in the darkness. The hug had been amazing but over so soon she was struggling to think it had even happened. How had he smelled? She remembered breathing him in, so familiar, but now it was disappearing from her grasp. She didn't go straight inside. She needed a moment to savour what had just happened. It was everything and yet it wasn't enough. Jaz hugged herself, trying to remember the pressure and feel of his strong arms around her. His skin had been warm against her face as she'd tucked herself against his neck.

Why had he done that? Was he just happy to see someone he knew? Did she look like she needed a hug?

Reefing open the door, she locked it and went back to the bar. Ryan, Stevo and Bud were standing up by the table as if they were about to leave. Jaz headed straight over there.

'You heading off?' Jaz said, moving to Bud's side.

'Yep, you need to close up,' he said with a wink.

'I'm going to give them both a ride home. I've paced my drinks, they didn't,' said Ryan.

'I can drive you home, Bud, if you don't mind waiting around?' Jaz guessed this might be dangerous territory, but she thought of what Bud might discuss with just the two of them and no one else. Jaz's mind was going crazy at all the possibilities, until she saw Ryan's face. There was a lot of black in his eyes, making them look less brown every second and more like thunderous clouds.

'It's okay, Jeni. I work with these guys, they're my problem not yours. You finish up and get home to bed.' Ryan's tone was soft and sweet but the hidden meaning in his eyes wasn't.

He didn't want her taking a drunk Bud home. Fair enough. For now Jaz let it go, but if the chance came up again and Ryan wasn't here to bail her out, she'd take it. No reward without risk.

She walked them out, chatting as they went. 'I'll see you guys later.' By the door she caught Ryan's glance and it was filled with so much longing it nearly crippled her right there and then. She felt exactly the same.

As they walked away Jaz wondered what had changed with Ryan, making him like this after he'd clearly tried to push her away at the wedding. Maybe it was just the fact that it had been a while since he'd seen her, seen anyone he knew.

Jaz couldn't even begin to understand how hard it must be to go deep undercover and give up your life as you know it.

After Jaz cleaned up the bar and knocked off, she eventually got home, walking into the gym and feeling a warmth spread over her. Home. Her life. Her friends. She thought of Ryan alone in his strange flat, or with Annaliese.

Annaliese. She didn't want to allow her mind to go there. At all.

'Is that you, Jaz?' came Anna's voice from the bedroom.

Jaz put her backpack on the kitchen table and made her way to her friend. 'No, it's a big bad burglar,' she whispered. Anna was curled up in her bed, on the opposite side of the room slept Tay, snoring softly. 'But no burglar would break in with that motor running,' she teased.

Anna giggled. 'I find it comforting. Lets me know he's still here and I'm not alone.'

'You could just snuggle up next to him and you wouldn't be alone,' Jaz teased.

Even in the dim light from the kitchen Jaz saw Anna's eyes enlarge. 'Jasmine,' she scoffed.

Jaz knelt down by her bed so she was really close to Anna. 'Guess what?'

'What?'

'I saw Ryan tonight.' Jaz couldn't keep the happiness from her voice.

'No way, really? Tell me more.' Anna moved closer to the end of the bed, their faces really close. 'Oh, you smell like beer.'

'Sorry.' Jaz didn't move away, she had exciting stuff to tell. 'He was surprised to see me, I could tell. We got to chat a little at the bar and then later, as I took out the rubbish, he hugged me.'

'Hugged you?'

'Yep, at least, I'm sure he did. It happened so quick, it all seems so hazy.'

'Did he look well? Do you feel better for seeing him?'

'He looked great. Maybe I'm biased but he looked amazing, and healthy. It's all I could hope for at this stage. And I feel heaps better after seeing him. Knowing he's still alive. He hopes to come to the pub more often, so I'll get to keep tabs on him.'

Anna sat up on her elbow. 'I'm so happy for you, Jaz. I really am.' She hugged her friend. 'Now go and get some bloody sleep, you have your last exam tomorrow.'

'You mean today?'

Anna groaned and rolled over. 'Goodnight.'

'Sleep well, Annabanana.'

Jaz moved off to her room: a quick shower and bed were in order. One thing she knew for sure is that she'd have no trouble getting to sleep tonight.

CHAPTER 19

JAZ LOOKED UP at the clock. Five minutes to go and her last exam was done. She had finished it as best she could and she couldn't be bothered going back over the questions she couldn't get. Frankly, she didn't care. She looked around the room: one boy was staring out the window, his pencil resting on his lip, either deep in thought solving a question or daydreaming. Most of the others had their heads down, pen hands moving frantically as they glanced at the clock and back to their sheet. Jaz could almost feel their angst. Poor kids, she thought, their mark was probably important to take them onto their chosen path at university. Not Jaz. No great score was going to help her. Why couldn't schools have classes for people like her? Self-defence, coded messages, weaponry, how to follow someone in secret, you know, the usual hands-on spy stuff. She was sure they were subjects she would have aced.

There were three others who had finished their exam, and they sat much the same as Jaz, glancing around the room at all the others. Jaz couldn't see Anna and Taylor as they were behind her and she didn't want to get pulled up for cheating if she turned around.

When the time was up, they all brought their exam papers forward and left the room.

'How do you think you went?' asked Anna when she caught up with Jaz and Tay.

Typical Anna, wanting to talk about the exam and no doubt go through each question again. 'As well as can be expected,' said Jaz with a smile.

'Isn't it strange that this is our last day at this school,' said Tay, and he glanced around as they walked the corridor.

'Yeah, no more using my secret escape route, no more canteen, no more fights to break up,' said Jaz.

'Ruin a good moment why don't you,' teased Tay. 'It feels weird, though. It's like we're free. What now?'

'Let's go to Molly's to celebrate end of school and the start of our new lives,' said Anna. 'Then we can figure out "what now",' she said quoting the air.

'Great plan. Best text Mum and tell her I'm done. She'll want to know how I went,' said Jaz pulling out her phone.

'Same here,' said Anna. 'I'll see what Cody's doing, he might come celebrate with us.'

'He might be busy,' said Tay with a frown.

'We need a real party where we can get drunk as skunks and let off steam,' said Jaz. 'Except I have work tonight.'

'We can still have one without you,' said Tay with a wink.

'Oh, great idea, Tay. We could have one at the gym and we'll be there when you get home, it'll just be getting started,' said Anna. 'And my mum will be none the wiser.'

'We could see if Bags or Tick wanna join us too. And your couple of mates from school?' Jaz said to Tay.

He shrugged. 'Yeah, I could ask. But it's weird, the gym is our place. I don't want to contaminate it with outsiders, if you know what I mean. We're going to make new friends from now on.'

They walked out of the school and turned around when they reached the bottom of the steps. 'Photo moment?' said Jaz.

'Definitely,' said Anna.

Jaz got a passing student to take a photo of them outside the school one last time.

'Thanks,' she said to the girl before checking the photo. 'Aw, look at us. Leaving this place behind and moving onto the next chapter of our lives.' Tay and Anna bent in close to have a look as students who'd sat the same exam left the school. Other classes were still going on as normal and that made everything feel even weirder, as if they had the run of the place.

They all jumped into her black Jeep and headed off to Molly's.

'Cody will meet us and he said he'll shout us drinks. Aw, that's nice,' said Anna.

'He can be a nice dude,' said Jaz, using one of his favourite words. 'Invite him to the party, get him to bring the drinks,' she said with a laugh.

They parked and walked into Molly's, heading for their usual table in the rustic coffee shop.

'Hey, dudes,' said Cody coming into the shop just behind them.

Cody was wearing whitewash jeans with black thongs and a singlet that had an ocean picture on it. His sunnies were stuck up in his shaggy blond hair, which was unlikely to blow off if he was walking in a strong wind.

'Congrats on the no more school.'

He high-fived Tay, and then hugged Jaz and Anna. He even smelled salty like the ocean. Probably went for a surf this morning.

'So, what'll you all have? My shout.'

After much deliberation they all got coffees and a slice of the to-die-for chocolate fudge cake. It's not often Cody paid, so they made the most of it.

'You know he's just paying us back for all the times we've had to shout him 'cause he left his wallet at home or in his car,' said Tay as Cody ordered at the counter.

'That man is the most forgetful guy I know,' said Anna. 'How does he not forget his gun when he's on a mission?'

'Because we bail him out he doesn't make a point of remembering. But no one can bail him out on a mission. I'm sure he has his priorities sorted,' said Jaz with a chuckle. They all fell quiet for a moment.

'So, now what,' said Anna with a dramatic flail of her arms. 'What do we do without school to go to?'

'Well, I've got my life sorted I think. Told Mum and Dad that I want to run the gym full-time, and then I can fit in with Agency life,' said Jaz.

'Yeah, well, that's all great for you but my mum is going to expect me to go to uni and be something she can brag to her friends about. I don't want to leave here,' said Anna.

'Who says you have to leave?' said Cody as he joined them again.

'Exactly,' said Jaz. Tay was agreeing too.

'Come on, guys, you know what my parents are like.'

'Yes, but you can still go to uni, just pick one close by and then you can still be here in between. Do something in computer science or something that can further your work at the Agency,' said Jaz.

Anna's face lit up. 'Oh yes, I could tell Mum I'll do uni but have it on my terms. I was thinking I'd like to become a qualified nurse.'

'What?' said Cody. Even Jaz was a little confused.

'Guys, I have the computer skills already and the Agency makes sure I have them up to date for what they need. But I'd like to be able to fix you guys up when you come back from missions with bullet holes and knife cuts all over you.' Anna turned to Jaz. 'I've been thinking, we could build a secret room in Pax's house and make it an ER of sorts. Have it kitted out with everything you'd need for trauma. Maybe I'll study to be a theatre nurse and see how the doc stitches people up, then you guys can be my guinea pigs.'

Anna seemed to have given this great thought. Jaz wasn't so sure about the guinea-pig part but it was probably no different to what Ryan and Tilly had done over the years. If they got in all the right gear it could make it so much easier, especially with Anna actually learning the right way.

'Why not just become a doctor?' said Taylor.

'Well, I did think of that, but it takes longer and I need to know how to help you guys now,' said Anna looking really pleased with herself. 'Well?' She turned to Jaz.

'I love the idea about the medical room at Pax's. We could fix up the old pantry in the kitchen that he never used, extend it out a bit and no one would have any clue. It would be hidden from the outside behind those big shrubs Pax planted.'

'Oh yes, fabulous. Who could we get to build it?'

'Tilly can do it, he did a bit of building work back in the day,' said Cody.

'And we have plenty of money to get it done,' said Jaz. She had money from Pax, as well as her own income from the Agency and now the pub.

'This is crazy, but good,' said Tay. 'And your folks would have to be happy with you doing something like that.'

Their coffees and cake arrived but Anna paid them no notice. 'I know, right? I'm going to find some courses and gather all my stuff so I can take it to them and they'll have to say yes.'

Jaz took a sip of her coffee, pleased that Anna was happy about her future. 'I hope you can move into Pax's full-time next year. Maybe I could do some courses as well to keep Mum happy.'

Anna burst out laughing. 'Oh my gosh, now you're sounding like Pax. You'll have certificates for all sorts of things.'

'At least mine will be real,' said Jaz.

'And if you can't finish them, I'll print you up a certificate anyway.'

'Perfect,' said Jaz.

Jaz loved these moments with her friends, sitting around the table laughing and joking. Her heart was swelling with love.

'What about you, Tay,' said Cody. 'What are your plans?'

'I don't know. I did think about seeing if I could get a job at the range.'

Even though the Agency was trying to take down the guys who had attacked him and threatened his dad, there was nothing Tay could do to resolve it and she knew it irritated him. He took his frustrations out at the range. As often as he could.

'You're there enough, they may as well pay you,' said Anna.

'Yep, but I need something with flexible hours so I can fit in with the Agency when I'm needed. I thought of starting my own business, like a repairman or a gardener so I can choose my hours, take time off when needed,' said Tay.

'That would work best. That's the hardest bit, having a job that's flexible. Nine-to-five jobs won't cut it,' said Jaz.

'Hey,' said Cody, waving his fork in the air. 'Just do what I do and surf full-time. It's got my dad stumped how I manage to live without a job. I think he thinks I'm selling drugs to pay for my surfing habit.'

'If only he knew you were trying to get it off the streets not sell it,' said Anna. 'I can't believe you don't mind him thinking that.'

Cody shrugged. 'You gotta do what you gotta do.'

They all fell quiet as Cody's words resonated. Lying to their parents and whoever else along the way was their sacrifice and they made it willingly to do a job they felt was important.

'For the greater good,' said Anna.

'So … party?' Jaz said, finishing her cake first.

'Party?' repeated Cody. 'I'm in.'

'Good, we were hoping you and Tay could bring the drinks. I'll bring the food,' said Anna. 'We'll have it at Pax's, a bit like what we did for Jaz's birthday. Except she'll be out working.'

'Sounds cool. I'm in. We can go grab the booze in my car if you want,' Cody said to Tay.

'And I'll leave you my awesome playlist on my iPod and I'll be back around midnight just as the party's winding down,' Jaz added with a pout.

'Nah, it'll just be hitting its stride by then.' Cody wiggled his eyebrows. 'I'll be still kicking and I'll save you a dance.'

Jaz was about to protest but decided against it. Why pop Cody's bubble. 'Sure. I'd like that.' She needed her friends. If she couldn't dance with Ryan, then dancing with Cody would be the next-best friend. She'd have to make sure he didn't push his luck, but if he did she'd have an excuse to drop him to the floor. And she had so much fun dropping Cody.

They all split off as they left Molly's. The boys for the booze and the girls went to the shop to grab food supplies and some decorations to make it feel like a celebration. Then it was time for Jaz to change and get to the pub for her night shift.

'See you when you get back. I hope you see Ryan again,' said Anna as she loaded the dips and cheeses into the fridge.

Jaz was so nervous all night, eagerly watching the door, waiting for Ryan to show up – but nothing. Not even Bud and his mates came back. Maybe two big nights in a row was a bit much. But Craig and Bert were and they kept her entertained with stories from their youth, Bert as a polo cross player and Craig a rodeo rider.

'He wishes, he was the rodeo clown, you know the ones that dress up funny and distract the animal,' said Bert.

'I did that once, Bert. Once. Only to help out a mate, the rest of the time I was riding broncos,' said Craig with a look that showed his mind was reliving the good old days.

'You okay, Jeni? You seem a bit flat?' asked Ted at one point, after describing the way he and Bert had met through their love of horses.

'Just tired,' she said, forcing a smile as she headed back into the kitchen to help with dishes.

The night seemed to drag on for ages, probably because she kept watching the clock and the front door. But eventually it was time to go home, and she hoped the party was still going because Jaz needed something to cheer her up. It was probably optimistic to think that Ryan would be back the next night, but hope did funny things.

Jaz parked in the small garage at the back of Pax's house. In the car park at the back of the gym she saw cars belonging to Taylor and Cody, plus Bags.

The party must still be going. Unlocking the back door, she headed into the house to dump her stuff. From here she could hear music blaring in the gym. It sounded like a club, dance music, probably Nero if Jaz was correct. She couldn't be bothered changing out of her T-shirt and black leggings, so she left her backpack by her bedroom door and headed to the source of the music.

What she saw inside the gym made her smile. Empty bottles of beer were piled on a table, like a trophy, next to empty chip packets, half-eaten dip, biscuit crumbs and cold party pies and sausage rolls. Her iPod was plugged into speakers and sat on the floor by the powerpoint. But it was her friends that had caused the smile. The only light came from the office and change rooms, creating mood lighting through the gym. They were all in the boxing ring, using it as a dance floor. Anna was dancing with Bags, who practically held her in his arms, her feet on top of his as they tried to waltz to the dance song. Then there was Cody and Tay, dancing with each other but bouncing off the ropes as they did twirls and then back again as they tried to copy Bags and Anna. Jaz stepped closer and started clapping. It was the funniest thing she'd seen in ages and exactly what she needed.

'Jazzy, come join us,' said Cody, pulling the ropes apart so she could climb in.

'Good party?' she asked.

'The best,' said Anna. Her cheeks were flushed and her eyes bright.

They all joined her in the middle and they started jumping up and down to the beat of the song. Bags picked her up and did his rag-doll dance with her. He was such a big strong man, you couldn't be anything but a rag doll in his arms. Bags swung her about before putting her down at the end of the song.

'Shit, you young ones have worn me out. I thought I could make it but I'm beat. Think I'll have to follow Niles' lead and head home,' said Bags, wiping the line of sweat from his forehead.

'Aw, do you have to? I just got here,' said Jaz, making a sad face.

Bags cupped her head and kissed her forehead. 'I must love you and leave you, my little one. But I'll see you tomorrow, if my head feels up to it,' he added.

Bags then hugged the girls and high-fived the guys before climbing down from the boxing ring and gathering his stuff.

'Bye, Bags!' they yelled in unison as he left out the back door.

'Five Hours' by Deorro came on and Anna started jumping up and down and dragged Tay over to her to dance.

As the beat picked up, Jaz closed her eyes and let the music take her away to another world. She didn't need alcohol, she'd probably inhaled enough at work. Sometimes she found music to be a better release.

Arms came around her and she leaned back into the body holding her, recognising Cody's salty fresh scent. They swayed together and Jaz took comfort in the contact, wishing it could be Ryan. Dreaming it was.

As the song changed to Adam Lambert's 'Ghost Town', Jaz opened her eyes and saw Anna and Tay dancing together closely. Anna had her head resting against Tay's chest and they were moving slowly. Tay leaned down and kissed Anna's head. They were in their own world.

Jaz grabbed Cody's hand and tugged him towards the ropes. Before he could speak she put her finger up to her lips to silence him. Like a well-trained puppy, he followed her down from the boxing ring and over to the office. Poor Cody probably thought she was leading him somewhere for a kiss.

When they were inside she let go of his hand and walked to the two-way mirror.

'Jaz?' he said, coming to stand beside her, his body pressed up against hers.

'Sh,' she whispered. 'Just wait.'

Sure enough, when Jaz looked back, Anna and Tay, arms still around each other, were kissing.

'Aw, it's about time,' she said softly. Jaz wanted to clap her hands in excitement but held back.

'Tay getting some action,' said Cody proudly. 'Nice.' Cody put his hand around Jaz and pulled her up against him. 'What do you say, shall we do the same?'

Jaz smiled, her mood was too good to be ruined. 'Ah Cody, you never give up, do you?'

'Everyone you don't ask for could be one you miss,' he said with a wiggle of his eyebrows. 'Look, I know you're taken,' he said with a wink. 'But I'm here if you need to scratch an itch.'

'Actually, you can,' said Jaz. She almost laughed at the shocked expression on his face. 'I could use a hug from a friend.'

Cody chuckled. 'Yeah, I can do that.'

He pulled her in tightly and Jaz held him just as hard. Sometimes a hug was all you needed, that connection, feeling someone's heartbeat against your own, that reassurance you weren't alone. She rested her head on his shoulder and they stood like that for a long time. And it was nice.

CHAPTER 20

JAZ WAS BACK at the bar a week later, after a very slow, long week of no school to pass the days, so she spent them sparring with the boys, shooting at the range, and visiting the paintball arena every other day. The guys who ran the paintball operation, with whom they were now on first-name terms, mentioned another paintball place north of the city, if they wanted to try another venue, plus some outside ones in the bush.

Cody came up with a brilliant idea of buying their own paintball guns so they could go to a block of land and hunt each other and set up targets to hit. Of course it turned out that Anna and Jaz would have to buy, thanks to Pax's money, a block of land, something still uncleared to use as their training area.

'Plus it could be a place to bury a body if we need,' said Tay.

They'd all stared at him, opened-mouthed.

'I'm kidding. Gee whiz,' he'd said with a belly laugh.

'I think it's a brilliant idea. Our parents will think we're using the money to buy an investment property,' said Anna. 'But we'll have a place to go to shoot whenever, even at night.'

'Oh, we could get night-vision goggles,' said Cody.

'I wonder who'll pay for that,' Anna had mumbled.

Jaz had been a little disappointed that Tay and Anna seemed to have gone back to normal after their big snog fest at the party. She didn't want to pry in case they were keeping it a secret from her while it was still new, but it was hard when she just wanted to see her friends happy. She had decided that if they took too long, she was going to talk to Anna and see what was going on. Maybe they'd blamed the alcohol for it happening and gone their separate ways? Who knew. It was a little irritating not knowing but Jaz was trying to keep her nose out of it.

Having work to go to was a blessing. It was a good distraction, and she was dying to see Ryan again.

As it turned out he didn't turn up on Thursday night, but the boys were there on Friday night and twenty minutes after Bud arrived so did Ryan. Jaz didn't think she could ever get sick of seeing him. Their eyes met briefly but so much passed between them. It was hardly a passing glance but they made every millisecond count.

'Hey, great to have you boys back,' said Jaz. She knew Stevo got a kick out of being included with the 'boys' even though he was the oldest. Jaz was really taking a shine to Stevo, which always came as a shock when she caught sight of the tattoo on his wrist. It reminded her that no matter how nice someone was, they could always hide a secret. Jaz did, but it wasn't a bad one like Stevo's. She couldn't help but wonder as she watched him: what did he do for the Shesha Serpents? Was it just keeping an eye out? Was he the gardener? Did he bury bodies? For all she knew, Stevo could be the one who killed unwanted people snooping around Jameson. Probably took to them with his gardening pruners. She shuddered and found it hard to believe. Surely she was a good judge of character? She got Ryan right. Her gut told her that Stevo had a soft heart.

She could only hope that he didn't prove her wrong.

'We come just to see you, Jeni,' said Bud with a smile.

Now Bud, she was uncertain about. He could have a crazy killer hidden inside. Like a switch, or a Jekyll/Hyde kind of thing.

'Awe shucks, Bud, you'll make me blush,' she said. 'So, who's for a cold bevvy?'

She got to glance at Ryan when he said yes to a beer. It wasn't much but another vision for her memory bank that she'd cherish along with all the others.

It wasn't until Ryan came to pay for the third round that she got to speak to him without his workmates around.

'Hey, Jeni, can I get another round?' said Ryan.

He smelled so sexy Jaz was having a hard time stopping herself from leaning over the bar to take a deep breath of him. 'Sure can, Reece.'

He held out his money between his fingers and as Jaz went to take it she noticed the small white slip of paper with it, tilted away from any prying eyes.

'Thanks,' she said taking it carefully. As she dropped her hand down to walk to the till, while hidden behind the bar, she slipped the note into her pocket.

Then she had to ring up the change and sort out the beer the whole time the note was burning a hole in her pocket like a hot coal.

'Here you go.' With a last glance at Ryan, she turned and served a few more people down the end of the bar before Ted came back and she ducked off for a toilet break.

She just about wet her pants with excitement as she sat down on the toilet in her private cubicle to open the note.

24-16-5, 66-33-12, 11-25-6, 102-53-7, 98-54-8, 41-17-22, 70-26-18

Damn, she should have guessed it'd be in code. What if he was searched at work? Maybe they were searched all the time. It was good that Ryan was playing safe; only, now Jaz had to wait until she could get home. Then she had to find the magazine he'd given her ages ago, which they communicated through. In a way it was nice to know he still carried the same magazine around with him, like their own personal phone for which only they knew the PIN.

The rest of the night dragged on, the note an even bigger distraction in her pocket. At least she got to sneak glances at Ryan, but she was too busy with a big crowd to spend any time with the guys who kept to their group of three, Wilkie not making an appearance.

Bud made a point of finding her before he left, when she was at the bar washing glasses and stacking them in the fridge.

'We're off now, Jeni. Just wanted to say goodbye.' Bud held his hand up and gave a little wave, which looked weird on his stocky form.

'Aw, how nice. Bye Bud. Sorry I was too busy to get a game of pool in with you.'

'That's all right. Maybe we'll try to come on a Thursday when it's quieter?'

'Yeah, that would be great.'

'Sweet. See you.'

Jaz waved and kept it going when she saw Stevo and Ryan looking her way. She tried not to let the longing and desire for Ryan end up in her eyes for all to see.

Half an hour later, Ted stood in front of her while she had the broom in her hands. 'You're like a cut bloody snake,' he said shaking his head. 'You really wanna get home, hey?'

Jaz did. She'd been going hard to get everything closed up and done. 'Yep. I do.'

Ted took the broom from her. 'Go on then. I'll finish up here.'

'Really?' Jaz leaped into his arms and hugged him. 'Thanks, Ted. You're awesome.' Then she grabbed her backpack and headed for the door at a jog before he could change his mind.

Jaz struggled to stick to the speed limit when she finally left the Agency house and made it to the gym in record time. She was so eager to get inside she cursed when the key wouldn't turn properly. In the end Anna opened it for her.

'You right? It was sounding like a big ol' rat trying to chew its way through the door, cursing as it went,' she said sleepily.

'Sorry, I got a note from Ryan and I'm busting to decipher it. Go back to bed and I'll tell you what it says in the morning.'

'Fine by me,' said Anna whose eyes had shut. She turned in her cow-print pyjamas and shuffled back to her bed, either by feel or she'd opened her eyes again.

Jaz went to her room, flicking on the light, and rifled through her drawers looking for where she'd stashed the magazine.

'Bingo.'

She found a pen and paper then flopped down on her bed, pulled the note from her pocket and worked through the numbers. Page number, line number, then word number. Slowly the message came together.

garden city ten jeans west middle change room

Jaz smiled. Was Ryan going to meet her, or would he leave her something hidden? Jaz was so excited she almost skipped to the bathroom to shower and then ended up lying in bed wide awake. The only thing that got her to sleep was not wanting to look like crap just in case she did get to see Ryan.

Jaz woke with a fright as Anna's face was almost pressed up against hers.

'Good morning, sunshine. Did you decode it?'

Jaz was about to curse her when she smelled the coffee. Opening her eyes wider she realised that Anna held a tray with a coffee and some toast with jam.

'Oh, thanks.' She sat up and went straight for the coffee, taking a good gulp. Now she felt more awake she could answer Anna's question.

'Okay, he wants to meet me at Garden City, in the Jeans West shop, middle change room at ten. At least, I hope I get to meet him and it's not just something he's left there for me.'

'What would he need to leave you? I think maybe he just wants to be able to talk to you freely,' said Anna before taking a bite of toast. 'Do you want me to come and keep a lookout?' she mumbled.

'Actually, that would be great. You could guard the change room.'

'I'll block my ears if any funny business starts,' she said with a wink.

Jaz saw an opportunity and took it. 'Like what happened with you and Tay?' She puckered up her lips and did air kisses.

Anna's eyes grew big and her hand went to her mouth. 'You saw that?'

'Yep, so did Cody, so we know it happened. But what's going on? You two don't seem to be together?'

'I don't know, Jaz. I thought it was just the alcohol making Tay kiss me. I mean I was rather merry and it was all very in-the-moment stuff. It was amazing and,' her face turned skywards, 'perfect and his kisses are … well … I've never had that before.'

'Did you talk about it afterwards?'

'No. I just said I had to go get a drink of water.' Jaz pulled a face. 'What? I was a little overwhelmed. I could feel my face burning and I didn't know what to do.' Anna shrugged. 'He hasn't said anything since, so I presumed we'd just went back to being how it has been. Friends.'

'Anna, maybe you should start looking at Tay as more than a friend. Personally I think he's crazy for you.'

'No. Really? Me? But I'm not …'

'What? Not what he usually dates? Did you think that maybe he's changed, he's found someone who really gets him and supports him? You are smart and beautiful, Anna. Why wouldn't Tay be interested?'

Anna's mouth opened and shut but no words came out. She was doing a great goldfish impersonation, though.

'Look, I need to get ready and you need to get out of your PJs.' Jaz glanced at her watch. 'Hell, we've only got half an hour and we need to be on the road.' Jaz cursed again before she skolled more coffee and reached for some toast. Late nights meant she usually slept in, but she couldn't do that this morning.

'Heck.' Anna took the tray back to the kitchen before going to change.

Half an hour later and they were in Jaz's Jeep on their way to Garden City shopping centre. After parking, they raced up the escalators to find Jeans West.

'Here, just up and around the corner. Good.' Jaz started walking at a slower pace to match the shoppers.

'You think Tay could really like me?'

Anna's face was confused and unsure, her mouth twisted.

'Yes. Why would he kiss you? Haven't you noticed how attentive he's been lately? You two have spent lots of time together.'

'We have, haven't we. But I thought that's mainly because you've been busy, you know. I love Tay heaps but I just never let myself think about us that way, just didn't think it would be possible.'

They got closer to the store; Jaz's heart rate increased and she searched the crowd for that familiar face. 'Just so you know, I'm happy either way. I love you both and just want to see you guys happy.' Jaz glanced at Anna quickly to show she meant what she said.

'Thanks.' Anna gripped her hand. 'We're here. I'll go look at the clothes and keep watch.'

She let her go and walked to the ladies' collection of jeans. Jaz headed to a nearby rack and found a top; it was probably not even in her size but that didn't matter, she took it to the back of the store to the change rooms. Through an archway there were three change rooms, all unoccupied. A large mirror was at the very end. Jaz put her hand on the middle door, her breath caught in her throat, her skin prickled with anticipation, as she pushed it open and stepped inside.

There was nothing inside except a mirror, a seat and a lot of hooks. Momentarily she was upset; no parcel, no Ryan, but then she realised maybe he was still coming.

She was a minute early. Jaz hung up the top and then sat on the bench, and waited. At five minutes past, the door opened and Jaz jumped up thinking it was someone wanting to use the change room, she hadn't locked it. Except it wasn't just anyone. It was him.

Ryan walked in with a shirt in his hand, turned and locked the door, then hung up the shirt on the closest hook.

Jaz stood there, totally lost in watching him move, the way his muscles rose when he hung up the shirt, his familiar scent driving her into a bliss-filled Ryan coma as his dark, simmering eyes latched onto hers. He was clean-shaven, wearing a black T-shirt and jeans. Jaz, funnily enough, was in similar gear, except her black top was a singlet.

'Hey, you,' he said, almost a whisper.

There was music playing in the shop and it would give them some cover if they kept their voices low.

'Hey, back,' said Jaz, her throat dry like a sandy dune. She was lost for words. This tiny change room was their little private oasis. They stood there like two cowboys sizing each other up before a fight. Only, this wouldn't be a fight, the look in Ryan's eyes said not today.

Then he brought out his sexy, melt-your-belly smile and the next thing she knew he had pulled her body against his. This time the hug wasn't rushed like the last one.

Ryan groaned as she sank into him. She latched her arms around him then, realising she could, snuggling into her Ryan pillow of heaven. God, he gave the best hugs.

She felt his lips against her ear, was he kissing her?

'I've missed you so much.' Another kiss. 'Jasmine,' he purred softly.

It sent her body into spasms of delight.

Ryan was now kissing down her neck. It was sweet torture as she tried to keep control of her thoughts. What was she about to say?

'Um, really? You missed me?'

He stopped with the kisses and pulled back. Jaz made a little noise of objection. She didn't want him to stop, ever.

His hands clasped her face as he tilted her to meet his eyes.

'Were you followed?' he asked seriously.

'No. Were you?' she shot back.

He smiled and shook his head. 'I doubt you could you even begin to understand how much I've missed you. Your spunk and quick wit. This hair,' he said as he reached for a handful, letting it slide through his fingers.

Jaz could feel him growing hard against her. Another shiver of delight racked her body.

'And those eyes, this jaw, these lips,' he said running his thumb across them as he licked his own lips.

Jaz was hoping he was holding her tightly because if he kept this up she wasn't sure how long before she went completely gooey. Her hand went to his face. 'I'm a little confused,' she said. And she was. Pushed away one minute and held closely the next. She let her hand slip across, so her fingers could play in his hair.

Ryan closed his eyes and smiled. 'I love it when you do that.' He bent his head so it was touching Jaz's forehead. 'Jaz,' he whispered, she almost missed it. 'You're what's getting me through this. The things I have to do. You are my torch.' He moved so he could place a kiss against her skin. 'I love you.'

What? Come again. Did she hear that right? She looked up and saw the truth in his eyes and his expression. 'You do?'

'I think I always have and I've probably fought it every step of the way, knowing that I shouldn't, but I refuse to fight it anymore. You are too important to me.'

She may have been looking at him in disbelief, her mouth open, shock all over her face, but that melted away the moment his lips found hers. Oh my lord, she had waited so long for this moment. To see Ryan and not be able to hold him and kiss him had near on ripped her apart, but now she finally got to lose herself in his warm kiss. He tasted of coffee. His tender kiss soon turned hungry and hot.

Jaz felt his need as much as her own fire burned bright. His tongue made her forget where they were. He owned her, she gave herself to him completely. She pulled away just long enough to say, 'I love you too, Ryan.' She found his lips again like a hungry lion to its prey.

Never in a million years did she think Ryan would tell her he loved her. She thought she was alone in the love department.

'I'm sorry,' he said pulling away. 'It seems wrong to tell you that and now I have to leave.'

Jaz had her hands all over him, trying to memorise the feel of every muscle. 'I understand. Quite frankly, I wasn't expecting any of this,' a little smile crept along her face as she flushed a little, 'but I'd do it again in a heartbeat.'

They hugged each other tightly one last time before pulling apart.

Ryan reached for the lock latch, paused, leaned back to Jaz to get one last kiss. 'I love you. Don't forget that.' Then he grabbed the shirt he was supposed to try on and left.

Jaz remained, waiting another couple of minutes. She needed to breathe.

'How's it look?' came Anna's voice.

The coast must be clear. Jaz grabbed the shirt and went out to Anna. 'It looks pretty good,' she said.

'I'm so excited for you.'

Anna did her little excited dance and Jaz felt her cheeks hurt from her smile.

They waited until they were back in the car before Jaz told her everything.

'He wanted to meet me so he could tell me he loved me,' Jaz said, still not really believing her own words.

'No way! Oh my God. Wow.' Anna was almost squealing with delight.

'I know. Big wow.' Jaz sat in her Jeep, basking in her own glow. Her heart was drunk on love and it felt swollen, twice its size as her chest ached with all the love.

It was plain and simple.

Ryan loved her.

CHAPTER 21

RYAN LEFT THE change room, his gaze passing Anna as he went to the counter and bought the shirt he didn't try on. As he paid, he struggled to keep his face plain and not show the pure joy he felt at that moment.

When he first walked into this shop he was a man on a mission. Then he'd spotted Anna, who wouldn't make a very good agent – she got all excited and almost waved at him. Luckily anyone watching might put that down to hormones. His 'man on a mission' feeling had started to crumble then, knowing Jaz was here. His steps faltered, he stopped to grab a shirt off the rack in his size while trying to calm the sensation gripping his body. Just the thought of seeing her, having her so close had nearly undone him. But he continued to where Jaz was waiting. To kiss her and hold her in his arms properly, not like that quick hug at The Duke. All that had done was make him crazy with want. It was strange how he could be in a moment of pure bliss and delirium, and then tearing his heart in two as he had to walk away.

Except today he was on cloud nine, maybe because he'd got to taste those plump lips, slide his fingers through her hair and tell her how much he loved her.

Ryan took his shopping bag and headed to the next store on his list, Annaliese's favourite, G-Star Raw, but his mind was still on the girl he left behind. Telling Jaz he loved her had been so freeing, as if he could walk away now she knew how he felt.

She'd surprised him by reciprocating his feelings. Maybe he'd hoped she felt that way but after the wedding, the way she'd marched away with so much strength, well, it had him second-guessing. Indeed it had left him pretty gutted. Was that the catalyst to realising how deep his feelings truly ran?

Hell, he felt like a giant today, striding through the shopping centre like a man who couldn't be knocked down. It was hard work to keep the spring from his step, the smile from his face and the urge to turn around and look for Jaz. Yet, he knew he had to. He'd already taken a big risk today by meeting up with her. Lucky this was his normal plan as Reece and Jaz had fitted in nicely to his movements. Ryan just had to get Annaliese her size-eight jeans then he was going to check out the Oroton store and see if they had that new purse she'd been eyeing off in the latest catalogue. He was trained to notice things and it came in handy when he had to do some sucking up to keep the boss's daughter happy. He couldn't afford for things to turn sour with Annaliese, so he made sure to shower her with gifts and surprises. He picked up on what she didn't like and changed to suit. He played her boyfriend like it was a character written for a *Home and Away* script.

He did all his shopping without ever spotting Jaz; he knew she was smart enough to leave straightaway and check she wasn't followed. He had faith in her ability to pick up on simple things like that; he'd love to think it was his training, but he knew a lot came from Jaz's own intuition. One of the things he loved about her, she was a quick learner, clever and level-headed, even if she was prone to taking too many risks. But didn't he do that too?

Over the noise of the shopping centre he heard his phone's ringtone. 'Hello, Mr Randall,' said Ryan, recognising the number.

'Are you free to come by the house now? I need to talk to you.' Randall sounded serious.

Ryan's breath caught in his throat. What could be wrong? He'd double-checked everything, nothing should be found out. He hadn't been followed. Yet a small part was worried he'd let something slip. Had he been followed to the shopping centre? How many eyes did Jameson have? 'Sure can. Do I need to be in work uniform?' he asked, hoping to get a better clue what this was about.

'No, not yet.' Randall hung up on him.

Shit. That had him even more confused. Ryan rushed back to Jameson's house, where a uniformed Bud let him in through the electronic gates.

'Hiya, Reece.' Bud waved with enthusiasm.

'Hey, Bud.' Ryan waved back as he drove through the house yard and straight to the workers' area.

Yep, Ryan had a friend now, he just had to work on Wilkie.

Randall appeared as Ryan got out of the car, standing there in his suit and shades like a *Men in Black* agent.

His purchases were on the passenger seat, Annaliese's purse and her jeans. Randall caught a glimpse and raised an eyebrow.

'Not for me, honest,' Ryan said with a smirk, while trying to gauge Randall's mood.

'I don't know, I think that colour goes with your complexion.'

Ryan stared at Randall in shock. The guy had a sense of humour? Who knew? That had to be a good sign. Right?

'I think you would be good fun after a few beers, Mr Randall,' said Ryan with a chuckle.

'Probably a good thing I'm not a big drinker, then. Come on, we'll talk in the staff lounge.'

They headed to the side of the car shed where the staff quarters were and into the end room, which housed the kitchen and lounge. It was clean and tidy, nothing second rate about these quarters, Jameson's staff were well looked after. Randall gestured to a chair and they sat.

'Sorry to call you in on your day off but we have a problem. A spew bug has taken out three of our good men, so we're left shorthanded.'

'That's cool. I'm all for helping out. I've been there before. Lay it on me. What can I do.'

'Well, here's the thing, it doesn't involve the boss. I mean, it's not looking after him. Today we need to help look after some important documents of his.'

'Righto. That's fine by me.' Ryan's eyes fell on some artwork on the wall. He frowned as he studied it. But he knew straightaway what it was. The Sesha Serpent logo.

'What?' asked Randall.

'I've seen that before. Yes, I think Bud has that as a tattoo, and Stevo now I think about it.' He tried hard to make it sound like natural inquisitiveness. 'What is it? A family crest or something?'

'I guess you could say that. Those loyal to Jameson all have the same tattoo as a mark of respect and trust.'

Ryan's eyes dropped to Randall's wrists on purpose. He already knew there was no tattoo there.

Randall reached up to his chest and pointed to it. 'Mine is here. We all select where we want them. I prefer mine close to my heart, shows my loyalty; Jameson is family. The boys prefer to put them on display, some use it as a trophy over the others.'

'Will I earn one? Or am I too close to Jameson by being with Annaliese?'

'Do you want to earn one?'

'I believe so, if it helps Jameson. I don't take my relationship with Annaliese lightly, nor that with her father. He could very well be my father-in-law one day,' said Ryan, letting Randall know his intentions.

'Then that makes it an interesting question. One that may be answered over time. By doing this job today it's a foot in the right direction. We'll see if you can be trusted, keep your mouth shut and that includes with Annaliese. The boss likes to keep her out of the business, you understand.' Randall's sunglasses sat on top of his head, his eyes were like giant anchors holding Ryan still with the seriousness of his words.

'I've been in security work for a long time, Mr Randall. I understand privacy, keeping my mouth shut to what I see and do. That will always stand, even if I am with the boss's daughter. I've never taken my work home with me, to any of my family or girlfriends over the years. I take my job and my positions seriously.' Ryan tried to return the same steely gaze. 'You can't expect people to take you seriously if you don't take your work seriously.'

Randall watched him for a moment before sitting back. 'Good. We could use more of that around here. Between you and me, I feel that Bud is a little lax on that part.'

'So, what do you need from me today?' Ryan asked, trying to remain calm and serious, fully aware that this could be another step towards Jameson's underworld.

'Come back this afternoon at five, in your suit, bring your weapon. We'll go from there.'

And that was the end of their conversation. Randall got up and left, mumbling something about having to get back to do a check around the house and interview new staff.

Ryan got up slowly, scanning the lounge area while he could for any-thing he could use later. There was a pile of drag-car magazines on the table: Who was into them? Wilkie? Might be a way to get to him.

With nothing else standing out as noteworthy, Ryan headed back to his flat to change before going to Annaliese's for lunch. He was worried she'd find a long black hair on him or some other telltale sign of Jaz, so for good measure he changed his shirt.

It was just them for lunch at her expensive flat, so Ryan could relax a little.

'Here are the jeans you wanted, babe, and I got you something else … just for being so amazing,' he said pulling out the Oroton purse from the bag.

His ears trembled at the squeal she let out as she dived for the purse.

'Oh my God, Reecie, this is just what I've been wanting. How did you know? Oh, I love it.' Annaliese held it like a baby, stroking it and smelling the leather.

What he'd paid for that purse would be enough money to feed the little girl he'd made friends with in Pakistan a few missions ago, and her family, for a year.

'I have just the dress for it. I'll have to wear it tonight when I meet up with the girls.'

'About that, sweetie. Randall called and wants me to be at work at five. I'm so sorry I can't make it.' He tried his hardest to look like he gave a damn.

Annaliese looked at her purse then back to Ryan. 'Well, best we make the most of our time.' She put the purse down on the table, trailed a finger over it lovingly one last time before stepping towards Ryan and reaching for the top of his jeans.

'We haven't had lunch yet,' he said quickly. He wasn't in the mood, especially after being with Jaz earlier. He didn't want to taint this day. He'd even left his shirt on his bed for tonight so he could lay beside it and see if he could still smell Jaz.

Annaliese slipped her hands under his shirt and ran her long nails up his chest. She had that look in her eye that said nothing was going to change her mind.

Ryan tried to dissect himself into two. He needed to be Reece now. With a deep breath, he gave into the situation and let Annaliese have her way.

A few hours later it was a relief to get back to his own flat, shower and lie on his bed by his shirt from earlier. His Jaz shirt. He picked it up with gentle hands and brought it to his face, the part where she'd rested her head.

Closing his eyes, he inhaled. And there it was—the faint scent of frangipani. It almost brought him to tears. The lump in his throat was agony as he fought it all the way. He couldn't give in to the loneliness, the aching, the wanting. This is why agents weren't supposed to fall in love. It was messing with his head. It had been torture with Annaliese earlier. All he wanted was Jaz.

Trying to stay in control, Ryan jumped off his bed, got dressed and went for a long, long run. When he reached a nearby park he did push-ups, squats, sit-ups and whatever else he could think of to fill his mind with pain.

By the time he got back to his flat, he was drenched in sweat and ready for another shower. Then he headed off to work.

'Good, you're here,' said Randall when he arrived back at the house for his 'special' job.

'Yes, sir.'

Ryan followed Randall to another car, one Ryan had never seen Jameson in. It was a similar car to the one Jameson used but an older model. Wilkie was at the driver's seat again but no words were exchanged as Randall opened the back door for Ryan.

They both got in and Wilkie drove out of the Jameson estate.

It was a quiet ride and soon Ryan realised they were heading to the warehouse by the port area.

'Stay here, and watch the outside until I come back,' said Randall as they stood at the front of the shed and he pressed in the pin.

200634

But it was useless to Ryan when he knew there was a camera inside, plus another code was needed for the secret door. It wasn't worth breaking in if he couldn't get to that inner door. Ryan had wondered about getting in through the back wall, cutting it open, but that would also raise suspicion and make them move whatever it was they were hiding.

Fifteen minutes later Randall came out with a locked case, black with a number lock at each end of the opening, which he passed straight to Ryan. But what surprised him the most was the young girl by his side.

Randall spoke to the girl in perfect Filipino, not something Ryan was overly familiar with except for a few simple words in greeting and enough to know that it was the language being spoken. The girl looked like she was Jaz's age, with darker skin, black hair and russet-coloured eyes that held great sadness. She nodded at Randall's words and went straight to the car, holding down the blue skirt she wore in the afternoon breeze. Her top was a white, almost see-through blouse with matching slip-on shoes. Who was she for, Ryan wondered.

Randall locked the door behind him. 'Let's go.'

Ryan went straight for the front passenger seat and Randall didn't correct him. He held the case on his lap and wished he had X-ray eyes. He bet it contained either money or drugs. Or maybe nothing at all, yet.

He couldn't see the girl, nor hear her; she remained quiet, as did the car's other occupants.

'We all clear?' asked Randall twenty minutes into their trip.

'No one following, sir,' said Wilkie.

'Nothing,' said Ryan as he glanced in the side-view mirror.

'Good,' came Randall's satisfied reply.

Wilkie was driving them into the wealthiest area of Perth. Peppermint Grove was not where Ryan had expected this trip to take them. To a brothel maybe, in some side street suburb, but Peppy? Wow.

They stopped by a big, gated fence and Wilkie talked through the intercom.

'We are here for the six o'clock delivery.'

No names, no details. This didn't help Ryan at all. He tried to keep the address in the back of his mind. If this girl was being left here, what for? This person's own plaything, or was the guy an owner of a few prostitution houses, or was she just going to be a housemaid? Ryan almost laughed at his last thought, so naive he should know better. The worst thing was Ryan couldn't save this girl, taking down this one man wouldn't stop the others. But he'd do his best, as would the other operatives he could put in place to watch this house and see where the leads could take them.

Wilkie drove through the open gates, up a paved driveway to the entry point of the house, which had a drive-through area like a hotel.

Ryan felt a tap on the shoulder and turned to see Randall. 'You come with me.'

So, no names were being used in front of the girl. Smart.

They got out, Randall took the case and pushed the girl to him.

'She's your responsibility, bring her but keep her five metres behind me. If I don't get what we came for we take her back. Understood?'

Ryan put his hand gently on the girl's slender arm and nodded. He'd vouch she hadn't eaten well in the past few months, by the feel of her.

Wilkie stayed in the car, Randall headed for the door, which a guard opened for them, and Ryan kept the girl at the requested distance.

They went inside through a huge, extravagant entryway of jarrah and plush carpets. The owner seemed to have a thing for stuffed animal heads – a game hunter maybe? A solid wood staircase swept its way up to the second floor in front of them and rooms spread out to the left and right. They were guided into a sitting room on the right with leather chairs and ottomans. The paintings in this room were edged in large gold frames and looked antique, the jarrah side table had crystal decanters filled with whiskey, with matching crystal glasses.

Another man in a suit came into the room. 'He will see you now.'

Randall nodded, then turned back to Ryan. From the silent look he gave, Ryan knew he was to stay here with the girl and to watch his back. Randall didn't trust these guards and so neither would Ryan.

For a moment he was left alone with the girl. He looked at her, releasing her arm. 'You're okay.' Then he remembered the man from Jameson's farm. 'Yanna?'

Her head shot up, face bright, recognition in her eyes. She started talking in hushed Filipino.

Ryan shook his head. 'Only English. Sorry.'

She fell silent then, her face back to the unfocused dread of before and Ryan wished he knew enough to tell her to be brave and that her father hadn't given up on her. But then she'd probably ask if her father was alive and Ryan wasn't sure what action had been taken in that department. Not without asking Randall, which could cause all sorts of problems. All he could do was smile at her and try to convey some hope.

Footsteps came and Randall appeared with a man beside him. The boss of the house, Ryan guessed by the suit, gold accessories and the cigar hanging from his mouth. No one else would dare smoke in a house like this.

Cigar Man stared at the girl, his thin moustache twitched and the thin hair on his head didn't hide the shine that bounced off from the light above. This guy was getting excited just looking at the girl and Ryan felt his stomach cramp with disgust. It took every bone in his body to resist the urge to pull out his gun and shoot the sick bastard now.

Randall gave Ryan the nod, as he held the case closer to his body. Yep, the payment had been made, the girl now belonged to Cigar Man. Ryan reached for the girl and, instead of letting her make the trek alone, he guided her to the man's side. Each step was like walking over shards of glass. His body wanted to resist it completely, his heart was aching in pain for this innocent girl, yet he had to continue. He was still a long way off being able to bring down Jameson's empire and reach. Saving one girl would sacrifice hundreds more. He had to keep thinking of the bigger picture.

He let the girl go and tried to avoid her eyes as she latched onto him for help.

'Nice doing business with you,' said Randall. He gestured for the door with a nod of his head and Ryan quickly led the way.

He couldn't look back. But his heart broke for what the girl was about to endure and he hoped she was strong enough to survive until they could make all these sick, twisted, money-hungry bastards pay.

In the car, Randall turned to him as Wilkie drove out of the Cigar Man's estate. 'Well done, Reece.'

'No worries. That seemed easy enough. No complications.' He tried to keep his voice even and hoped the injustice he felt wasn't noticeable.

'Can we call on you again?'

This was a test. It was more than just a simple question. Randall was asking if he was up to this kind of business. This was his chance to run if he hadn't liked what he saw, it was his out.

'Yes. I'm your man for the job.' Reliable, trustworthy and confidential Reece was the one he tried to portray.

Randall's lips twitched and he nodded. 'Good.'

Ryan glanced out the back window, looking for tails, but he really needed a moment. The only thing that kept him going was Jaz and the fact that the Agency would take every little detail he could gather to sink these bastards. He just hoped he was there when they took them down.

CHAPTER 22

'JENI, YOU'RE GOING to wear away the wood if you keep that up,' said Ted.

Jaz looked down at the bar top. Her hand had been rubbing circles with the cloth while she'd been staring towards the front door in a daze. It had been over a month since she'd kissed Ryan in the change room, and he'd only come to the pub twice since then.

Jaz was feeling worn out. Mainly because she was training hard to let out her frustrations. She would have taken on that fight that Cody suggested, but the problem being if she won it could mean some attention and right now she couldn't have that. What if Bud saw her bruises, or Ted? She had to stay low-key. Besides, the way she was feeling she'd win that fight hands down. She was itching for a fight. A pub brawl, anything! But the facial bruises might not bode well for work.

Anna had suggested she try a meditation class by the ocean, to give herself an hour of reprieve. She declined, but the comment had given her an idea and, making the most of the summer weather Jaz had asked Cody to teach her to surf.

'Sure thing, shark bait,' had been his reply.

That was three weeks ago and even now Jaz couldn't wait for tomorrow morning. Cody was right, there was something amazing about the power of a wave, the salty water and fresh air.

'Can I get a beer, love?' said Bert. 'You okay, Jeni?'

Jaz threw the cloth over her shoulder and moved to get a glass. 'Yeah, I'm good thanks, Bert. Just a bit preoccupied today.'

She gave him his beer and then got his change.

It was at the end of the night, hopefully that would be Bert's last beer before he left and she could close up. Bud was still over by the pool table, waiting for her return.

She'd been spending a lot of time with Bud when he was at the pub. He hadn't asked her out yet, she wasn't sure why. She was hoping tonight she could drive him home for a chat. Just thinking that made her check the door again, waiting for Ryan to come striding in to save her from doing something dangerous. But he didn't. It worried her that he hadn't been in much, but on his last visit two weeks ago he'd managed to say a few words.

'It's harder to get to the pub now I've got some extra work finally happening,' he'd said quietly, but with emphasis.

It had just made Jaz more scared for him. It drove her nuts not being able to ask him what was happening. And if he couldn't get to the pub, then there were no more chances for them to meet up. Their declaration of love seemed so long ago.

'Hey, here's my favourite girl,' said Bud as she picked up the pool cue.

'I thought you'd be home by now,' she said with a coy smile.

He stumbled as he walked towards her. 'Hmm, I'm not sure I want to leave just yet.' He held out his hand and Jaz slipped hers into it.

'Would you like me to call you a taxi? Or drive you home?'

Bud's eyes shone with drunken happiness. 'You'd do that for me?' He put the pool cue down on the table and reached up to touch her hair. 'It's like silk. Black as a pearl and silky.'

Jaz couldn't help but step away as she covered the move by hanging up the pool cue. She couldn't bear Bud to touch her hair like that. That was reserved for Ryan. From now on she was going to plait it or keep it in a topknot.

'Come on, let me drive you home. I make a mean coffee,' she said with a smile.

Bud threw his arm over her shoulder and she was doused with his strong deodorant, something like Brut, as if he were compensating for something.

'You're too good to me, Jeni. I do like you lots,' he said, blinking slowly.

'Just wait outside for a bit while I see if I can leave early.' Plus it would sober him up a fraction so hopefully they could have a bit of a conversation.

'Ted, is it okay if I knock off early? I've emptied the bin and cleaned up out back already.'

'Sure, I can handle Bert.'

'Thanks.' She kissed his cheek before grabbing her backpack and heading outside to Bud. 'Right, where's your car, Bud?'

'This way.'

It was a warm night. Jaz enjoyed the fresh air and didn't feel cold at all in her shorts and black singlet. The streetlights led them to a car parked on the side of the road. It was a black Pontiac Trans AM. 'This is yours?' It was beautiful.

'Yep. Always wanted one.'

'Oh my God, Bud. It's gorgeous.'

Bud had a grin from ear to ear.

'You sure you want me to drive it?'

He fished out his keys and handed them to her. 'I trust you, Jeni.'

A little voice in her head said maybe he shouldn't.

They got in and Jaz started the car. Its rumble was loud so late at night, but it did sound pretty cool. 'Where to?'

Bud gave her directions and soon she was pulling up at a house not far from Jameson's house. She'd hoped he lived on the main estate, giving her access to see more. But this brick and tile home would have to be it.

'This your place or do you rent?' she asked Bud as she parked out the front. The lawn off to the side looked neat and tidy.

'Nah, work provides it. I stay here with two of my workmates. Stevo's here too.'

'Is he the gardener or you?' she asked.

Bud laughed and laughed. Eventually he stopped to reply. 'Nah, that's all Stevo. He's the groundskeeper and that includes this place. The boss is all for appearances, so the place has to stay neat.' Bud opened his door. 'So, you gonna make me that great coffee?'

There was her invite inside.

'Sure. Let's go.'

After a few attempts to open his front door, Bud gave up and handed her the keys. 'Quit while I'm ahead, hey,' he said with a chuckle.

His hand rested on her back as she opened the door, and then he led her to the kitchen, still holding her. Together they got their coffees sorted while whispering so as not to wake up Stevo and the other housemate.

'Let's take this into the lounge. We can shut the door.'

Careful, her head screamed in warning, but she was sure he just meant for the noise.

Jaz didn't want Bud to think he had a chance tonight. She didn't want to have to knock him back, or knock him flat on his arse if he wouldn't take no for an answer. She'd set back whatever progress she'd made with him.

'So, how long you lived here?' Jaz asked, sitting beside him on the blue sofa so they could talk quietly.

'Three years. I've got a good job, it pays well, I'm happy,' he said. His eyes were still glazed and shining from the lamp by the sofa that threw soft light across the room.

It was a plain room, no personal photos. Just the main items: TV, wall art, magazines on the table and someone's clothes draped over the nearby chair.

'So, you have a good boss, then. Ted's a good boss. I'm quite fond of him,' said Jaz before sipping her coffee. She'd watched carefully to make sure Bud didn't slip something into it. Can never be too careful.

'Yeah, Jameson's okay. Don't get to deal too much with him. He has a guy who looks after all of us. Randy, we call him,' said Bud with a smirk, as if he'd just defied someone.

'Has this Randy been to The Duke?' she asked.

'Nah, he's hardcore, hey. Takes his job too bloody seriously.'

'I haven't seen much of Reece and Wilkie at the pub. Those guys still working with you?' Jaz looked into her cup, less to give away if he couldn't see her expression.

'Yeah, they're still around. Randy has them doing extra stuff, so they're busy when we go to the pub. Kinda sucks that Reece is new and gets jumped up the food chain and he doesn't even have one of these,' he said, holding out his wrist.

'What's that? It's cool,' said Jaz, putting down her cup on the coffee table so she could hold his hand and take a better look at the tattoo. 'I've noticed it a few times. I love the circular snake design. Which tattooist did it?'

Bud shook his head. 'It's a special guy they get in to do it so it can't be replicated. Boss don't want this to get out in the public,' said Bud slowly.

His eyes were closed as Jaz was gently massaging the skin near the tattoo.

'Hmm, you have magic hands, Jeni,' he mumbled.

He was falling asleep. Jaz took the cup from his hand and put it on the table.

His eyes sprang open as her hands left his. 'Hey, where are you going?'

'Home, it's been a big night. Thanks for the coffee.' She didn't want to pump him for too much info, just in case the others in the house could hear them.

'But I have so many questions for you!'

'Huh, you've asked me just about everything at the pub while we play pool. It's you who I know nothing about,' she said.

'You wanna know more about me?' He smiled. He wasn't bad looking when he wasn't trying so hard.

'Yes. That would be nice. All I know is you have a job and you drive a Trans AM.'

'I have a brother who's in prison, the family don't talk about him much. My parents live up north in Geraldton. I had a pet dog call Chester but he died two years ago and I miss him. Not much else to know.' He smiled sheepishly.

Jaz grinned back at him. Then rested her hand on his leg as she leaned over and kissed him on the cheek.

'What was that for?' His eyes were fully awake now.

'I like you, Bud. You're a nice guy. But I need to get home before my flatmate worries.'

'Here, take my car home,' he said, trying to stand up to see her out.

'It's okay, I'll get a taxi.' She called one and gave the address before Bud could fight her on it. No point taking his car unless she could bug it and she didn't have any gear for that. But she did have access to his house now, so it was a possibility for later.

Bud was sweet and waited with her outside until the taxi turned up. Gave him a bit of time to sober up too.

He held the taxi door open for her. 'Hey, Jeni. Would you think about going out with me sometime?' he asked as he pressed a fifty-dollar note into her hand. 'For the taxi,' he added.

Jaz gave him a hug as she said, 'Thank you. And Bud, I don't need to think about it. I'd like to go out with you sometime.' She got into the taxi and he closed the door.

He watched her depart, not moving from the spot by the kerb and wearing the goofiest grin. Jaz wondered what would happen from here. And, as usual, she felt that stab of unease at leading Bud on and using him like she had done to Marcus. Sometimes her job was hard.

The next morning Jaz was up early as per Cody's instructions. He'd picked her up in his beat-up Jeep, her new surfboard strapped to the top next to his, and they headed north up the coast to Trigg Beach.

Cody parked and then they got their boards down. Cody's was a nice fiberglass board with sharp fins and a sharp nose, while Jaz was still using an eight-foot softboard. He'd said the thicker board provided more floatation, which made paddling and catching a wave easier. So, in theory she could catch more waves and become a better surfer. 'You can get a fiberglass one like mine when you're past the stage of hitting yourself in the head with it while you're learning,' he'd said.

Jaz tucked her blue board under her arm and looked out to the ocean, a slight breeze flicking her hair about her naked shoulders. She wore a black triangle bikini and her wetsuit was bunched at her waist, ready to pull up.

'Isn't it the most perfect thing you'll ever see this time of the morning?' said Cody, coming to stand beside her in the same pose. His body was bronzed from the sun, his abs conditioned from the surfing and fighting.

'Yeah, it's not bad. Race you there,' said Jaz, taking off down to the beach. Cody yelling out behind her, trying to catch up.

There were only a couple of other surfers at the beach this morning. Cody said that wintertime the conditions were the best and this place 'went off'. Jaz hoped that by wintertime next year she'd be up to riding some of those great waves.

Sinking her feet into the wet sand, she put her board down to do up her wetsuit and strap on the leg rope.

'You ready?' said Cody. His blond mop brushed across his face.

She could see the passion in his eyes, just how much joy surfing brought him. Jaz hadn't understood it before, but after all their surfing together she was starting to get it.

They paddled out and sat on the boards floating, waiting for a wave. The strength of the ocean current moved around her, the salty water building into a wave. The briny smell and the squawk of nearby seagulls added to the tranquillity as the sun started to rise from the city side. Jaz realised just how much she needed this moment, this time out to recharge her batteries. She'd been working hard lately, training and getting closer to Bud. And while that was happening she was thinking, more like worrying, about Ryan. If she didn't have these moments to appreciate life she'd end up run-down mentally.

'Switch on, Jaz, this ride has your name on it. Paddle hard and pop.'

Jaz did as she was told. Having strong arms made the paddling easy and her balance was already good due to her fighting and core strength. Seawater splashed in her face as she paddled hard, caught the wave and jumped up. It was thrilling, riding a wave, and Jaz tried to move her board about, getting familiar with the movements and trying to stay upright.

She could hear Cody cheering her on. He was getting such a kick out of seeing her surf and having someone to share it with.

Jaz and Cody caught as many waves as they could until she was feeling exhausted. That desire to wait for the next great wave was a hard thing to give up, but eventually they headed to shore. As usual, because their stomachs were groaning for food.

'Not a bad morning of surf, hey?' said Cody as he pulled off his wetsuit. He stood in a pair of black surf shorts that clung to his wet legs.

'It was awesome. Did you see me on that last wave? Think I'm really getting the hang of it.' She couldn't keep the smile from her face, or her voice.

'You're a natural sportswoman, Jaz. I doubt there's anything you couldn't pick up quickly.'

'Cooking and computers. I'm shit at both,' she said with a chuckle.

'Yep, I'll think twice if you invite me for dinner, then.' He winked. 'I'll get our stuff.' He jogged back to his ute, returning soon with their towels and an esky.

They sat on their towels as the full sun dried them. The beach was busier now, with beach walkers and sandcastle builders.

Cody opened the esky and pulled out a cold ice coffee drink, which he passed to Jaz. 'I also packed your favourite.'

Jaz took the long paper-wrapped roll he held out, her mouth instantly drooling. 'Bacon and egg wrap? Damn, Cody, you are a man of many talents. When do I get to go to your house for dinner?' she said while undoing the brekkie wrap.

'I do breakfasts well, the rest not so much. I kind of stick to the three Ps: pasta, pies and potatoes.' He opened his drink and took a big skoll as Jaz laughed.

This was becoming a ritual for them, surf then eat together while lying on the beach. She could see the appeal to his lifestyle. 'Were you on duty last night?' she asked him.

'Yeah. Stayed out till midnight then Jack took over.'

'Jack?'

'Good bloke, mid-thirties. I'm sure you'll meet him one day.'

'Seems like there are so many working for the Agency that I don't know.'

Cody shrugged as he unwrapped his breakfast. 'It's the way they like it. But over time, with different ops and missions, you end up meeting the main ones. There are still heaps who just do simple observation jobs. Ears-on-the-ground kind of dudes who bring in information we can run with.'

Jaz nodded as she finished her mouthful. 'So, nothing happened at the warehouse?' Cody had been sent to watch over a warehouse/shed that Ryan had notified them about. It belonged to Jameson and was something new to keep an eye on. Jaz like the fact that they were all working to bring down Jameson.

'Nah. We have to watch for a guy who keeps an eye on the place for Jameson, but he didn't show. And there was no light coming from the back of the shed this time. My guess is no one was staying there.'

Cody had mentioned light he could see from a hole in the wall when he did a sweep around the shed a while back. You had to get up close to see it, but it proved that someone was inside. Which was funny for a building like that, positioned so close to port.

'Word is that Jameson is trafficking girls in. We just have to find out how, when and where,' he added.

'Why does the world have to be full of shit people who do shit things,' said Jaz. Her bacon and eggs churned in her stomach.

'I don't know, Jaz. Be nice if everyone could live safely, with only good things to offer. How do people like Jameson and Salvatore get into these positions in the first place? Are they born that way or shaped into it?'

They were some deep questions from Cody, ones Jaz had asked herself from time to time. Especially if Salvatore was her father. Jaz had been trying to push Salvatore from her mind, using the mission and Ryan's absence to focus on instead. She was determined to forget what she'd found out about him but then there were moments like this, when his name came up and she had to admit she was curious about him, about his family. Did she have some of his traits? His tendencies? Is this why she was like she was? Did having a father in the killing business and a spy for a mum mean she was always going to be this way inclined? Would she end up going bad? Maybe it was possible;

sometimes people who saw so much death and destruction ended up becoming what they fought against. She'd seen it in TV shows, mercenaries were once good guys who jumped ship and end up working for the highest bidder.

'You okay, Jaz?'

'Yeah, I guess. I was just wondering if I could ever end up going bad. What sets people off on the wrong path?' she said, confiding in Cody. They'd grown close over this last month, surfing and talking. He was more than just a cheeky ratbag with shaggy hair.

'This is a deep convo, hey? And some deep questions. Jazzy, you don't ever have to ask that, 'cause I don't think there is a bad bone in your body. You are all for helping people. I'm a hundred per cent sure you can rest easy. If not, you have friends who will make sure you don't go rotten,' he said, reaching over and punching her shoulder.

'Thanks Cody.' It was nice to be reassured. But Cody didn't know the whole story. Would his answer be different if he knew Salvatore was her father?

CHAPTER 23

Jaz stood on a bar stool as she tried to hang up the green tinsel.

'Careful, Jeni, I can't afford for you to break your neck over bloody Christmas decorations,' said Ted.

Jaz stuck the last bit in place before climbing down to check her handiwork. 'But Ted, look at the place. It's so cool.'

'I don't think the regulars who come here will even notice,' he said with a shrug and walked off.

Jaz didn't take it to heart, she'd seen Ted smiling when she'd put up the 'Merry Christmas' sign she'd brought. It was December, after all. If you couldn't get festive what else was there to look forward to?

'Place looks great. Is this your doing, Jeni?'

She turned to see Stevo walk in with Bud. 'Sure is. If you like it, make sure you tell Ted. He thinks I shouldn't have wasted my time.' Bud came up to her and slipped his arm around her and kissed her on the lips.

'Hello, pretty lady. I've missed you,' said Bud. 'It's a long time between drinks,' he added.

It had been three weeks since she'd kissed him at his place. Since then they'd started a slow kind of relationship, which started with swapping phone numbers so they could text and talk in between the pub visits. It was still at the *getting to know* you stage. She'd been on one date with him, going out for fish and chips in Fremantle, and then they caught a movie one Sunday. But between Jaz working nights at the pub, and Bud's work, the relationship had been slow and steady. Which Jaz was happy about.

'You texted me half an hour ago,' she said, poking his chest with her finger. It was at that moment that she realised someone else had stepped inside behind Stevo.

Ryan.

Could Bud tell she'd gone limp in his arms? Could he tell her heart had begun to race and her breath had caught in her throat? Could he tell that her body was screaming out for someone else?

'Hi Jeni,' Ryan said casually. His eyes flicked to Bud's arm around her. 'Bud mentioned he'd caught the barmaid, but some of us didn't believe him.'

'Told you I don't lie,' said Bud.

'It's good to see you back, Reece. It's been a while. Thought you must have found another local to drink at,' said Jeni, hoping Ryan understood how much he was missed. The little muscle in his jaw was pulsing, as if he was clenching his teeth. His eyes shot to Bud's fingers that rested against her waist. She needed to do something. Standing this close to Ryan after such a long, long time was asking for trouble. Already his aftershave was wafting and that blue button-up shirt was undone enough to drive her insane. 'Can I get you all a beer?' She stepped out of Bud's embrace, waiting for their answer.

'Yes, thanks Jeni,' said Stevo as he moved to the table, grabbing the basket of nuts.

'I'll get them,' said Ryan pulling out his wallet.

That was when Jaz noticed the unfamiliar mark on his wrist. The Sesha Serpent tattoo. In that moment she was scared, it felt like all the blood had drained from her body.

'Thanks Reece.' Bud kissed her cheek, oblivious to her inner turmoil. 'Come see me when you can.' Then he went and joined Stevo.

Ryan moved to Jaz. 'Shall we go to the bar?' he asked, snapping her out of her sudden freeze.

She nodded, then followed him. As she poured the three beers she studied Ryan. He looked tired. Dark shadows sat around his eyes and he seemed thinner. Fitter but thinner, as if he wasn't eating properly or maybe overdoing the exercise. Combined with that tattoo, she was as worried as heck but couldn't say a damn thing.

'New artwork,' she whispered as she put the beers on the bar in front of him.

Ryan shuffled his watch so it covered the tattoo. 'Yeah. Bound to happen. You and Bud?'

'Yep. It's all good. We do what we have to, hey?' Jaz didn't know why she felt so suddenly angry. Because Ryan was dragged into the Sesha Serpents? Was she angry that they couldn't be together? She knew it wasn't possible, that it wasn't Ryan's fault, but yet she felt angry. She wanted to be able to hold Ryan, hug him in public and she wanted that shitty tattoo off his skin. It was like he'd been branded as someone's property, and Ryan didn't belong to anyone. Maybe that's what was making her so grumpy.

'Have you been well?' she said softly. She was kind of amazed she'd managed to get anything out at all. But she needed to make the most of their time together.

'As good as can be expected, I guess. This is driving me a little crazy,' he said as she handed him the change.

As she did his hand clamped over the money and her hand, holding, touching, the power of that simple touch felt like a thousand Christmases. He let go and with shaking hands put his change back into his wallet. Jaz knew exactly how he felt. She felt like crying from the pure pleasure of touching him and the torture of not being able to have more.

'You look good,' he whispered. 'Browner maybe.' Deep dark eyes drank in her skin, they dropped to her arms and chest.

'I've been surfing nearly every morning.' This made her smile. It was a pleasure to spend her morning in the ocean.

Ryan frowned. 'I hope he behaves,' he said as he collected up the three glasses in his large hands.

Jaz knew he was talking about Cody, and it was sweet he was a little worried.

'I'll be over later,' she said for theatrical purposes, but needn't have bothered as the closest person was four stools away along the bar and Ted was chatting to him. 'Can you believe it's nearly Christmas,' she added.

He gave her a smile that was Ryan all over and for the moment it was enough to satisfy her cravings. She could do this. She could put on an award-winning performance too.

The rest of the night was busy with a full house, but she managed to pass by Bud's table on a few occasions. Once they all stopped their hushed talking as she approached and she was curious as to what they were talking about. Shesha Serpent stuff?

'Here Jeni,' said Bud, gesturing to his lap.

Jaz shook her head and put her arms around his neck so she could whisper to him, 'I better not. Ted will get grumpy if I play favourites. Might make the others think they'll get the same service.' Plus she didn't like making it more uncomfortable for Ryan. She was sure he wouldn't rub Annaliese in her face if he could help it.

Ryan spent a lot of time looking into his beer. Was that so he wasn't caught glancing in her direction?

Jaz was back behind the bar when she saw Ryan head to the bathroom. She ducked into the back room and out the side door, which opened into the same corridor that led to the toilets and the outside door. She reached for a rubbish bag on her way out, it wasn't even half full but she needed something.

'Here, let me get the door for you,' said Ryan as she stepped in behind him.

'Thanks, that'd be great.'

Jaz flicked the light switch off, the one Ted had finally got around to fixing, and stepped outside into the dark. The bag dropped from her hands the moment she felt Ryan reach for her, pulling her to him. His hands caressed her face as he kissed her. Hot, warm lips that knew what they wanted.

Jaz clung to him as they opened their mouths, kissing and tasting with a feverish need. It was red-hot and she was burning with desire.

Ryan pulled back a fraction, his breath coming in shallow pants, caressing her face each time. 'I gotta go. I love you.'

'I love you too. Be careful,' she said before stealing another kiss.

Ryan groaned, then pulled away as if it pained him to do so.

She knew just how he felt. Ryan turned the light back on for her as he went inside and she found the light rude and intrusive. She wanted to revel in the kiss, in the dark where the memories lingered, yet the bright light forced her to pick up the rubbish bag and put it in the bin.

When she went back inside she locked the door and went to the toilet. She needed to splash water on her face, her cheeks felt like they were on fire. Maybe it was her whole body? As she stared at her face in the mirror she wondered if they'd all notice the flushed cheeks and sparkly eyes. Maybe Bud would think it was for him.

Jaz had to endure the rest of the night but it was worth it to have Ryan so close. She had to make the most of it, because it could be another month before she saw him again. Ryan stayed until Stevo and Bud left. They'd all come together, apparently.

She hugged Bud goodbye but her eyes were only for Ryan and she tried to take in as much of him as she could. It was strange to have her arms around one bloke while staring at the man she loved.

'Text me tomorrow,' said Jaz as Bud headed to the door. 'Bye Stevo, bye Reece. Come back soon.'

Then they were gone and Jaz had to stop herself from running outside, or from bursting into tears, or throwing a chair. She couldn't decide which would make her feel better.

'Hey, trouble. Seems like the decorations better stay,' said Ted. He put his arm around her shoulder and led her back to the bar where only six people remained, having their last beers.

'I told you people would like it, even if they mightn't say so.' She gave Ted a nudge in the ribs. 'You're an old softy, I'm sure of it.'

'Nah, I think you've got me mixed up with someone else,' said Ted. 'I'm a grumpy bar manager who's gonna sack your arse if you don't get this place cleaned up.'

He tried to frown but it came off looking like a soft teddy bear with a monobrow. Not that she'd ever tell him that.

By the time Jaz had cleaned up, caught the bus, then driven back to The Ring, she was exhausted. Seeing Ryan had flipped her emotions and she felt drained and a little sad.

It wasn't until she crawled into her bed after her shower that she realised she had company. The bed did feel warmer.

'Hey you,' said Jaz. She snuggled up to Anna, wrapping her arms around her friend. 'You get scared?'

'Maybe. Tay went home so he could see his dad in the morning and I didn't want to be in my room alone.'

Growing up they'd often shared a bed, like best friends do. Like a comfort teddy or blanket. Which was exactly what Jaz needed now.

'I don't want to be alone either,' said Jaz as tears sprung from her eyes. She couldn't help it. The more she thought about Ryan, the tattoo and how tired he looked, the more the tears came.

Upon hearing her sniffles, Anna rolled over. 'Oh, Jaz. Are you okay? Talk to me. What is it?' Her voice no longer sounded sleepy.

'I'm sorry, it's just me being silly. Go back to sleep.'

'No.' Anna brushed her hair back and waited. 'Did something happen with Bud?'

Jaz shook her head. 'Ryan came tonight. He has the Serpent tattoo and he looks different, unhealthy I guess. It was good to see him but I don't know why I'm crying. I'm being a baby,' she said feeling ridiculous, but unable to stop the tears or the sobs.

'You miss him. That's not silly. He's probably feeling just as bad right now. You need to be strong for him. You guys will get through this. You'll be together soon. I know you will.'

Jaz smiled through her tears and took her first steadying breath. 'You think?'

'I know so. I know everything, after all.' Anna rubbed her hand up and down Jaz's arm. 'Come on, it's late and you're probably tired. You'll feel better in the morning. Try to sleep.'

Anna was such a mum, but Jaz loved her for it. Sometimes it was needed.

'I'm glad you're here. I love you, Annabanana.'

'I love you too, Jazzy.'

Somehow Jaz managed to get off to sleep, thanks to Anna. Her steady rhythmic breathing drew her mind into the darkness where her dreams of sand and waves took over.

CHAPTER 24

RYAN PULLED OUT his gun and checked the clip of bullets. It was habit. And his gun was needed more with his entry into the Shesha Serpents. He rubbed the tattoo on his wrist as if it had been done with pen and he was trying to smudge it; only, the ink that was etched deep in his skin wouldn't budge. It felt awkward, like he was wearing a dress or something that just wasn't him. Every time he looked at it he felt bad, not wanting to be associated with such scum, but he tried hard to use the tattoo as a symbol of his determination to bring the gang down. It was his reminder of how far he'd come, the sacrifices he'd made – Jaz's face flashed before his eyes – and just what was at stake.

Oh, Jaz. How he missed her. That night in the pub was just what he needed to keep his spirits up. She was his prize, if he could see out this mission he got to be with her, which was something he reminded himself of constantly. Her face alone was enough to keep him going. But stealing that kiss … it curled his toes just reliving it in his memory. How sweet she tasted and how warm she felt against his body when he felt so cold and alone. Jaz made him feel human, made him feel like Ryan. If only he had the time to tell her that. He shouldn't have risked a kiss; if they'd been seen it could have caused all sorts of trouble. It was a selfish need that took over his body and his common sense, but hell, it had been totally worth it. He couldn't wait for when it could be just them together with all the time in the world to explore and get reacquainted.

Ryan tucked his gun into the glove box and rubbed at the tattoo again. It was like a mozzie bite, irritating and itchy but he knew it was just his mind taking a dislike to it and what it represented. Even Jaz. He's seen the shock, the horror and the sadness all flash through her eyes when she spotted it. He'd have cut the tattoo out there and then if it would have brought her smile back. He lived for that smile, those lips. Closing his eyes, he tried to picture them without groaning out loud.

Wilkie was driving them to the airport for another pick-up. Randall was in the back. It was business as usual.

It had been Wilkie who pulled him aside one night to tell him he'd been accepted into the Shesha Serpents if he wished to join. Of course Ryan had asked what it meant and what it entailed.

'It means being loyal to Jameson, it shows that we are his trusted men and we do what is required with no questions asked, and total secrecy,' Wilkie had said. 'It also means a bonus pay rise and a few perks. And a word of warning: Don't take this position lightly. You can't change your mind or back out. No one ever leaves the Shesha Serpents.'

'So, Jameson's the one who gave the okay for this?' Ryan had asked. He needed to know who really led this rebel group.

'Yes. If you agree to join, you'll need to meet with Jameson. Others only talk to Randall but the boss man wants to see you personally. Could be due to a family conflict,' Willkie had said with a smirk.

Ryan had said he'd join and so the next step had been put in place. A meeting with Jameson. It was inside the house, in his study and Randall had delivered him personally with no words of encouragement, which was to be expected from Randy.

Jameson had been wearing a suit, Ryan was yet to see him out of one. He'd wondered if his pyjamas were similar in style.

'So, you want to join the Shesha Serpents and you've heard what it entails,' Jameson had said, cutting right to the point.

'Yes, sir. I'm prepared to serve you and your business for Annaliese's future,' had been Ryan's reply.

'Good. I like you, Reece, you are good for my daughter. She cares for you deeply, I've never seen her this interested in anything before. If you're the man she marries, then you will be the only son I have, and eventually I'd like to integrate you into the family business and hopefully have you run it when I'm gone. Does that interest you?'

'Yes, sir. I love Annaliese. She is my future and so is working in the family business.'

And with a nod from Jameson, it had been confirmed. He would join the Shesha Serpents.

Randall had come for him then and he'd been taken straight to the tattoo artist. Ryan knew it wasn't going to be a walk in the park. Men like Jameson didn't just give people a business, Ryan was on trial and would be for a long time before he was trusted with any part of the Jameson empire. But for now he was allowed to take the first step towards that future by joining the gang. With it had come access to the back room at the warehouse.

Ryan was sure Wilkie, Bud and the others didn't have the clearance that Ryan now had, but nor were they being groomed as Jameson's protégé.

What he'd found in that back room had been cells, cages for girls, plus a small office where the documents for this side of his business remained hidden away. Ryan was yet to get his eyes on anything of substance but he knew he just needed time. Drugs were also stacked in a locked vault, which, going by the girl who had been in the cell, they used to get the girls addicted so they had control over them. Was it ice, meth, cocaine? It didn't really matter, it was all the same to him.

Trying to keep his anger locked inside wasn't helping his health any. Fitness was his only release, punishing his body until the pain cleared his mind. Annaliese loved his lean muscled body, but it only made Ryan hate himself. Some days he even tried to do the yoga Jaz had taught him, to be closer to her and to try to free his mind. It was probably the closest he came to being relaxed.

Wilkie stopped the car at the airport short-term parking, and Ryan and Randall got out and headed to the international terminal. As they waited at the arrivals gate, Ryan fished out the bit of paper in his pocket and unfolded it. It had the name of the girl they were waiting for: Alexa Brillantes.

Ryan had been completely surprised to find out that the girls came into the country like everyone else. Mind you, they probably had forged passports but they came in on visas to be housemaids. Not that any of them became housemaids. Ryan had asked Randall why they came in this way – he'd assumed they were smuggled into the country illegally by boat; wasn't that what the warehouse was all about? – and Randall had explained that it was too costly to pay off all the corrupt police. This way the girls came in legitimately, approved by the government on working visas, and then,

Ryan figured, Jameson farmed them out to pimps who were no doubt on his payroll. 'It's all too easy,' said Randall.

After ten minutes, a small girl, hardly seventeen, came to stand in front of him and pointed to the sign. 'Me,' she said. Her long dark hair reminded him of Jaz and he felt the urge to grab this girl and make a run for it. But it wouldn't save the others.

'Follow me,' he said to the girl. She wore a simple white T-shirt and black shorts with thongs. She carried only a small backpack that had seen better days. He wondered how she got mixed up in all this. How did they get the girls? By promising a great life in Australia? Were they sold to pay off family debts? Were they threatened? Ryan would find the answers to these questions in time, no matter what it took.

He led the girl out to the car, Randall behind them both to make sure the girl didn't run.

Once inside the car Wilkie took them back to the warehouse. This was Ryan's sixth trip to the airport to collect a girl. And she would be the sixth one he'd have to deliver to some pimp or rich man wanting a plaything. Each one wore him down and made him more desperate to put an end to all the suffering.

At the warehouse it was his job to put the girl in the cell. It wasn't nice. Just a simple bed in the corner and a toilet, much like a prison cell. This room stank like a men's toilet at a dirty pub, and mould. The girl started to cry when she saw it, yelling out in Filipino.

'What are you doing? I was told my family would be waiting. Why am I here. Don't put me in there.'

At least he was pretty sure that's what she was saying. After his time with Yanna, Ryan had started studying Filipino in his flat in secret. He wanted to learn more, to reassure them a little, maybe enough to talk to the girls to get information about the other side of the trafficking.

Ryan grabbed the girl now, holding her shoulders.

'It's okay,' he said. Randall had gone into the office but could probably still hear him. 'Just relax, have a rest.'

'Fuck you,' she said. Obviously she knew some English. The girl started yelling again in Filipino, too fast for him but he got the gist of what she was saying. While she was rambling, Randall came out with a needle and jabbed her in the arm. Ryan tried not to wince as Randall pumped her with the sedative. Next would come the drugs. Ryan was getting all too familiar with the routine. She started to go limp and he gathered her up in his arms.

He hated this part of the job. Shooting the bastards like Randall and Jameson was much more fun. Since Ryan had been helping Randall with this line of work, Randall had become reserved. Maybe it was because he didn't mix work with friendship, or maybe it was because Ryan wasn't doing a good enough job at hiding his distain. For whatever reason, his distance was purposeful.

'You set her up. I'm going to get Wilkie to pick up more sedative from our supplier and check that her screaming didn't alert anyone.' Randall left the room, the door clicking shut.

Ryan dragged the girl to the bed and laid her down on it. Quickly he darted out of the cell and locked the door, then headed to the small office while he had a chance. From previous visits he had identified one camera that was set up facing the cell, and another one facing the vault, but he wanted to check out the office. If he could get some names and details to pass on to the Agency, then this would all seem worth it.

He stepped into the room, still holding onto the doorknob. First he looked to the tall filing cabinet against the corner wall, then the desk with a computer and printer set up, then more filing and a big shredder machine on the floor. Where to start? How much time did he have? Ryan stepped to the desk.

There was a sheet with flight details on it and meeting times. The meeting for the buyers? Ryan took out his phone and took a photo of it. He'd be shot if they found this on his phone – but, risk for reward, he reminded himself.

Quickly he sent the photo to Tilly then deleted the photo and message. Did he go for the filing cabinet next? He went to open the top drawer but it was locked. Damn. Where would they hide the key?

He ran his hands under the desk, down the back of the cabinet and even behind the door. Nothing. Maybe Randall kept the key on himself at all times.

Ryan went to the other filing cabinet on the floor, it too was locked. It was like being in a maze full of dead ends.

Clang!

He jumped up, his heart racing as he darted from the room. Glancing about, he found the door still shut. His eyes passed over the girl in the cell, her shoe had come off her foot and fallen to the floor. Jesus, it had scared him to death.

With no time to waste he went back into the office and rifled through the shredder, picking out strips of paper and looking for anything that made sense. He pulled out one that had more flight details. Quickly he tucked it into his pocket. It was all worth checking out. As long as he didn't get caught with it on him.

'Reece. What are you doing?'

Fuck! Randall. Where had he come from?

Now what?

He was kneeling on the cream carpet, in a room he wasn't allowed in, and Randall was behind him. How did he not hear the door? Had this been a test? Would Randal believe anything he was about to say?

'I've lost my contact lens,' he said quickly.

'I didn't know you wore lenses,' he said slowly.

'It's not something I go around telling people,' he said as he pretended to pick it up and put it in the bin. 'I needed a new one anyway.' He got up, Randall watching him the whole time.

'What were you doing in here anyway?' demanded Randall.

Shit.

Ryan was drawing blanks. Heck, had he just blown his cover? Think, Ryan, think, his brain screamed.

'I was chasing a tissue. She spat on me.' God, he hoped this was enough. 'I couldn't find one and was trying to wipe it from my eyes when my contact fell out. We really could do with some antibacterial wipes or something,' he said, wiping his face again for good measure.

The silence from Randall was deafening. He only had to ask Ryan to empty out his pockets or hand over his phone, and he would be in deep shit.

He itched to put his hands in his pocket and screw up the bit of paper until it resembled something that had gone through the wash. He also wanted to try to turn his phone off. But Randall was watching him, waiting for him to sweat. It was taking all his effort to remain calm and appear innocent, which was hard when his body was screaming to fight and flee.

'The thing with all this, Reece, is ... it's plausible, but I've had this feeling about you these last few weeks and I wouldn't be doing my job right if I didn't double-check.' Randall almost smiled as he pulled out his gun. Ryan was left to his mercy.

Would Randall shoot him here? Now?

'Normally I'm a shoot-first-ask-questions-never kinda guy, but with you it's a bit sensitive. The boss has a vested interest in you. He has things to consider. But I'm going to take my concerns to him. And we'll go from there. Maybe you are innocent, maybe not.'

He motioned with the gun and Ryan stepped out of the office. His heart was racing like a million machine guns.

'You're barking up the wrong tree but I understand you gotta do what you gotta do.' What else could Ryan say. He didn't want to plead innocent and then be caught with the paper in his pocket, or if they went through his phone and managed to extract that photo he'd deleted. The only thing he could do was play along and be cooperative as if he was innocent. Randall only had to check Ryan's eye for his other contact lens, which Ryan could say he'd lost earlier. Maybe he'd say he took both out as it messed with his head only having one contact. That could work, just. Maybe.

'How about you come and wait in this cell and keep the girl company while I go and speak to Jameson.'

Ryan headed to the cell with the gun at his back. Stay calm, he told himself. Don't give anything away yet, it could be salvageable still. He couldn't throw away just how far he'd come with Jameson on Randall's over-active mind.

'Just know that when Jameson finds out that I'm legit, you may find yourself working under me.' Ryan allowed a little smile to appear. He made sure it was cunning, as if he'd just set a trap and Randall had walked straight into it. If he could make him think that this was maybe his plan all along, it might make Randall think twice.

Randall's Adam's apple bounced as he swallowed hard. His eyes shifted uneasily around the room. 'Unlock the cell,' he demanded, trying to take back control.

Ryan did as he was asked and stepped inside.

Randall locked him in and then asked him to hand over his key. 'Just make yourself comfortable while we sort this little situation out.' His hand remained outstretched. 'Phone, too please.'

Fuck. He handed it over and hoped it took them a long time to find the things he'd deleted.

Ryan shrugged, trying to portray a calm that he didn't feel at all. 'It won't be for long,' he said without a care as he sat on the end of the bed, moving the sleeping girl's legs.

Randall's neck jumped with his pulse, his skin moving like something was crawling under it. Ryan never did like Randy Randall.

Without another word, Randall left the room, locking the main door.

Ryan sat there, trying to think. He had to hide the bit of paper without anything showing up on the camera watching the cell.

How much time did he have? What would happen when Randall came back? Would he be tortured or spared due to Annaliese? Jameson was a hard man and if he thought Ryan was a spy and had used his daughter to get to him, well, he'd surely be sliced and diced into little bits of shark bait. He just hoped Jameson's daughter meant enough to him that he'd make sure to give Ryan a chance to prove himself.

There was a lot of if's and un-answered questions. Ryan couldn't predict what was about to happen next. If he died, he hoped Jaz would move on and be happy. Maybe he could get word out through the girl in the cell with him? Even if it was a goodbye message to Jaz. One last, 'I love you.'

Shit.

It was all turning to shit.

CHAPTER 25

JAZ WAS AT the gym, cleaning some mats, when a shadow passed over her. For some reason it felt like the grim reaper as her body shivered involuntarily. Something had her senses on edge. Maybe it was the nightmares she'd been having about Ryan mixed up with the Shesha Serpents, his face all gaunt and looking like a junkie on Ice. It had been a hellish week and a half, and no sign of Ryan again did nothing to ease her frustration and despair. She just hoped that he'd turn up in the next few days at the pub. It was all she seemed to live for, not even the morning surfs could deter the feeling of dread that followed her around.

'Jaz?'

She looked up at the shadowed figure, his voice familiar but so out of place at the gym. 'Tilly.' Jaz left the sponge on the mat and jumped up. Tilly was at the gym! Something must be up for him to risk coming here. 'Hey, what are you doing here? What's going on?'

Tilly's face was normally grave-looking, so it was hard to get any sense of what was coming. He still looked like a scruff in torn black jeans, white T-shirt and a red check flannel shirt even though it was hot outside.

'Is there somewhere we can talk?' he asked glancing around.

There was no one else but Jaz here, but she locked the front door and took him into Pax's house so they couldn't be disturbed. The whole time her heart was racing. Was this about Ryan? Or did Jaz have new orders? Was James back and wanted to meet? Had she been compromised?

'Can I get you a drink?' she said feeling uneasy.

'No, let's sit.'

Crap. Never a good sign. Tilly hated to sit still.

Chairs scraped against the old lino as they sat, and then silence. Jaz was about to chew right through her nail to her finger if he didn't hurry up. 'Tilly!'

'Sorry. I'm not sure how to put this. When was the last time you saw Ryan?'

Shit. Not good. Not good at all. 'Last week at the pub. Why?' Had they been caught kissing? Had someone got suspicious?

Tilly put his head in his hand and massaged his temples. 'He hasn't been back to his flat all week,' said Tilly softly.

'What? What do you mean?' Jaz reached out for his arm and shook it, maybe a little too hard. 'Tilly?' He sat up, his pupils like pinheads.

'Every morning Ryan does a drop out the front of his flat. Sometimes there's nothing to report, but our man is always waiting and sees Ryan come and go. But he hasn't been back since Saturday.'

'He could be on a trip?' Jaz offered hopefully.

Tilly shook his head. 'Annaliese hasn't been seen with him either. She's still going on as normal, so she either knows where he is or has been told something different.'

'I don't get it. What are you trying to say, Tilly? Is Ryan okay?' Jaz felt completely confused. She just wanted a simple explanation.

'I think he's in trouble.'

Her belly dropped to her feet and she started to feel light-headed. 'Say what?'

'Saturday afternoon I get a text from Ryan, a photo actually, that listed flight numbers and meeting times. It was big, Jaz. Great intel we can use. But because no one has seen or heard from Ryan, I'm wondering if this intel he collected got him caught.'

'Oh.' What else could she say. This was just Tilly's opinion, he could be wrong. But in thinking that, Jaz knew Tilly was right. She'd had an awful feeling all week and now, with Tilly coming to her with this, it just made sense. 'How can we find out for sure? What can we do?'

'It's what *you* can do, Jaz. You have the connections with the gang members. You need to pump them for information about Ryan. They have to know something, or noticed his absence. They should have some sort of clue. Can you do that? Have you got close enough to them to get this info?'

'Yes, I think so.' Jaz was already thinking about how to extract info from Bud.

'I hate to say it but pillow talk works best.' Tilly wasn't smiling, nor teasing her. He was stating a fact and going on past experience.

Jaz knew if it came to that, she'd do whatever she had to in order to help Ryan.

Heck, what if he was already dead!

Her thoughts must have been written all over her face, because Tilly leaned over and gripped her hand.

'Jaz, don't fall to pieces on me. You need to be strong and not think the worst. We don't give up on anyone until we have proof. Right now we have nothing except my gut feeling.'

He was right. Jaz pushed her fears away, burying them deep down. 'It's not just your gut feeling, Tilly. I've had this bad feeling all week since I last saw him.'

Tilly frowned. He didn't like that news one bit. His reaction didn't make her feel any better either.

'When's your next shift at the pub?'

'Tomorrow night.'

'Good. You know what you have to do. If you have information for me, wear your hair up when you go surfing, then I'll stop by.'

Jaz raised an eyebrow at Tilly. He'd been keeping tabs on her? Or maybe he'd been talking to Cody? No, he must have seen her surfing to know she always left her hair out.

'Righto, will do,' she said as he got up.

'Out the back?' he asked.

Jaz nodded and let Tilly out the back door so he could slip away undetected. Ever the cautious one.

Jaz locked the door, leaned against it and then slid down to the floor. Tomorrow's shift couldn't come soon enough. Until then, the worry was going to eat her from the inside out.

Jaz walked into the pub the next day full of jitters, like it was her first day and she was about to be tested on everything. So much depended on her coming away with information, but what if Bud didn't come? She'd have to endure another day! Just the thought threatened to drive her insane. As she started work, she was all fingers and fumbles. A glass slipped from her hand and shattered all over the floor.

Jaz felt like that glass, so close to shattering into a heap of bits.

'Leave it, Jeni. I'll get this,' said Ted who'd turned up with a dustpan and brush. 'Go serve the thirsty lads.' He pointed to the end of the bar.

'Hi guys, what can I get you,' she asked the two blokes waiting with their money in hand. She almost missed their order as more patrons walked into the bar area. Part of her was hoping it was Bud and the other hoped it was Ryan.

All night she prayed for Ryan to walk into the pub. *Please, please,* she begged to the universe. But he never came. Bud did, though, only because Jaz texted him to make sure he was coming by, and to sweeten him up she said she'd got an early knock-off if he wanted to take her for a drive.

Sounds great. I'll be there in ten, he'd texted back.

Then Jaz had to beg Ted for an early knock-off.

'You're just lucky it's a Thursday and I like you,' he said with a frown.

Jaz put her hand on his shoulder. 'I like you too, Ted. And you know I'll make up for it.' She smiled and he shook his head.

'More like I can't afford to have you here breaking all my glasses,' he said with a grin. 'You're a bit out of sorts today. Is everything all right?' he added, throwing his bar towel over his shoulder.

'Yeah, just a few family issues, nothing to worry about,' she said with a shrug.

When Bud came in, he stayed for one beer and then she grabbed her backpack and they left for his car.

'You just want to drive my car again, don't you?' he asked. 'Tell me the truth – is it my car you're after?'

Jaz pushed Bud back against his car, holding him there with both her hands on his chest. 'Bud, I don't care what car you drive,' she said before leaning in to kiss him. Jaz made it the best kiss she could. She closed her eyes and thought of Ryan. She'd do whatever she had to, even if it meant going all the way with Bud, or even if she had to kill the whole lot of them. Nothing was going to stand between her and her soulmate.

'Wow,' said Bud as Jaz stopped for air. Bud's hands were on her waist and he seemed moulded to his car. His eyes shone in the streetlight, his smile dopey and drunk-looking.

'Shall we go for a drive?' she asked. 'To the beach?'

'Sure. Hop in.'

Cottesloe beach was quite busy, with people out for an evening meal or stroll. Jaz climbed into the back of his car, and Bud followed suit.

'That's better,' she said as she slid close to him and snuggled up against his chest.

'I agree. This beats sitting at home listening to Stevo try to sing in the shower and Tyson entertaining his lady friend,' said Bud.

'Sounds as exciting as my flatmate.' Jaz held his hand in hers. His fingers were short and stubby, his hand wide. Nothing like Ryan's strong long fingers, so capable and tender even though they were calloused. 'Do you find it hard working all day with them, then sharing a house as well?' she asked, moving into phase one of her plan.

'Yeah, on occasion. It's not too bad. Sometimes I can go all day and not see Stevo or Tyson.'

'And Wilkie and Reece?' she added.

'Thank God I don't live with Wilkie, he gives me the shits enough at work. He stays at the staff quarters on the estate. I think because he likes the housemaids who stay there too,' said Bud. 'He's all drag cars and conquests.'

'Reece hasn't been around much. Is he still busy with work? Seemed like you guys all got on well enough,' said Jaz, dipping her hand between his legs. If she could keep his concentration on what she was doing and not her questions, then he might not realise what she was up to.

'Reece, is um …' Bud struggled to make a sentence as her hand worked its way up his thigh. 'He's actually not around anymore.'

'Did he get fired?' Jaz reached for his hand and rested it against her breast. She knew Bud would like this, he stared at them enough. 'What did he do? Shoot someone?' Jaz had talked with Bud before about his bodyguard job and getting to carry guns. She always carried on as if it was such an exciting job, wanting to know if he'd ever shot anything. Due to her interest Bud usually tried to talk up his line of work, telling her stories of Randall shooting someone, or Reece tackling a bloke to the ground who'd been about to attack Jameson. In trying to impress her he'd inadvertently given away snippets that Jaz had clung to.

'Or did he get shot himself?' Jaz said stopping her hand just before it reached the zipper on his jeans.

'No, no one got shot. But I did hear he's in trouble with the boss. He's done something to piss Randall off. Wilkie loves it, he has his old job back and now there's a new kid driving the car.'

Jaz didn't like the sound of this one bit. How much more could she probe? Did Bud have any more answers? Jaz went for his zipper, and Bud's hand found its way under her shirt to her breast.

'Oh Jeni.' He groaned.

He glanced out the window and she could tell he like the danger of this, of being in a public place.

'You like it dangerous, don't you? Bet you'd like to see my gun too?' he said with a smile.

Jaz leaned over and kissed him, then whispered against his ear. 'You know I do. Tell me more,' she said panting a little and increasing her strokes. 'What do they do with Reece? Does he get punished if he's not fired? Is it like the gangster movies and he gets buried somewhere,' she said.

'Oh, he'd be getting punished for sure. You don't double-cross the boss.'

Bud was wriggling in ecstasy while Jaz felt like she was working. Is this how those poor girls who were forced into prostitution felt? Jaz tried to put it to the back of her mind, as if this was another job like scrubbing the toilets or mopping floors. Every job had a shitty part.

After Bud had reached his happy end they sat in the car, watching the moon glisten across the water.

'Well, I wasn't expecting that to happen tonight,' said Bud, holding her hand.

'Surprises are good, hey?'

'Yep. Do you want to go get something to eat? My girlfriend,' said Bud, nudging her shoulder.

'That sounds like a plan.' Jaz felt sorry for him, the fact that she was stringing him along and would dump him the moment this mission was over. It was hard not to be conflicted. He wasn't a mean person, that she'd seen, and he had always been sweet to her.

As they walked towards the road lined with pubs and restaurants, Bud was chatting, wondering about what to eat, but Jaz's mind was on other things. Well, one thing: Ryan. From what Bud had said she got a good feeling that Ryan was still alive — for the moment. Maybe he wasn't in a good way, but he was alive. She had to hope that things weren't clear-cut, because if Ryan had been caught red-handed he'd more than likely be killed on the spot. Guys like Jameson didn't play games, they didn't get to where they were by being nice. Salvatore wasn't nice, he'd killed Ryan's friend Chris the moment they realised he was a spy. Jaz shivered as she imagined the same happening to Ryan. God, she hoped not.

'Jeni? Is pizza okay?' Bud asked again.

'Oh, yep, sounds great, Bud.' Jaz mentally kicked herself. She had to pay attention, even though all she wanted to do was run and find Tilly and then demand they do something to save Ryan. She didn't want to sit here playing nice with Bud when Ryan could be suffering. It had already been more than five days, how much longer could he hold out? Would the Agency send in a team or would they not compromise the mission? Maybe Ryan could survive the questioning and be trusted again. It all relied on unknowns. Jaz hated unknowns. She needed to know now.

She would scoff her pizza and then feign feeling sick and ask Bud to drop her back at the pub, saying she'd accidentally left her keys there. She didn't want him to know the address of the Agency flat just yet. If it could be avoided, all the better. They didn't need Bud turning up at all hours trying to see Jaz when no one actually lived there.

Until then Jaz had to sit through dinner with Bud, while her body churned with thoughts of Ryan and what he could be going through. One thing was a plus: she didn't have to feign feeling sick, because right now she felt downright horrible.

CHAPTER 26

JAZ TIED HER hair up in a bun the moment she got out of bed, just in case Tilly was watching. It had been a shit night's sleep and she was up at six, so she went into the gym and did a gruelling set of push-ups and speedball work.

Anna and Taylor staggered in at seven, after another marathon TV night of watching *Black Sails*, messy haired and in their crumpled pyjamas holding cups of coffee.

'Jaz, stop trying to kill yourself and come and get a coffee,' said Taylor. He stood in only the black shorts he wore to bed.

Anna was right by his side, her face full of concern. 'Was it bad?'

Jaz grabbed her towel and started to wipe the sweat from her body as she walked towards her friends. 'It wasn't good news, but I believe he's alive.'

'Oh good,' Anna said with relief. 'Come, sit and tell us all.'

They all went back to the kitchen, where Anna sat beside Jaz while Tay made her a coffee. She told them everything Bud had mentioned. 'So, what I'm thinking is he's hidden away somewhere under interrogation. Bud would have told me if he was dead.' Jaz shuddered at the word. 'At least I think he would. The gang seems tight, so he'd know what happens to Ryan.'

'So, now what?' said Taylor. 'Wait and see?'

'I'll see Tilly this morning and hope he has a plan. Then we go from there.'

Tay and Anna glanced at each other and Jaz knew what they were thinking. What if Ryan wasn't alive? What if they couldn't save him? What would that do to their friend? She knew they were worried for Ryan and for Jaz but she couldn't think of how to reassure them that she'd be okay, because truthfully Jaz didn't know if she would be okay. So, she offered them something else.

'Life can be short, you never know what's around the corner. If I've learned anything it's to love and to not waste time. To take risks, live to the fullest and smile.' Jaz reached out to hold her friends' hands. 'I love you guys. It'll be okay.' She hoped. She had to because it's all she had. Hope.

Down at the beach Jaz let Cody go in by himself. 'Don't become shark bait,' she yelled as he splashed into the cool waves. Jaz was too agitated waiting for Tilly to even contemplate surfing. Instead she sat on the sand with her board and scanned the beach.

She didn't realise the man walking up the beach with a surfboard and boardies was Tilly until he was practically standing beside her.

'A man of many disguises,' she said. With his sunnies and bronzed chest he looked like he belonged among the sand and surf.

'I make a living from it. Gotta be good at it.' Tilly put his board down and sat beside her. The beach was empty and only about five surfers in the water, including Cody. 'So. How's our Ryan doing?' Tilly said as if he was asking about the weather instead of something of this magnitude.

Jaz quickly filled him in, every little detail in the hope that Tilly might pick up on something she'd missed.

'What do we do?' she asked afterwards. Surely Tilly held all the answers.

He scratched his chin. 'Not much we can do. We don't know where he's being held. No one has noticed anything from the estate or warehouse. I'm going to go straight out and watch the warehouse, that's my first bet as it's new and the most likely place, but they could have moved him. It's so hard to know. We can't go storming into every building Jameson owns. We just have to keep watching.'

'That's it!' Jaz almost yelled. 'Watch and wait? What if they're torturing him?'

'He knows how to deal with that. He won't give away the Agency. If they *are* torturing him, he'll die before he gives himself up. Best chance is they end up believing him and put him back on duty.'

'Yeah, and if not they kill him. Great.' Jaz was furious. Surely the Agency could send a man in there to get him out. Then reality hit Jaz: they really didn't really know where he was. 'So, we watch and wait.'

'You could keep pressuring Bud, he might be the only way to find out where Ryan's being held.'

Great. 'Is it worth trying to get to know Annaliese and see if she knows anything?'

'You could try. But you run the risk of working both sides and having them meet. You know too many of the gang now, they could place you.'

Tilly remained calm, his voice even, while Jaz felt ready to scream and throw fistfuls of sand in frustration.

'Ryan wouldn't want you to endanger yourself. Let's just take things easy, don't rush into anything.'

Tilly shot her a look as if Jaz was well known for this. Well, maybe she did have a track record of jumping into the deep end.

'I'm no good at just waiting, Tilly. This is Ryan.' Her heart was in her mouth and she forced the well of emotion back down. She would not cry in front of Tilly.

'I know, Jaz,' his voice was barely a whisper. 'We need to use our heads. No one will be sitting idly twiddling their thumbs. I'm going to leave here and put a task force together to watch every building, worker, you name it. Jameson won't be able to take a shit without one of our guys knowing about it. We'll find out where Ryan is and then we can work out our next plan of attack.'

He was right. Even when they did find Ryan, getting him out could ruin everything. But when it came to his life, maybe blowing the mission was the right thing to do. Jaz just hoped Ryan saw it that way. Maybe they'd be able to get a signal from him, he would know if he needed to be extracted.

Suddenly a thought popped into her head. And she wondered … maybe it would be worth trying? She didn't tell Tilly, because this idea fell into the 'don't rush into anything' category. Seriously, it probably needed a good week to think on it, but Jaz didn't have a week. She needed action now. This plan might just be crazy enough to work and she was desperate.

'I'll stay in touch.' Tilly got up, unaware of Jaz's busy mind planning its own scheme. Before he left the beach he said, 'Tell Cody to meet me asap at our meeting place.'

Cody came back to shore, shaking water all over Jaz. 'What's the verdict?'

Jaz relayed the conversation and told him about meeting Tilly.

'Well, what are we waiting here for?'

Cody didn't bother drying himself off. They headed to his Jeep and he drove Jaz back to the gym before heading off to meet Tilly. Jaz, on the other hand, went inside and changed into baggy green cargo pants, her hi-top Converse and a loose shirt with a hat she could hide under, with her reflective aviator sunglasses.

'Where are you going?' asked Anna as Jaz was heading for the door.

'I'm out for a while. Not sure how long I'll be, but I'll text.' Anna frowned. 'It's okay, just doing some watching for Tilly.' It was a white lie; she didn't want to tell Anna the truth, not yet. If she told her what she was about to do, Anna would need to know all the stuff she'd kept to herself. Stuff that only Ryan was privy to. The only reason Anna didn't know about it was because Jaz wasn't sure how to tell her friends. That and the fact she'd buried it to the deepest part of her mind as she tried to move on.

Until now she'd done a great job of forgetting Salvatore. But right now he could just be the key.

Jaz left the gym and headed to Salvatore's place. She sat in her Jeep parked outside but it drove her insane waiting for something to happen, so she went to his plane hangar. She knew what car he drove and was excited to see it parked by the large building. Jaz did a drive by, and then left her car hidden in a car park up by the small airport. Walking back, she tried to figure out how this was going to work. Would his men shoot her? Would they even remember her? What would she say and do?

Before she knew it she was opening the office door. Last time she was here, Ryan was by her side. It was the day after they'd made love. Just that thought alone strengthened her spine, and inside to the lion's den she went.

No one was in the office, and she wasn't here to snoop, so no paperwork was of interest to her, so Jaz took a deep breath and walked out the back. She knew the way.

'Hey, what do you think you're doing back here!' yelled a man over by a workshop bench. Not far from where the black plastic had been rolled out last time.

'I'm looking for Salvatore,' she said. Her voice almost cracked at his name. What the hell was she about to do? Had she gone completely nuts? Maybe.

'That doesn't mean you can just waltz in here. There are safety protocols,' the man told her, walking closer.

Jaz could tell by the way he walked that there was a gun tucked into his pants at his back. She didn't bother to ask about his so-called safety protocols. 'Is Salvatore here or not?' she asked.

'What's up, Jim?' said another guy who came from the back of the work-shop behind a couple of vehicles parked inside. This guy wore jeans and his hand was stuck behind him, no doubt ready to train his gun on Jaz if need be.

Jaz tried looking around the shed. Salvatore had to be here. His car was. Shit, what if it was just here to be serviced by his staff? 'I'll wait until Salvatore turns up. I have an urgent message for him.'

'I don't care who you are, lady.' The man in jeans came closer and tried to look under her hat to see what he was dealing with. He glanced at the other bloke. Jaz could see them trying to decide what to do. 'You need to leave this area. Go make an appointment like everyone else. Salvatore is a busy man.'

'No.' She stood her ground. Jaz moved to take off her sunglasses and the guy to her right reached for his gun.

'Jim,' the other guy groaned. He rolled his eyes, unimpressed with Jim's jitters.

But it was probably not surprising after the big gun fight they had here months ago. Jaz never thought she'd be back here. Jim might have been one of the guys she'd shot at.

With the gun now in her face, Jaz raised her hands. She didn't think they'd be stupid enough to kill her without asking questions. 'Don't shoot. I just want to see Salvatore.'

'Who do you think you are?' The gun came closer, resting against her chest.

'What is going on out here,' boomed a voice from a door by the back corner. 'I'm trying to conduct business and you're in here making all this noise,' said Salvatore as he strode towards them.

Jaz kept her head tilted down, hidden by her hat as her heart raced. This was her dad; man, that was so weird. She could only hope he didn't want to kill his own daughter.

'Jim, what's going on,' Salvatore said as he got closer and realised there was a situation.

'This girl just waltzed right into the shed and is demanding to see you,' said Jim. 'After last time, I thought ...' His voice dropped away.

'What do you want?' Salvatore asked Jaz.

She slowly reached for her hat, pulling it off as her eyes tilted up to meet his. As her hair dropped out and fell around her shoulders, she saw his eyes widen.

'It's you.'

At Salvatore's words his men realised who she was, and now she had both men pointing their guns at her.

'You're stupid coming back here,' said Jim. His smile indicated how much he wanted to pop a bullet in her chest.

Jaz flicked her eyes back to Salvatore. 'I've come to talk and I'm sure you've got some questions for me, don't you?'

Salvatore stood there, black slacks, leather shoes and a pin-striped shirt, with gold cufflinks that matched his gold necklace. Jaz noticed her medallion was around his neck. It sent a weird sensation through her body. It was his, after all, but it had belonged to Jaz for so long, had been something she'd treasured. Now she felt very confused. Salvatore saw her eyes drop to his medallion, he reached for it, feeling the inscription with his thumb just like Jaz always had. Even weirder, she thought.

'Drop your guns,' he said to his men.

'Sir?' They stared back at him blankly. 'I think we should keep them here while you talk, just in case she tries something.'

'I haven't come here to fight. I've come to talk to you. I'm not even armed,' she said.

'Well, you're a bit stupid then,' said Jim. 'Want me to tie her up then, boss?'

Both of his men stood with their guns aimed, waiting for Salvatore's direction. Jaz didn't dare make any sudden moves; they both seemed trigger-happy and likely shoot her on impulse. 'You don't have to worry about doing that. I'm not here to hurt anyone and you won't be hurting me either,' she said calmly.

'And why is that, missy?' said Jim.

But Jaz targeted her reply straight at Salvatore.

'Because I think I'm your daughter.'

CHAPTER 27

'WHAT?'

All three men said the same word. It echoed around the big shed, bouncing off each wall like surround sound at a cinema.

'Um, boss?' said Jim uncertainly.

'How can I believe that?' said Salvatore, his arms crossed at his chest.

'You already know something's up otherwise you wouldn't have stopped your men from shooting me last time,' she said.

'I was confused,' he said reaching for the medallion again. 'This is mine. How did you get it?'

'From my mother.'

'But …' He paused. 'I gave this to only one person.'

If he thought any harder, Jaz was sure smoke would seep from his ears. 'Yes, my mum. Look at me, see the resemblance? Now, if you give me some of your time, I'll try to tell you what I know. But I want something in return. Just know that I'm only here telling you this because I'm in a jam. Before this, I was quite happy to pretend you didn't even exist.'

'I'm seriously confused.' Salvatore stared at her.

Jaz could tell that he saw something about her that was familiar but he wasn't sure he could believe anything. If Salvatore had come to her saying he was her father she'd probably have told him where to go. Luckily, he was giving this some thought.

'All right. Let's talk.' Salvatore reached past the gun for her arm and gently tugged her towards the door he came from.

'Ah, boss, what do you want us to do?' the guy in jeans asked.

'Go back to work,' Salvatore replied.

He let her arm go but kept glancing at her. Was he trying to spot the similarities or just checking she didn't make a run for it?

Through the door was a small office. It had a large oak desk with a new computer on it and some matching filing drawers against the wall behind the big leather chair. On the opposite wall was a long black leather couch with a pillow and a throw rug. Jaz got the feeling he slept in here sometimes. Maybe he had no reason to go home?

'Please, sit,' he gestured to the couch and they sat.

Now she was facing Salvatore and had time to study him. His hair was the same silky black as hers, and their skin tone was similar. But it was the lines around his eyes that fascinated her, and the deep rich nutmeg of his eyes that shone with an uncertainty as he searched her face.

'Your eyes, they ...' His words ended but he kept studying her.

'They're just like my mum's, so I'm always told. I'm not sure who you knew her as but she was with you about twenty years ago. Fairer than I am and had brown hair back then. She said you were in love.'

He put up his hand to stop her. 'Julie?' His head tilted, face shocked. 'I've only ever loved one woman. The same woman I gave this medallion to. But she left me, disappeared completely. I searched for her but she didn't exist.'

Right then, in that moment, Jaz felt sorry for Salvatore. His face was so raw with emotion and a tiny bit of hope.

'No.' Jaz shook her head and prepared to tell the story as she knew it. 'Back then she was a spy, sent in to gather information about your family and the bad business they were into. Her name and backstory would have been made up.'

'A spy? But—'

Jaz put up her hand and shushed him. 'Let me finish.' Jaz never thought she'd see the day when she 'shushed' a big bad drug lord. 'Now, from what I know, she actually fell in love with you too. So much so, she told her brother she believed you were different from your family, that you were good. Anyway, she fell pregnant. She couldn't tell her family because they would have wanted me gone, as would the Agency she worked for, and she didn't want to tell you and have me brought up into your family. Especially when she saw how tied into drugs they were. So, she disappeared to WA and raised me. Only thing was, her one connection to the Agency – the man who helped her create a new life, is also what connected me eventually to the same Agency. It's who I now work for trying to take down people like you. So, it's a freak of nature that we actually got to meet and for you to recognise this,' she said pointing to the medallion. 'Without that, I'd never have known who you really were. Mum refuses to talk about you.'

'Wow.' Salvatore blinked rapidly. 'That's a lot of crazy.'

Jaz almost smiled. 'I know, hey.'

'Do you have a photo of her, I really need to see to believe.'

Jaz got out her phone and found a photo that didn't give away any other details. She held it out for him to look, but not touch.

'Oh my God. Julie,' he said as his hand came up to his mouth. 'She's a blonde now? Still so beautiful. I knew I recognised your eyes.'

Salvatore stared at that photo until her arm hurt and she dropped it. She saw the loss splash across his face. She understood that loss.

'I never knew what happened to her. There were no records, as if she'd never even existed. It did my head in.' Sal shifted in the couch. 'So, Julie is okay?'

Jaz had no intention of telling him her real name. He loved her as Julie, so she would forever remain that girl. 'Yes, she's okay. She's happy. She married. Had another kid. I've had a great life.'

'She did the right thing giving you a new start. My life is not what I would have wanted for my children either. But I wish she'd given me the chance to run with her. I would have given up my family for Julie. She was my everything. And yet here you are, mixed up in this lifestyle she wanted you away from.'

'I know. Funny how it worked out. But I've always had this yearning to do something worthwhile and good. It's just a shame to find out my biological father is one of the bad guys I'm trying to put away.'

Salvatore actually looked shocked.

'I'm having trouble finding out Julie is still alive and well, let alone the fact that she had my child.' He held up his hand, wanting to touch Jaz's face, but she moved out of his reach. 'I'm sorry. You actually look a lot like my sister when she was young.' They sat in silence for a few seconds before Salvatore spoke again. 'I believe you. As crazy as it seems. But seeing Julie and you, and you filling in the blanks, plus the medallion – I believe you.'

It was hard to dispute the medallion.

'So, you already have a father?' he asked.

'Yes, I do. He's been there for me since I was two. He's an amazing dad and he works hard making an honest living to support us.'

'I guess I must be a disappointment to you,' said Salvatore.

'I don't know anything about you besides the drug selling and killing,' Jaz said harshly. It was good to remind herself. She didn't need any fanciful ideas, especially while having this oddly normal conversation.

'Firstly, I've never killed anyone, not by my own hand,' he added when he saw her expression. 'I have a gun and know how to use it but I've never killed anyone.'

Jaz didn't feel like pointing out that she had killed someone and seen her fair share of death already, but that was nothing he needed to know.

'And I don't do drugs. It's something my father always drummed into us with his business. We only sell to those stupid enough to take them.'

'Yeah, except sometimes it's kids who don't know any better and have been pushed into it by friends or drug dealers. You're still the catalyst for many deaths, killings, thefts, addictions, etcetera, etcetera.' Jaz wouldn't let him get away with sugar-coating his life.

'I know. I never wanted anything to do with my family's business, but I truly lost my way after Julie left. I moved to WA in search of her because she once told me she thought it was a beautiful state and we dreamed of a carefree life in Perth. But I eventually realised I was never going to find her, and finally my father forced me back into the business. You know nothing of family pressures. I'm guessing you have a very supportive and loving family?'

Jaz didn't reply, just a small nod of her head. Yeah, Jaz had it pretty darn good but she wasn't about to rub it in.

'Are you willing to tell me your name? Can we stay in touch? Is it too much to ask to be in your life?' His words were spoken with care, almost a plea.

Jaz didn't even think about him wanting to see her, or get to know her. It had been the furthest thing from her mind. Even now, it was all about Ryan. What would he think about her doing this?

'I guess you can call me Jaz. And yes, it's my real name. I'm not sure it's good for us to be anywhere near each other while you're still dealing in drugs and murder. Otherwise it might be me putting a bullet in you at some stage.' A touch melodramatic but realistic, she thought.

'Seriously, how can you be a spy when you can only be ...' Salvatore paused to do the sums. 'What, about eighteen?'

'Yeah, but I can take care of myself. You don't have to worry about me.'

'It's not every day you find out you have a daughter. It changes everything.'

'You have no right to be my father. You're far from it. But I come to you with an offer to take a step closer to that position.'

Salvatore leaned forward, his frown serious. 'I'm listening.'

'Do you know Jameson Figlomeni well?'

His brow creased as he paused for a moment. 'You're mixing with the wrong crowd, Jaz.'

The sound of her name on his lips was weird. Was this all getting too familiar? Would he want to hug her goodbye next? Would Jaz like that? Her emotions were so mixed up. She'd detested this man for what he did and the stories she'd heard from Ryan, yet here on this couch he was just a man. No, he was actually her biological father, which only complicated things more.

'Just be thankful we've gone after him at the moment. But a word of warning: you might want to cease your drug operation if you plan to have any sort of life.'

'Who do you work for? Who did Julie work for? Is it the police?'

'You don't need to know that. Just know we have a lot on you and Jameson and we won't stop until we topple you all.'

Salvatore scratched his chin. 'What do you need on Jameson? I do know him. We've done business together, but we generally stay out of each other's way. I don't like his side business, what he does with the girls. That's not on.'

He meant it but Jaz wasn't going to let him off the hook, she would not allow any humanity on his part to infiltrate her.

Jaz took a deep breath. This was her chance. 'We had a man undercover in Jameson's gang, the Shesha Serpents.' Salvatore's brow went up, obviously impressed. 'But we think he's in trouble. I was hoping you could reach out to Jameson and see if our man's still alive and where he might be holding him. We have eyes on all his buildings that we know of but have nothing.' Her heart was racing again, just thinking about Ryan stranded.

'You must be pretty desperate to come to me.'

Salvatore was smart.

'Yes, I am.'

'This man means something to you?' he asked. 'You don't need to answer that. I can see it all over your face.'

Jaz's hand went to her cheek and she felt silly for being so readable. But she was here for Ryan, his safety was driving her.

'Sure, I'll do it.'

'What?' Jaz wasn't expecting this, nor was she ready for it. Sure, she'd hoped he'd help and that being his daughter might sway him but she didn't really know how he'd react to any of what she'd told him. He could have pulled out his gun and shot her if he hadn't believed a word she'd said.

'I said I'd help.' He thought for a moment. 'I can get in contact on the pretence of a deal. Maybe tell him I'm getting out of the business and see if he wants to buy in. I'm guessing you'd like me to do this asap?'

Jaz could only nod. She was barely breathing, let alone able to make a sentence.

'Right. Did you want to wait here while I call him? Or do you have a number I can reach you on?'

Heck, she had to think. 'I can wait. And how about you give me your number.' That way she could call him on a burner phone.

'Righto.' He stood up and went to his desk. He grabbed a business card and wrote down a number on the back. 'This is my private number. Feel free to use it anytime.' He held it out to her. 'Anytime, Jaz. For anything.'

Again she felt a weird sensation when he said her name, especially sounding all sincere-like. Jaz went over to grab it from his fingers. Then he pulled out his mobile and made a call.

It was a quick one. 'Hi, it's Sal. Can we meet?' And then a few *Yeps* and it was done.

'We meet in an hour. Call me in two hours' time and I'll hopefully have some information for you.'

'Do you think he'll tell you anything about Reece?'

'Reece? I can only try. We usually only discuss necessary matters we have to deal with. I asked him not that long ago about one of my men who went missing.'

Jaz almost choked; lucky she wasn't eating. 'Yeah, about him. He's dead.'

Sal's mouth opened but no words came out. Just as well. 'I won't ask how but at least now I know for sure now. Did you?'

'Long story, I was there and it wasn't meant to happen,' said Jaz. 'So, I'll go and call you in two hours?'

'Yes. I know you don't know me, or even like who I am, but I won't do wrong by you, Jaz. I know I have to earn your trust. A lot will change from now,' he promised. 'I'm glad you came to me.' He smiled, his face pulled in funny places as if he hadn't smiled like that in a long time. 'You are a gift from God. Not only do I find out that Julie is alive but I have a daughter. Family.'

They were far from family in her mind but she'd let him think whatever he wanted if it meant she'd get Ryan back.

Jaz was still on the fence with her decision to seek Salvatore's help, unsure if this was the right thing to do. She'd put herself at risk now that Salvatore knew about her. She'd have to be extra careful he didn't have her followed, find out where her mum lived; you name it, Salvatore could destroy it all. But looking into his eyes now, she felt the strangest urge to trust him, or to at least give him a chance. Maybe she was too gullible or too much of a romantic to hope that Salvatore could do something good. Was it a flaw? Was she setting herself up to be hurt? All she had to go on was her gut feeling. And right now her gut just wanted Ryan safe.

CHAPTER 28

'Um, say that again?' said Anna.

Jaz took a deep breath and tried not to let her words rush out. 'I was just with Salvatore and he's going to try to find out where Ryan is being held and if he's okay.'

'What the hell were you thinking, he could have killed you!' said Tay. His arms flapped by his sides like he was trying to launch into space. His face was red and there was a glint in his eyes that said maybe he thought Jaz had gone a little mad.

Jaz sighed. It was time she shared her secret, they wouldn't understand otherwise. 'He won't. I just recently found out he's my biological father.'

Tay rocked back on his heels as if she'd hit him with a leaf blower. 'What?'

'Um, say that again?' repeated Anna.

For the next twenty minutes Jaz told them the whole story about how she came to work out that Salvatore was her real dad. All their interrupting questions made the task much longer than it needed to be.

'The medallion was the key. Without that, you'd still be none the wiser,' said Taylor.

'Yep. Only, I was happy to just ignore it, carry on as normal, but now with Ryan in trouble I thought Salvatore might be able to help,' she said.

'How? By having a drug-lord-to-drug-lord chat kind of thing?' said Anna sceptically.

Jaz shrugged. It was pretty much what she'd thought.

'Shit, Jaz. So, now you're waiting to call him? This is crazy.' Tay paced around Pax's kitchen. 'How did Salvatore take the news?'

'He was a little shocked, I guess.' He'd reacted the way a normal person would, and to Jaz that seemed wrong. Shouldn't a killer and drug dealer not really give a shit?

'How are you feeling about it?' asked Anna. Always so thoughtful.

'To tell you the truth, it's a little weird. I'm not sure how I should be feeling about it. Speaking with him just made it all the more confusing.'

The sound of his voice as he called her name still rolled around in her mind, along with the look on his face as she left his office. Jim and the other guy had stopped work to see if they were needed but Salvatore had waved them away.

'She is never to be harmed, you understand?' he'd told them sternly. 'Ever.'

Salvatore had walked her to the front door and then they had an awkward goodbye. Jaz got the feeling Salvatore was scared to let her leave in case he never saw her again, and it made her think of her mum. To have someone you loved just up and vanish.

'I'll call you in two hours,' she'd said to reassure him before walking out. She'd snuck back to her Jeep, making sure she wasn't followed, and then parked in another spot, waiting to watch Salvatore, who left half an hour later. She followed him from a distance, and only when he pulled into a park next to a big black car did she go back to the gym and her friends. She had half a mind to follow the black car, but she knew lots of Agency people were watching his every move. If they couldn't find Ryan, what chance did she have?

'Do you think he can be trusted?' asked Tay, bringing Jaz back from her thoughts.

'I honestly don't know,' she said before checking her watch again. 'Time will tell.'

Time had passed quickly talking about Salvatore and their meeting. And as always, it was a relief to have it off her chest, no secrets from her friends, and they helped share the burden. Jaz pulled out Salvatore's card from her pocket and played with it while Anna brought out one of the Agency's untraceable phones from her special room.

Anna had spent the past week redoing the room – a fresh coat of paint, new carpet and fancy-lockable storage cupboards – and it looked fresh, modern and more like Anna's place. She'd also designed the special medical room and had Tilly and Cody on the job. Slowly they were gathering build-ing supplies, which they stored in the gym ready for construction.

'Time to call?' asked Tay.

He was as eager as Jaz. Tay had grown close to Ryan too, the training, the mateship. It was nice to know she wasn't alone in this crazy plan to get Ryan home safe. Both her friends backed her without a second word. Sure, they probably thought she was nuts but they truly understood Jaz and knew she'd probably do it without them if it came to that.

Jaz dialled the number and Salvatore answered after one ring.

'Very prompt,' he said.

'I try to be,' said Jaz, who felt relief at the playful tone in Salvatore's voice. Was it good news or was he just in a good mood?

'Reece is alive,' said Salvatore, getting straight to the point. 'Jameson has him at the port warehouse. He's unsure what to do. At the moment he's waiting for his men to finish their background checks to see if he is who he says he is. Jameson's worried he might even be working for another dealer. He asked me if he was one of mine but I swore that he wasn't.'

'So, you don't think they'll kill him?' Even saying the words made her stomach roll like the choppy sea.

'I've kept my head with Jameson because I don't trust him. He's like a slippery snake. He could say one thing and do another. No one double-crosses him. The fact that Reece is still alive is only because of Jameson's daughter, but he knows he has to make a decision soon. He has men sifting through Reece's flat and checking every detail. If that comes up clean, then your man may be safe. But like I said, I wouldn't trust Jameson.'

Jaz wondered how long before Jameson's men came across the fake details. The backgrounds made were never meant to withstand a deep check. If they called the schools or the police about Reece's assault charge … anything like that could reveal the lies. It could be any moment. They had to act fast.

'Jaz, let me help. Let me lend you some of my people,' said Salvatore.

'No,' Jaz replied quickly. 'I don't want to be in debt to you. I already feel bad about coming to you in the first place.' Then she realised she should be a little nice about it all. 'Thank you, though, for finding out this information. It means a lot.'

And it did. If this whole thing wasn't some sort of trap.

'The door code is 200634, he took me to see him, just to make sure he wasn't one of mine or if I'd seen him before. I said I didn't know him.' He paused for a breath. 'Be careful, Jaz. Please think about staying in touch when you get Reece out. I'd like a chance to get to know you.' His voice was melancholy.

Jaz memorised the number before she spoke. 'You'd have to go straight before I'd even consider it.' Then she hung up and relayed it all to her friends.

'Do you think it's a trap?' asked Anna, while Tay called Cody and Tilly. They needed all the help they could get.

'I'm not sure.'

'What's your gut telling you?'

'It wants to trust Salvatore, but I don't know if that's just foolishness. A small part of me hopes my drug-lord father has some sort of a kind, loving side. Do you think I'm pathetic?' Jaz felt pathetic. More the fact that she didn't want to be hurt or made a fool of.

'No, not at all, Jaz. You wouldn't be human if you didn't wish for that. We want our parents to be good people. Anyway, right now I don't think we have the luxury of not believing him. It's all we have to go on. Let's hope Cody and Tilly are on board with the plan.'

'And what plan is that?' Jaz asked. From where she sat they hadn't planned anything yet.

'The "get Ryan back" plan.' Anna slammed her hand down on the kitchen table.

'Right,' said Tay as he put down his phone. 'Cody and Tilly are on their way, plus Tilly is contacting the Commander.'

Jaz winced. She hoped they all wouldn't get into trouble for this.

'Don't stress,' said Tay. 'Tilly said the Commander wouldn't want to miss it.'

Just how much trouble would she be in with the Agency, Jaz wondered. But this was Ryan, so she didn't care how much hot water she got into.

'We have to go about this right,' said Jaz when Cody and Tilly turned up and they all sat huddled around the kitchen table. The boys leaned forward on their elbows as they tried to work out the best plan of attack. 'I don't want anyone hurt. Everyone must come home safe.' Ryan wouldn't like it if someone ended up dead because of him.

'I agree,' said the Commander as he followed Anna in through the back door of the house.

'Sir,' said Jaz. She was a little starstruck and momentarily forgot his name was Ian.

'So, what have we got?' he said sitting next to Tilly.

All eyes went to Jaz.

Anna threw down some photos Jaz had asked her to print. Everyone looked at them as Jaz spoke. 'This is Jameson's warehouse, where Ryan is being held. The main door has a code.' Jaz repeated the code and they all nodded, confirming they each had it stored in their mind.

'And there's also a camera,' said Cody. 'But that's easy to black out.'

'Good. You can be in charge of that,' said Jaz. 'Now, we don't know what we'll be facing on the inside. So, once we get that door open I want Tilly and Cody left, and Tay and Ian right.' Jaz wanted Tay protected and the best way to do that was to put him with the best. She was yet to see the Commander in action but from the stories Tilly and Ryan had shared, there was no better agent.

'Best time is just on dark,' said Ian, his voice strong and sure.

This was probably a walk in the park for him. Ryan had told her once how he'd taken down an opium grower overseas, killed all his men, set free the slave-labour kids, and with hand grenades had decimated the plantation. Just listening to the story had seemed like an action movie. It made her wonder if these so-called fictional stories were actually based on real events and truths. Who would really know?

They talked and planned for hours, pausing only for coffee and the Subway rolls that Anna grabbed for them. When Tilly's stomach rumbled people from two states over could hear it.

Soon they had the operation planned out as best they could.

'So, is everyone right on their positions,' said Ian.

'Yes, I wait in the car in case we need a fast getaway,' said Anna.

Her face was flushed and her teeth clenched. She was as excited as she was scared to death. Jaz knew that feeling.

'You don't get out of the car,' Jaz said to her softly. Anna may be a good shot but she wasn't prepared for one-on-one combat. 'I can't have anything happen to you. Okay?'

Anna nodded almost as fast as a woodpecker hammering its beak against a tree. Her friend was not going to stay at the gym and wait. She'd demanded she have a job. 'But you get to go,' had been her reply. 'I promise I won't get in the way.'

Sitting in the car was the best Jaz could come up with, and Tay had backed her up on this after initially wanting Anna at the gym.

So, the three of them would ride this mission together, a first. In a way it was comforting and yet it scared the hell out of Jaz. These were her closest friends, and she couldn't live without them. Yet they had watched her go off on missions and supported her. She couldn't now try to wrap them up in cotton wool, she couldn't protect them or prevent them when they wanted to help. It was a large, ugly pill to swallow.

'Right. I'm going to go and get ready,' said Cody standing up. 'I'll get the spray can. And I'll meet you all at the rendezvous point.'

'I'll bring cable ties, tape and extra bullets.' Tilly pushed back his chair and reached for the last Subway roll. He smiled. He was ready for a fight. 'See you all soon.'

Tilly walked out whistling a tune, as if he didn't have a care in the world.

The Commander stood next. 'I always did like Pax's place. It always felt like a home, or a shelter, I guess.' His eyes took in every detail of Pax's kitchen. 'It still feels like he's here, and I keep expecting him to walk out from the back room with one of his Godawful shirts on.'

Jaz and Anna glanced at each other. Yeah, they knew exactly how he felt.

'You've been here before?' asked Jaz.

'I spent quite a bit of my younger days here, before you were born. Then in later years I'd stop by mainly for papers and a quick catch-up with Pax. He was one of a kind.'

Ian's words were spoken with so much admiration Jaz felt like hugging him, but she didn't. Instead she watched him walk to the back door with no further conversation or goodbye.

'And then there were three,' said Tay. 'Is anyone else pumped?'

'And shitting bricks?' said Anna.

'I'm doing both,' said Jaz. 'I have so many worries. What if we're too late? What if someone gets hurt?' She couldn't say die. But that was what she meant. What if someone died? It could even be her. Save Ryan only to die in the process. How very Romeo and Juliet.

'Jaz, you have to stay positive. Remember what the Commander said. You need to see our plan working, visualise it coming together, being prepared for anything. We can do this,' said Tay as he got up from the table to join his friends.

'Besides, there might only be one guy holding Ryan. This could be a walk in the park!' Anna was so optimistic it was adorable, so much so Tay couldn't resist putting his arm around her.

'Exactly,' he agreed.

Anna could have said the moon was green and that tomorrow the Martians would land and Tay would still agree with her.

'Okay, so we need to make sure our alibis are in place, we get our guns ready, leave mobiles at home, change into black, pick up the getaway car—'

'Oh, that sounds so James Bond-ish,' said Anna.

'No, it's more like *The Blues Brothers* or *Gone in Sixty Seconds*,' said Tay.

'I would LOOOOVE an Eleanor to drive.'

Jaz clapped her hands together, making her friends jump. 'Are you guys listening,' said Jaz gruffly. 'Focus. Bullets, blood, mayhem. It's all about to get serious.'

'We know that, Jaz,' said Tay. 'It's just nerves.'

Tay did look a little green around the gills and he still hadn't taken his arm away from Anna.

'We know what's at stake.' Anna reached out and pulled her into a three-way hug. 'I want you both to be careful. I love you so much.'

As Jaz hugged her friends, she wondered what the outcome would be. To get Ryan, would she lose someone else? Would this moment be the last with her friends? There were no answers and there was no point thinking this way. Jaz couldn't predict the future, all she could do was trust in her team, believe they could do this and see it through till the end. Jaz just hoped she could keep her head if and when she got to see Ryan.

Stretching out her arms she hugged her friends, enjoying their warmth, their security and their love. And she prayed it wasn't the last time they got to do this.

CHAPTER 29

THE METALLIC SCENT of blood stirred his consciousness, along with a damp mustiness that reminded him of a cold cave. Ryan drew a breath; the movement caused a sharp pain to radiate through his chest. Broken ribs? Other parts of his body ached and throbbed, but at least he knew he was alive. Death wouldn't be this painful. Ryan wanted to open his eyes but they felt stuck together like bad conjunctivitis. He'd taken a few hits to the face, how many exactly he'd lost count, but they would have caused the swelling. He must look amazing if how he felt was any indication.

He breathed again, less painful now as he grew used to the familiar pain, but this time he noticed a hint of something sweet. Like the last remains of perfume days after it was applied.

Something cold and wet touched his forehead and he flinched, causing himself more pain. What the hell was it? Suddenly he felt water rolling down his face as if he'd been crying.

He felt the air shift and felt the presence of someone else in the room. Where was he? For a second he panicked.

'Stay still,' came soft feminine words. 'It's okay,' she added. Her Filipino accent was thick.

Then it came to him. He was in the cell. Jameson's cell that he used for his girls. This poor abused girl was helping him. It only made Ryan feel worse. It should be the other way around.

'Thank you,' he mumbled through cracked split lips that were dry and tasted like blood.

As if she had read his mind, he felt a wet cloth dabbed across his lips, making them feel better. Then the cloth shifted back to his eyes and around his face. He must be a right bloody mess.

'You take much pain,' she said. 'You hurt?'

'A little,' he said truthfully. Actually it was a lot, but with all of the pain from different parts of his body competing to be felt, everything almost dulled it into one ache. He focused his mind on Jaz, as he always did when things got too hard.

He'd taken the beatings, the questions, and stuck to his guns, repeating the same story. Only he knew that it was just a matter of time before Jameson dug deep into his identity and found some anomaly. He was trying everything in his power to win Jameson over, to prove he was loyal. He could tell Jameson was unsure but it was Randall who was taking control of things. The big man took great delight in pounding Ryan's flesh, trying to get him to confess.

'How long have I been out?' Ryan asked the girl. The days were hard to keep track of.

'Long time. Other girl taken,' she said softly. 'Can you sit up? Drink?'

Ryan felt his chest; his clothes had been taken off except for his pants, his skin was slimy and crusty at the same time. 'I think so.' He pushed himself up into a sitting position, his hands protesting as they pushed against the manky bed. The girl sat beside him and he felt a cup pressed against his lips. He drank the whole lot. 'Thank you.'

Ryan dragged his body backwards until he could lean against the wall. He tried to use his legs but the muscles screamed out, his feet felt like they were cut.

Overall his injuries were ones that could be hidden later. If Jameson found nothing, maybe he would let Ryan go back to work and his daughter. If that was the case he couldn't go back too damaged. Missing fingers and other body parts would be hard to explain. For now Jameson and Randall were keeping it all above board – well, as much as you could with torture.

'Will they come for you again?' she asked.

'I reckon so.'

'You strong man,' she added as her tiny hands touched his chest as she continued to clean him up.

Ryan almost laughed. He didn't feel so strong right now. He wanted Jaz. Holding her again was the only thought getting him through at the moment.

He would suffer whatever Randall inflicted as long as he could kiss Jaz again. Nothing else mattered.

He wished he could pry open his eyes and see the girl helping him. Did she have raven hair like Jaz? 'How long have you been here?' he asked her.

'Two days. They come for you then I clean you. So much blood,' she said. 'What you do, Mister?'

'I'm not actually sure what I've done wrong,' he said. Ryan wasn't taking any chances. For all he knew they could be watching him now, recording him, you name it. The girl could even be a plant to get him to talk. 'Thank you for your help,' he said, trying to find her hand. It was so slender. 'How old are you?'

'Nearly sixteen.' Her words were whispered.

Oh my God, thought Ryan. His stomach turned and he felt the worst he had in days.

The sound of a door shutting echoed nearby and Ryan felt the girl's hand tense against his skin. She moved away from him and he felt the bed move as she sat at the end. Good girl, she was already learning that she needed to distance herself from him. He hated to think what she'd been through already. Without even seeing her he got the feeling she was a fighter.

'Hey, he's awake.' Randall's voice was playful. He loved his job far too much.

Ryan heard the shuffle of more feet and keys jangling as the cell was unlocked.

'He looks like shit, Randall,' came Jameson's voice.

'He's a tough nut to crack, sir. But I will. One way or another we'll have our answer by tomorrow.'

Shit. Ryan knew what that meant. They were making a decision soon. Ryan didn't like his chances with Randall, who would love to kill him, or Jameson, who hated any little blip in his plans.

He hoped if they killed him the poor girl wasn't around to see it. She'd been through enough already.

'Come on then, time to get reacquainted,' said Randall.

Randall's big hand wrapped around Ryan's arm, gripping it like a vice as he pulled him up off the bed. Ryan clenched his teeth, refusing to cry out in pain. He stood on his tender feet and went where Randall pushed him, each step feeling like it was on broken glass. Putting out his hand he tried to feel for a wall or a door, instead finding the cold metal of the cell. He tried to keep track of where he was going, if only he could prise open his eyes. The water the girl had washed them with was helping, he felt the blood that had helped glue them shut starting to soften.

He worked out they went through the door to the other area of the warehouse, where he'd been taken each time for his torture. This is where they had the pulley chains that hung from the ceiling, which they tied his hands into. Randall had enjoyed lifting him off the ground for hours on end, his wrists bruised to the bone from the heavy chains.

Before the beatings had started Ryan had seen the area they'd taken him. It was behind a half wall that segregated the open space. This was where the sorting of fish was done, the other side was where the forklifts brought the crates in from a locked sliding door on the side. So, if anyone happened to come in they were still hidden from view. Ryan wondered if the crew ever noticed his blood on the floor, or did it just mix in with the fish? Maybe Jameson had given them the week off? Ryan did recall hearing noises, the beeping of machines and the squeal of forklift tyres on the concrete floor, so he assumed they had worked some days. Maybe it was only when the boats came in with the fish.

Maybe Randall had one of the Sesha Serpents clean up after he'd spilled Ryan's blood all over the floor.

Even though Ryan couldn't see, he knew exactly where he was. His wrists were bound together again, the cold chain instantly causing pain and he wasn't even lifted up yet. Jaz's face came to mind as he tried to escape to another place where the pain wouldn't touch him.

The clang of the chains rattled through the shed as Randall had the pulley lift Ryan's arms up above his head.

'Have you got anything to tell us, Reece? Is your name Reece?' said Randall.

'Yes, my name is Reece Lancaster. I want to see my girlfriend. Is she here? Can I see her?' he said, starting his usual tirade. He tried to think like an innocent person. What would they say? 'I've told you, Randall, you're barking up the wrong bloody tree. You'll see,' he said confidently.

And that's when Randall hit him in the chest on one of his broken ribs. Ryan fell forwards, struggling for breath and wondering if it really was blood he was tasting in the back of his throat as a wave of nausea hit him.

Randall always got mean when Ryan spoke so confidently. He knew he was pushing his buttons, but he wanted Randall to see him as sure and smug. He wanted Randall to second-guess what he'd seen but if he wasn't careful, Randall might just accidently kill him so the boss never found out if Randall had been wrong. It was a deadly game of cat and mouse to play but Ryan was confident with Jameson around.

'Reece, I hate seeing you like this,' said Jameson. 'I know Annaliese would like to see you again but you understand we have to be sure.'

'I understand, sir. I don't know who Randall thinks I am but I do love your daughter and I'm loyal to you. Randall is just threatened, scared I'll take his job,' said Ryan quickly, before he felt the next blow. He needed to put the doubt into Jameson's mind, had been working hard on it over the last few punishments, but he couldn't tell if it was working.

'If we can't find anything, if you are who you say you are and you're not working for the police or my enemies, then you have nothing to fear. And to compensate for this unfortunate situation you find yourself in, I will make it up to you, buy you and Annaliese a new house and cars and you will have earned my trust.'

Jameson sounded sincere but Ryan couldn't bring himself to trust him. If he'd learned anything over the past few months working for Jameson, it was that he was slippery like oil. No wonder the police couldn't find anything on him, it was hard enough for the Agency to gather information on him. But Ryan had collected bits to put him away, if only he survived.

Jaz watched from the dark shadows as Tilly hoisted Cody up onto his shoulders. Cody was armed with a spray can and coated the camera in seconds. It would only be noticed if someone had been watching the camera, but they were counting on them being busy with Ryan. Tilly waved them over, so they ran through the darkness in silence, guns in their hands, loaded and safeties off. They all wore black, Jaz wore her hair up and under a hat as a disguise.

Jaz nodded to them all: Tilly, Cody, Tay and Ian. They knew their parts in the plan. They all signalled back and Tilly pressed in the code. It unlocked and he slowly opened the door as quietly as he could. When the gap was big enough, Ian and Tay scooted through to one side and then Tilly and Cody the other. Jaz crept down when she got inside and made sure the door shut behind her silently – until the lock clicked back into place loudly causing her heart to pound in her chest. She looked to Ian, who signalled all was okay. Soon she realised why. Just as the door had clicked shut a rumble of chains had masked the noise. A moment later she heard the chains rattle again and voices.

Ryan! She'd know his voice anywhere. He was alive.

Right then Jaz felt the most amazing euphoric high. They weren't going in to retrieve a body like Ryan ended up doing with his mate Chris. Thank God because Jaz didn't think she'd be able to handle that. Ryan was alive. He was bloody alive!

With her pulse racing, she followed Ian around behind the forklift where they hid, Cody and Tilly circling the other side behind some crates. Jaz saw a tall man step into the light at the last second, one of Jameson's men. Jaz managed to catch her gasp before it gave them away when she recognised Wilkie.

When Wilkie turned around Tilly was behind him within seconds, his hand over Wilkie's mouth and the glimmer of a blade at his throat. For a split second Jaz didn't want Wilkie to die, she'd come to know him through the pub and the thought of his blood shed made her uneasy. But she shouldn't have worried, for Tilly just made him pass out then dragged him back slowly into the dark where he would then tie him up with the cable ties in his back pocket, and tape over his mouth for good measure.

She was relieved. She'd rather Wilkie go to jail and have a second chance than be slaughtered.

Ian and Taylor crept forward, getting closer to the voices. Ian indicated that he saw three men and one was Ryan. Jaz trembled with excitement. Ryan was so close. She slowly moved forward so she was near Ian, she needed to see Ryan for herself. Her gun gripped firmly in her hands, ready to maim or kill.

Ian moved back so she could take a quick peek around the corner of the freezer they hid behind. It was level with the half wall that separated the room. Jaz moved her head out as far as she dared, just enough for her to see Jameson, another man and Ryan.

Oh my God!

She moved her head back and took deep breaths. Ryan looked like death warmed up, his chest a canvas of blood patterns and purple to black bruises.

He was strung up like a cow for carving, his arms stretched out above his head. Jaz could cry at the state of him, the pain he must be in, but she bit down on her lip and glanced to Ian.

He gave her the nod then signalled to Tilly that they were to move in three seconds. It was the longest countdown Jaz had ever experienced. Each millisecond seemed like hours as she waited to save her soulmate.

Just as Tilly and Cody stood up to move, the main door opened and two guys walked in. There was a moment where Jameson's men and the Agency operatives just looked at each other, trying to determine friend from foe, and then guns were drawn.

'Who are you?' one of them shouted.

Jaz cringed as she heard Jameson and his man go silent as they listened. She hoped they didn't decide to shoot Ryan then and there. Ian signalled to her, his aged face serious and almost scary in the half-light. He wanted them to act now.

Ian and Tay rose with their guns drawn and aimed towards Jameson. 'Don't move!' yelled Ian.

This caused confusion with the men at the door, who were trigger-happy and fired off bullets, causing Tilly and Cody to dive for cover. While this went on the man beside Jameson went for his gun and sent bullets in their direction. Tay cried out and ducked behind another freezer while Ian and Jaz went back to their hiding place. The stench of fish clung to the freezer as she pushed her body against it for protection.

Jaz signalled to Tay, asking if he was okay. He lifted his arm, it was bleeding.

'Just a flesh wound,' said Ian, putting her mind at ease. Ian had practically yelled as the firing of guns and pinging of bullets made for a hell of a racket in the warehouse.

She tried to see how Tilly and Cody were going. They were hunkered down behind a box with nowhere to go. Jaz rose enough to see the two men by the door, and took aim. She fired just as she realised one was Bud. He was flung backwards and to the ground.

Oh shit.

Bud.

She didn't have time to contemplate the nature of his wound because bullets were now coming her way. She dropped to the floor and found Tilly and Cody by her side.

'Nice work,' said Tilly. 'Drawing their fire.'

'Thanks,' she said back, while her mind was worrying about Bud.

'Who are you?' bellowed out a voice.

Jaz risked a glance at Jameson's man, who had his gun pointed in their direction. Jameson was hiding behind Ryan with his own gun poised.

Cody stood up, thinking he was hidden from the man at the front door and Jameson, when a bullet slammed into his shoulder, sending him sliding to the ground.

'Shit.' Jaz was stunned momentarily. Where had that shot come from?

'The corridor,' said Tilly, pointing to the opposite side, and he grabbed Cody's good arm and dragged him to their shelter.

A man, with a bald head and looking like Vin Diesel, had appeared from another area. Jaz could see sectioned-off rooms. Damn, how many were hiding back there? Were they outnumbered? This wasn't good.

Tilly lay on his back, Jaz unsure of what he was doing, then he pushed himself along the ground so his head and gun were sticking out from behind the freezer. He took aim and shot the Vin Diesel man before he even saw Tilly slide out. Jaz grabbed his feet and yanked him back to safety.

'Cheers,' he whispered before moving to check Cody's wound.

'I'm okay,' she heard him say.

Ian motioned to Tay to take down the guy at the door. Tay nodded and shifted behind them all, trying to make his way back down the warehouse towards the door. Jaz was shit scared for him but she knew it was his test, his time to learn and grow.

At the same time Ian and Tilly stood up, aiming their guns at Jameson and his man. There was a round of bullets fired, she could hear them fly past and through the tin wall behind her. Jaz wanted to stand up and scream at them to stop before they hit Ryan, but she had trust in Ian and Tilly's aim.

The only thing on their side was that Jameson and his man were cornered. They couldn't get out from where they were without getting shot. All they had was Ryan to hide behind.

The warehouse went quiet as they stopped to reload.

Jaz heard the click of a gun. For some reason it made her skin prickle.

'Move and I shoot this man dead,' said Jameson's man.

CHAPTER 30

Jaz snuck a peek, and sure enough a gun was now pressed against Ryan's temple, and his body used as a shield. Shit. They had figured out they were here for him.

It was then that Ian and Tilly stood, guns aimed. Jaz did the same and now had the time to really assess the situation. Ryan hung from the chains, his eyes looked like overripe plums and his body even more so. His pants were torn, his feet were red with blood. She couldn't fathom what he'd endured, it took all her energy not to rush to him. The smell of blood, his blood, that stained the concrete near his feet, turned her stomach. There was a table against the wall to the side, on it was a collection of knives, ones that looked like they'd just cut up hundreds of fish, yet there were no fish in this warehouse, not today.

Ian and Tilly stepped closer.

'Stay where you are, or I'll pop him right now.'

'There's nowhere for you to go,' said Ian.

Jameson glanced towards the corridor where Vin Diesel man lay. Was he still alive? Was Jameson waiting for more men?

'Those shots will have caught someone's attention. It's only a matter of time,' said Tilly.

Jameson's man, the one with hands like a rugby player, kept his gun on Ryan's temple while he unhitched his hands from the chain. Then, carrying him like a sack of potatoes against his chest, he shuffled towards the front door and possible safety. Jameson crouched behind them both, a double shield.

All three of them stepped a bit closer so they could keep their guns trained. Backing towards the corridor. Jaz glanced behind them. It could be a trap, but Vin was still lying where he fell, blood pooling out from underneath his body.

'I'll check the rooms,' said Tilly, and disappeared to do a sweep.

It was more important that Jaz's gun stayed aimed at Rugby's hands as he kept shuffling back towards the door. Where was Tay? All had gone silent. Was he okay?

She felt a wave of panic. What if he wasn't?

'Put your guns down,' came another voice. One Jaz knew.

She turned to see Salvatore walking towards them from the corridor, Tilly in front with his hands up and Salvatore's gun resting at the back of Tilly's skull.

Jaz felt her mouth drop along with her gun. What the hell?

She'd been so wrong. The disappointment stabbed at her, like a million knives that Salvatore had just imbedded in her back. How had her gut got this wrong? She should have known you couldn't change a person overnight. Shit just didn't happen like that in real life.

'Great timing,' said Jameson with a smirk on his smug face.

Jaz just wanted to kick him where it would hurt like hell.

Jaz and Ian watched as Salvatore led Tilly towards Jameson, using his body as a shield. Jaz watched his every move, the way he held his gun, and then she caught his eyes.

Salvatore recognised her but he didn't flinch; his eyes took in the gun in her hands and she saw something weird flash across his eyes momentarily. It seemed like disappointment. But she was too pissed at him to figure it out. He told her he'd never killed anyone. He'd lied to her, but what did she expect. That being his daughter would be enough to change his spots? She felt like such a fool and her face burned with the shame.

'Everyone okay?' asked Salvatore when he reached Jameson's side.

Now that they had the upper hand, Rugby guy was more relaxed, even smug like his boss.

'Yes, thanks to you.' Jameson nodded, clearly impressed with Salvatore.

Jaz wanted to scream and stomp her foot, but only because she couldn't kill them both without risking Ryan and Tilly. Goddamn was she pissed.

'We don't need this one now, he'll only slow us down,' said Jameson as his gun moved back to Ryan's head.

'Noooo!' Jaz screamed. She could see it all happening in slow motion.

Not her Ryan!

A shot was fired.

A body slumped to the ground.

Jaz felt like throwing up.

But Ryan was still standing.

More shots were fired.

Another body dropped.

What had just happened?

Jameson was on the floor with a bullet in his head, smack bang in the middle. But how?

She looked across and Salvatore had his gun still aimed at Jameson, not Tilly.

Ian stepped forward, his gun had been on Rugby's hands and Jaz knew then that he'd shot him. Which meant that Salvatore must have killed Jameson.

Salvatore stared at Jameson on the ground with an expression of disbelief. It really was his first kill. She could tell by the rigidness of his body and the slight shake of his gun hand.

'Thank you,' said Jaz as she walked to his side. She reached out and put her hand on top of his gun and gently lowered it. His eyes found hers, and he nodded.

'You better go before the DEA turns up,' she said.

Salvatore nodded again and headed for the door.

'What just happened?' said Ian as he watched Salvatore leave.

'That was Salvatore De Luca. Have I missed something?' said Tilly. He rubbed his forehead in confusion.

'I'll fill you both in later,' she said. There were more important things on her mind. Like holding Ryan.

'Jaz. Is that really you?' Ryan's words were like hot fudge during an Antarctic winter.

Jaz caressed his face gently. She wanted to hug him tightly but she didn't want to hurt him anymore than he already was. 'Yeah, it's me.'

Ryan's chest expanded as he breathed. 'I knew you were here even before you spoke. I could smell you.' His lips curled into a smile. 'And besides, who else would risk coming here to save me?'

Jaz laughed and his smile grew wider. 'You know me too well, Ryan. Come on, let's get you home.'

Jaz and Tilly put Ryan's arms around their shoulders and helped walk him to the door. Ian was going to stay behind to talk to the DEA.

'Oh my God, Ryan look at you,' said Anna, who was just inside the door. She had a strip of her shirt in her hands.

'I would, Anna, if I could see,' said Ryan.

He was in good spirits. He wasn't the only one. Jaz couldn't keep the smile off her face, even with her friend out of the car she wasn't supposed to leave.

'Anna, what the heck are you doing in here?' she tried to say gruffly, but it didn't work. She was just too damned pleased to be holding Ryan.

'She was saving me,' said Tay.

Jaz followed the sound of his voice to the floor. He was holding his waist, blood seeping past his hand. Anna knelt down and pressed her shirt strip to his wound.

'There, that should help. It's not too deep,' she said, before kissing Tay's forehead.

Jaz's eyebrow shot up at this open display of affection.

'Do tell?'

Tay smiled. 'I was fighting with him,' Tay gestured to a body on the other side of the door, face down, arms at funny angles. Further up was Bud, face down. Jaz had to look away.

Tay continued, 'We'd run out of bullets, didn't have time to reload so we went fist to fist, only he had a knife. I was doing all right until he cut me. I lost it for a moment.'

Jaz could understand that. Tay's first major fight, and a knife one at that.

'I was off balance and unprepared. I knew I was gonna get cut again and just before he went to strike he fell down like a tonne of bricks. Anna smacked him across the head with a tyre leaver.'

'You did *what?*' said Jaz, in awe.

'Did I hear that right?' said Cody as he staggered towards them; his hand was pressed against his bullet wound in his shoulder and he wore a grimace. 'A tyre lever?'

Ryan and Tilly chuckled.

'That is gold,' said Ryan after he finished laughing. 'Anna has a knack for knocking people out with unconventional things.'

'We might make a field agent out of you yet, Anna,' said Tilly with a smirk.

'No,' said Tay. 'Not this one.' He reached out and pulled her to him, kissing her lips. 'This one is too special.'

Anna traced her thumb across his lips, it was so sensual and heartfelt. A tear rolled down Anna's check and Jaz felt her own eyes water.

Somehow this crazy mob of friends had survived. Jaz couldn't be happier.

'Well, this is all lovely, but I'm bleeding,' said Cody. 'Where's my love?'

Tilly reached over and kissed Cody's cheek. 'Feel better?' he asked.

'Not really.' Cody shook his head, his lips giving away his amusement.

'What say we head back to the gym and get everyone cleaned up?' said Jaz. 'I think Pax has some aged scotch hidden in the kitchen for these kind of moments.'

Ryan squeezed her shoulder. 'You're speaking my language. Let's go home.'

CHAPTER 31

Back at the gym, Tilly and Anna set about fixing Cody and Tay while Jaz jumped in the shower with Ryan. The water stung his cuts but it was the only way to clean him up. Watching the red blood-stained water drain away was awful but at least Ryan could now open his eyes.

'There you are. You'll never know just how much I missed you,' he said touching her wet hair.

'I think I have a fair idea.'

It looked like a massacre scene in the small bathroom. Blood still ran from his fresh wounds and old ones that had opened up again. Towels were stained with red splotches and everything Ryan touched or stood on got smeared red.

The sight and smell of the blood didn't offend Jaz. She was too busy basking in the excitement of having Ryan back and taking care of him.

After he was patted dry, Jaz started patching up his injuries. 'What about your ribs?' she asked worriedly.

'They'll be okay. James knows someone I can see for an X-ray.'

Ryan took her hands after she'd finished half mummifying him and brought them to his lips. 'I love you. Thanks for coming to get me.'

Jaz looked at her beaten-up man, he was still so gorgeous even with the bruises and cuts. He'd just added to his collection of scars. Jaz wanted to hold him, touch him all over, make love to him, but now was not the time.

'You keep looking at me like that and I might tear off my bandages,' he said teasingly.

Not all of Ryan was injured but his ribs weren't up to anything too physical.

'We have plenty of time,' she said threading her fingers through his hair at the nape of his neck. 'But I won't be leaving your side anytime soon. I think you need to stay with me until you're a hundred per cent.'

His lips curled. 'I very much like the sound of that.'

He pulled her towards him and kissed her again. Soft and gentle.

'Come on, let's get you dressed before we get sidetracked.' Her gazed dropped to his lower half. 'I'm going to find you some of Pax's nice shirts for you to wear,' she teased.

'Oh no, surely not?' he pleaded. 'I'd rather walk around in a towel.'

Jaz came back with some clothes for him and he sighed with relief when it was a pair of baggy jeans and T-shirt from Taylor, who had half his wardrobe at Pax's just like the girls. This place was fast becoming their home.

Together they walked back to the kitchen where snacks had been put on the table, along with glasses of Pax's finest scotch.

'Here, sit,' said Tilly, jumping up from his chair and offering it to Ryan. 'Thanks mate.'

Cody and Tay were all bandaged up and kicking back in their chairs, the scotch already working wonders. Cody had a sedated smile on his face but he wasn't the only one. Anna gave up her chair for Jaz, and Tay pulled her onto his lap.

'I don't want to hurt you.' Anna only just got the words out before Tay cut her off.

'You won't. You're my medicine.' He tucked his arms around Anna and held her against him.

'About time, you two,' said Jaz.

Tay and Anna looked at each other and smiled. 'I know,' said Anna as she dropped a kiss on his lips.

'Is anyone allowed to join this party?'

All heads turned to the voice. Ian and James stood there watching. James was dressed casually in jeans and a black T-shirt. Jaz had never seen him out of a suit before, it made him look like one of the team.

No one had heard them come in. Ian had been shown where the hidden key was, so had Tilly and Cody. All were welcome here. But no one was expecting James. You could have heard a pin drop.

Jaz cleared her throat. 'Of course, grab a stool, it's all we have left sorry. Cody, more scotch please.'

The two newcomers joined them around the old table with its mismatched chairs.

'Are we in trouble?' asked Tay.

Jaz was thinking the same thing. Why was James here?

'I have a few questions. I'm not angry over this, Ian had kept me filled in from the beginning,' said James.

Good to know, thought Jaz. Then why was he here if not to bust them for a secret rescue mission?

'What I want to know … Well, what I don't get is why Salvatore shot Jameson? Was it over his business? Was it about claiming more power? But if it was, then why did you let him go? I also hear it was Salvatore who gave us information to help plan this mission. Jaz, I'm drawing a lot of blanks.'

She guessed it might come to this.

Jaz turned to her friends, who nodded, then she turned to Ryan, who smiled and reached for her hand. 'It's okay, baby,' he said.

Jaz took a breath and turned to James. 'I trust everyone here, and I guess it's better if you all know the truth.' Salvatore had saved Ryan for her, shooting someone for the first time just for her. It's not what many daughters would want from their father, but for Jaz, he'd given her the best gift. Ryan. And because he'd done that, she wanted him unharmed by the Agency. Maybe he'd spoken the truth about going straight just so he could get to know Jaz. Only time would tell. Until then she didn't want him killed.

Which led her to telling the Agency. 'Salvatore is my father.'

'What the hell?'

'No way?'

'You're shitting me.'

The last comment came from Cody.

'I don't understand,' said James. 'How is that possible?'

'Many years ago Salvatore fell in love with an Agency girl called Julie, your sister Natasha. What he didn't know is that she fell pregnant and ran away to WA under the protection of her friend Pax. She did it to save her child. Me.'

Jaz watched James as he tried to make sense of her words.

He jerked up, face white. 'Natasha was pregnant? To Salvatore? She moved to WA? But that would mean …' James stuttered as he stared at Jaz.

'That I'm your niece? Yes, it does. And your sister is very much alive and well and has no clue that I ended up with the Agency.'

James staggered and Ian helped him back onto his stool.

'Cody, I think we're going to need more scotch,' said Ian with a chuckle.

'I agree,' said Tilly, shaking his head.

'I'm totally lost, but I'll get the scotch.' Cody's chair scraped against the floor. He stepped to the special cupboard and retrieved another bottle.

'Lucky we have lots of scotch,' said Anna with a smirk.

Cody paused by Jaz's side, his shaggy hair looking like he'd rubbed a balloon against it. 'You might have to start this story from the beginning Jaz.'

'I second that,' said Ian.

'Me three,' said Tilly.

James was just openly staring at Jaz. She saw the moment he realised something.

'My God,' he said.

'I know, I have her eyes.' Her grin was ear to ear.

Then, in the comfort of Pax's kitchen, with her old and new friends around the table, Ryan lovingly by her side, and her uncle, Jaz started her story from the beginning. And she started it at The Ring where she first met Ryan.

Thanks for reading The Crescendo. I hope you enjoyed it.

If you'd like to know more about me, my books, or to connect with me online, you can visit my webpage www.fionapalmer.com, follow me on twitter @fiona_palmer, or like my Facebook page

Reviews can help readers find books, and I am grateful for all honest reviews. Thank you for taking the time to let others know what you've read, and what you thought.

You've just read the fourth book in my MTG Agency series. The other books in this series are The Recruit, The Mission and The Deception.